MW00879326

TENG RONG

Brilliant White Peaks

Copyright © 2021 by Teng Rong

All rights reserved. No part of this publication may be reproduced, stored or transmitted in any form or by any means, electronic, mechanical, photocopying, recording, scanning, or otherwise without written permission from the publisher. It is illegal to copy this book, post it to a website, or distribute it by any other means without permission.

This novel is entirely a work of fiction. The names, characters and incidents portrayed in it are the work of the author's imagination. Any resemblance to actual persons, living or dead, events or localities is entirely coincidental.

Teng Rong asserts the moral right to be identified as the author of this work.

If you enjoyed this book, please consider donating to The Wolf Conservation Center at https://nywolf.org/donate/. Your donation helps them fund the species recovery programs for the endangered Mexican gray wolf and red wolf.

First edition

ISBN: 978-1-7778585-0-6

This book was professionally typeset on Reedsy.
Find out more at reedsy.com

To my parents, who always believed in me.
To my mate, who supported me every step of the way.
Thank you.

Chapter 1

I first saw light when Ma left the safe place. I opened my eyes, and there was a tiny and bright crescent of light in the distance. I didn't like it, so I squeezed my eyes shut and shrank back into the warm, earthy depths to wait for Ma to come back. I longed for her warmth and her scent—the scent of home and safety.

Time passed, and I felt the chill of the emptiness all around me. There were fewer heartbeats in the safe place. My favourite brother was gone, and I didn't know where he went. My big sister too. But I wasn't alone: there was one more heartbeat. I heard a quick and trembling breath, so I nudged her. She whimpered. I opened my eyes again and saw her white-tipped ears and terrified face.

She was small and weak. When she trembled, the safe place didn't feel safe anymore. I bit her on the shoulder and told her to be quiet, and she retreated and pressed herself against the dirt at the back.

I laid down and stared at the dim crescent of light and waited for Ma to come back while White-Ears continued whimpering. "Shut up," I hissed, but she didn't answer. Her breath came quick and shallow.

Whine. Whine. Whine.

I stood up and walked over with my teeth bared. A growl ripped from my throat. White-Ears froze and closed her eyes. I stood above her and waited for her to look up and defend herself, but she never did. A few moments later, the whimpering started again. She was scared. Ma was gone, and I was scared too, and I didn't want to bite her anymore.

I nuzzled her neck with my nose. I felt her body relax, and we fell asleep together.

Ma smelled like many different things. Good and curious smells, but also unfamiliar and scary smells. I climbed her head and mounted her snout and tried to get a better sniff. Sometimes she was patient with me, but other times she shook me off with a grumble. When that happened, and it happened often, I left her alone and played with White-Ears.

I pinned her on the ground and pretended to bite her neck. She whimpered, and eventually, I let her go. White-Ears wanted to play more, so we did. We ran around each other until I pinned her to the ground again. Then we stopped to catch our breaths. Light filtered into the safe place, and her ears glowed faintly.

For the next few nights, I let her sleep next to Ma.

I heard voices, paw steps, and the rustling of danger that made my fur stand on end. White-Ears hid at the back and shook and whimpered, so I stood up and walked over to her. I licked her face until her breathing calmed and she opened her eyes again.

"Come meet the family!" Ma's song was low and calm, and the wind of the outside brought her scent.

"I'm scared," White-Ears whispered.

"Don't be," I said. "It'll be an adventure."

We stepped out together. It was very bright outside. The light hurt my eyes, so I closed them. The air chilled my body, making me shiver. I didn't want to go any further. I took a step back and shrank into the dirt, where it was familiar.

Something pressed into my back and pushed me forward. Grass tickled the bottom of my paws. Scents of earth, wind, trees, flowers, muddy sour wisps, soft sweetness, and sharp fragments made me inhale twice. A gust of wind blew my eyes wide open, and I saw the blue sky and brown trees and their shiny green tips. The air buzzed, and the trees trembled, and I heard the breathing and heartbeats of Ma and White-Ears and the others.

I looked up, and Ma was smiling, and her mouth was open, and her tongue dangled. She nuzzled me. Her body was vibrating with energy, and it was contagious, and I smiled too.

"The forest is alive. You are alive. Do not be afraid. You are here, and nothing will hurt you," Ma sang. She backed up, and we took a step towards her, and the safe place receded behind us. The world was bright and beautiful, and I knew that we were going to be okay. Ma took another step, and I leapt forward, straight into her outstretched paw.

Someone stood behind her. I flinched, fell to my side, and closed my eyes as I whimpered. "I'm here," Pa said. I felt his cold nose against the top of my head. His scent was familiar. I opened my eyes and saw him, a great white wolf behind Ma's slim grey figure. Behind Pa stood a big white wolf with a bright yellow mane and a pair of scruffy, patchy paws. He called me little brother and smiled a great big open-mouthed grin.

I took in their scents. It was safe. I was still in the safe place. The safe place had simply gotten bigger.

They danced all around us, yipping and yelling, inviting us to join. I felt my paws tap against the soft, spongy earth, and soon enough, I was running in circles. I tackled White-Ears and pushed her to the ground. She growled and pushed me off, and she chased me until we both climbed up Ma's huge paws.

The adults gathered in a circle and Pa gently grabbed us by the neck and pulled us off Ma's soft, warm fur. Together, Ma and Pa and Scruff-Paw and White-Ears and I stood on the ground of the safe place, and we sang our songs as a family.

The days were long, and they became hotter every day. The adults napped on the leafy ground, sometimes under a tree, sometimes in the hot sun. Their ears twitched as they slept. They didn't seem to mind the heat.

When the adults left in the afternoon, I adventured around the safe place. White-Ears was too scared to take more than a few steps, but I didn't need her. I went by myself, but without White-Ears, the world seemed a lot bigger.

I went as far as the stump before the trees started to close in. I felt small, and I didn't want to keep going without White-Ears. I brought back a bitter, piney branch for her to smell. She sniffed it, far away at first, then closer and closer until her shiny nose was pressed against the bark. Her face slowly lit up. We ran around each other, then around a tree, round and round until I fell over. I bounced off the forest floor and rolled around the leaves and rubbed myself against the dirt. When I got up to shake myself, I saw movement and in the corner of my eye.

White-Ears froze and leaned her head forward with her ears perfectly straight. My eyes darted around, and I sniffed the air. Hints of fur wafted into my nose as the ground rustled, and I leapt towards it. I jumped at the same time as White-Ears, and we crashed into each other, stumbling. The tiny, brown rodent scurried away between bushes until it scaled a thick tree trunk. I charged at it, but it just climbed higher.

We circled around the safe place, from the stump to the big rock to the huge oak tree to the south. There, I sat down on a mound of dirt and stared at the shimmering lake in the distance.

"I'm going to go there," I said, pointing with my snout.

"I'll come with you," White-Ears said. She smiled, and her tongue dangled from her mouth.

"No, you won't," I said. "You're too scared to explore."

"Please?" she whined.

I shook my head and turned around and ran back to the safe place, but the sound of her pawprints followed closely. "Please please please?" she said, and she wouldn't stop bugging until I relented.

Ma brought us different types of meat, and some of them tasted sharp, others sweet and mellow. I licked the corners of Ma's mouth until she heaved, and the scent of meat overwhelmed my nose. Chunks of bright red meat came out of her mouth, and I pounced on it, and it was delicious.

White-Ears was a slow eater, so I took her meat. But only sometimes, and only when Ma wasn't looking.

☁

"Come, my children," Ma said. She nudged us away from the safe place with her soft, cold nose. I leapt off the dirt and onto the grass, step stepping all the way out to the old oak tree, and just as I was about to take off running, she told me to stop and wait.

I turned around. Ma walked slowly, and White-Ears hid under her belly. Ma nuzzled her and whispered to her, and they shuffled up to the tree together. I jumped on Ma's legs and rubbed myself all over the wet, sticky clumps of fur. She smelled like meat.

"Where are we going?" I said.

"Follow me closely," Ma said. "We saved the best meat for you." She bent down and nudged White-Ears, who whined loudly. "Shhh, it's okay."

White-Ears looked at me, and then up at Ma, and nodded. "Adventure," she said. I stuck my tongue out at her and licked her face.

Ma stepped past the old tree first. Her paws squished against the mossy earth, and it went plop, plop to the same beat as her tail. The black tip of Ma's tail swished in front of me, and I followed it, feeling the bounce in my steps.

I heard White-Ears stop, so I turned around and saw her staring at the sky. The tips of the trees rustled in the wind. A branch crackled, and a black bird flew from it, squawking loudly.

"They're good animals," Ma said.

"Have you eaten them?"

"No, ravens are not for eating," Ma said. Her eyes followed the path of the raven as it flew west. "They lead you to the food."

We walked along the moist and soft ground, and all along the trees, it smelled like family. Ma took us southwest, under bushes and over fallen trees. When the sun was covered by a thin layer of clouds, we took a break near a patch of water, then kept going.

Meat wafted into my nose, and I tilted my head up to get a better sniff. "We're here," Ma said. She sang, and we joined her, and two low voices answered our songs. Ma nudged us to go to Pa and Scruff-Paw, so I leapt into action. Ears folded back and wind brushing against my whiskers, I ran as hard as I could. I was faster than White-Ears.

The scent of meat and family became stronger with each step until I crashed through a thick bush and straight into the open chest of the carcass. There was bright, sticky blood all over the forest floor and all over my fur. I reached into the belly and pulled out a chunk of meat, and I ate it whole, feeling the tender strands pop in my mouth, mashing against my teeth before sliding down my throat. Meat was sweeter when it was fresh.

White-Ears squeezed herself in beside me and lunged at the same piece of meat I was chewing on. But it was mine! I got here first, and I wasn't done, so I bit her on the neck. I didn't bite very hard, but she screamed and stumbled.

Ma growled, and I whimpered. I told White-Ears I was sorry and that I wouldn't hurt her again. She said, "Okay," and we

7

kept eating.

☁

When the sun was low, the sky darkened and cracked and screamed. Ma hurried us back to the safe place and stayed with us. We hid in the depths of the safe place, and Ma stuck her head in and blocked the rain from coming in. It was dark and comfortable. She spent the evening telling us stories about the ocean and the fish. For the whole night, lightning flashed and the smell of rain was everywhere, but I wasn't scared, not even a little bit.

☁

"Lake?" I nudged White-Ears. Her fur was uncomfortably warm from the sun.

We left for the lake and stuck to the base of the trees, where it was cooler. As we walked south, the trees became more sparse, and eventually, the sun started shining through. I slowed down, and so did White-Ears.

"It's too hot," I said, "and the lake is very far away, and it'll be dark by the time we get back."

"I don't mind the dark," she said.

"You will," I said. "It will be dark and scary."

I found a tree with a thick knot at the base and laid down in its shadow, nestling myself in the shade and putting my head on the ground. She laid down beside me, and we napped until Ma's song echoed between the trees. It was dark then, and we started heading back to the safe place. Her eyes glowed in the dark. She pulled on my tail as we walked.

"I'm not scared," White-Ears said. She was right, and it wasn't so scary. The dark wasn't so dark, and with the moonlight, I could see almost as far as I could during the day.

I swung my tail to detach her jaws and turned around to face her. "I'll race you," I said. And before she said anything, I bolted away. It felt good to run at night. I loved the cool air against my face and the sound of White-Ears struggling to keep up behind me.

This time we ran all the way to the lake, far past the great big stump, through the wet sticky marsh, and then a great windy field filled with white flowers. The lake sparkled in the sunlight and the air buzzed with bugs, up and down and all around me, and everything smelled like freshwater.

The surrounding shore was full of large rocks that made my paws hurt, so we walked slowly, feeling the crunch of rocks under our paws, careful to avoid the sharper stones until we got to the pebbled sand near the water. Cold, clear water lapped the sand, pushing up tiny bubbles and receding, leaving a shadow that slowly disappeared before the next wave.

The sun was directly above us, and I was overheating. I bent over to drink, and as I did, White-Ears jumped on me and pushed me into the water—splash!—cold water rushed in my face.

"Hey!" I growled. She laughed with an open-mouthed grin, so I got out of the water, shook myself dry, and chased her, feeling the burn in my chest with each step. And with each turn, I closed the gap until I was right behind her. Her tail flicked in my face as she turned, and patches of grey and white fur brushed against my whiskers. I opened my mouth and grabbed White-Ears by the tail, and we tumbled in the dirt together.

We napped in the shadow of a boulder. I fell asleep to the sound of water splashing up against the shore. This was a different kind of safe place. It only smelled faintly of family, but it was fun, and it was mine.

In the afternoon, when clouds came to cover the sun, we played a game of tag. White-Ears was slower, and I came close to catching her, and as she slowed down at the eastern edge of the shore, I lunged for her. She jumped into the water and swam away. I jumped in, and I snapped at her tail, flopping in the water, but I didn't have enough strength to actually grab on.

White-Ears was fast and agile in the water. She darted forward, nose first, parting the waves as she went. I followed behind. I could feel the force of her kicks, but I wasn't about to give up. I lifted my head out of the water and kicked harder. I was going to win this round, even if I had to chase her to the other end of the lake.

White-Ears turned and disappeared beneath the surface, so I dived after her. The water rushed into my ears and my face and all around my mouth. I opened my mouth and the water flooded in. I tried to breathe, but bubbles came out of my mouth. I thrashed. Water surrounded me, and it was dizzying, so I opened my eyes. It stung, but I could see the cavernous depth of the lake receding into the blackness. With all the strength I could find, I kicked out my back legs and pushed myself to the surface.

White-Ears stood on a large rock not far away, looking down at me with her tail held high. "Loser," she said.

I snapped my teeth at her and swam to the boulder. The bottom ledge was green and slippery, but my claws soon caught a grip, and I pulled myself onto the ledge. I leapt on the rock, feeling my wet spongy paws against the hot and sundried surface until I caught up to White-Ears. I stopped at the tip of the rock, and I bit her nose and told her I caught her and that she was the loser. She laughed and laid down on the rock, and I shook myself dry and did the same.

"Do you see that?" she said.

"See what?"

"In the water. Look."

I looked and saw only bright ripples of light against a dark blue basin. "You're stupid," White-Ears said, "look over there." She had pointed with her snout, and I followed her line of sight. There, on the shaded side of the rock and buried in the blue water, were silhouettes of fish. They were still and then they moved. I lifted my head to smell the fish, but they had no smell—or at least they were no different from the smell of the lake.

I stood up and jumped down to the lower ledge. As I landed, I stumbled and slipped on the surface. My claws cracked a piece of rock, which flew and splashed in the water. The black shadows darted away. I balanced myself and stood and watched motionlessly. Slowly, one at a time, they swam back and became perfectly still again.

"I want them," I barked as I turned my head towards White-Ears.

"Go get them, then."

I looked down at the shapes in the water. They glimmered. I couldn't take my eyes off them. The sounds of the air and the buzzing of the lake disappeared, and all there was was the fish in the water and their tiny movements. They had tails and mouths and beady little eyes, and I wanted them more than I wanted anything else.

One shape started to move. I took my aim, lowered my body until it was almost flat against the ledge, and leapt. I came into the water with a thundering splash, and there was water everywhere, against my fur, in my face and ears and mouth. My eyes snapped open, and I saw the fish there, just a few paws below me. I curled my body down and kicked with my legs and opened my jaw and felt the smooth, slimy shell against my teeth, and I bit down.

It was strong, wiggling in my mouth, thrashing, its powerful tail kicking whirls in the water and pushing water up my nose. I bit harder, feeling my teeth sink into the cold, throbbing flesh. Blood burst into the water, and the thrashing lightened. I shook my head in the water, feeling the lack of air. Kicking. Pushing water aside, pulling with my paws. The moment I burst from the water, there was an explosion of scents. The fish smelled like old earth and cold blood and the underside of meat on the wet ground.

I swam back to the boulder and dug my claws against the rock and pulled up. Above me, claws clicked against rock as White-Ears jumped up and down. I leapt up the first ledge to a face full of sunlight with the fish still flopping in my mouth. Her tail went wild. I climbed the boulder until I found White-Ears. She stood eagerly waiting, so I set it down. The fish flopped weakly, and White-Ears put her paw on it and sniffed it.

Then she bit its head off.

Chapter 2

Ma woke us up and told us to follow her. It was dim. Dewdrops covered my snout, and a blanket of tiredness hugged my body, but I got up and followed. The air was fresh and wet and had a coldness that made me shiver. Ma trotted with her head down, and I did the same, and every time I brushed against a tree, I felt the wetness gather on my fur. White-Ears stayed behind me, as she usually did.

Ma took us north, up, and away from the lake. We passed through the forest to the sounds of birds waking up. Then, when the sun was bright again, we huddled behind a dense brush near the treeline of a vast meadow that stretched all the way from the forest to the grey mountain peaks.

Deep in the bushes, I heard a rustle and I growled at it.

"Shush," Ma said. "I'm teaching you how to hunt. There is a herd of elk on the other side of the meadow." And as she said it, Pa and Scruff-Paw came out of the leaves. The two big white wolves stood side-by-side and stared into the distance intensely. Pa turned around. "Watch us and follow what we do," he said.

Scruff-Paw lifted his head and sniffed the air, so I did the same. The air smelled of wildflowers and family, but there was a distinct scent that I hadn't noticed. I turned to Ma, and she nodded without saying anything. The elk smelled strong, like rotting grass and poop. My ears perked up and I jumped beside Scruff-Paw and nuzzled him on the cheek.

Then we took off. Pa first, and Scruff-Paw followed on his left side, and Ma on his right. We jogged at first, and then as the scent became stronger, the adults started fanning out. I followed Scruff-Paw down the lower slope of the meadow. Ma and White-Ears took to higher ground. Pa ran down the center.

The morning mountain wind brushed against my face and chilled my ears. I folded them back and tried to focus on the hunt. With each step, I could feel my heartbeat get faster, and soon I was gulping air. I was flying. Gliding over the patchy grasses behind Scruff-Paw.

"We attack from top and bottom," Scruff-Paw breathed, turning around to glance at me. He turned sharply, and I did the same. I could feel the ground shift beneath me, and I gasped. My claws dug into the soft ground and I swung my tail around and around until I found my balance again.

Scruff-Paw dashed for a ridge, and I followed.

When I came over the top of the ridge, the elk had already started running. Scattering. Like a cloud of mosquitoes in the distance. They were huge, brown, smelly, and there were too many to count. We paused for a moment, and I saw them moving as one massive herd. I didn't know which one to go after, but Pa was focused on a single animal near the back of the herd, so Scruff-Paw and I raced after it, panting and heaving.

On top of the hill, Ma's slender figure burst out of the trees, and White-Ears followed. "Hurry," Ma breathed as she ran, "focus on one and ignore the others."

Focus on one. There was a single elk that limped as it ran. It was patchy and brown and smelled sour. Pa gained on it, and Scruff-Paw and I weren't far behind. I pushed my paws as hard as I could, but the adults were faster.

Twenty wolf-lengths.

Pa faked a leap in our direction, startling the elk and forcing the animal up the slope. The rest of the herd turned and ran down the hill but we ignored them. Scruff-Paw kept running forward. Ten. It tried to turn away from us, but Pa blocked the other side. It was running straight uphill now. Away from its herd. Slower.

In the distance, Ma barked low and loud. This sent the animal tumbling towards us. Pa was no more than a wolf-length from the elk now, and Scruff-Paw was gaining fast on the side. Suddenly, a burst of speed from Scruff-Paw left me behind in the dirt. Grass flew in all directions, and I saw from a distance that Pa had leapt onto the back of the elk.

He bit and clung on. The scent of blood, panic, and meat punctured the air, and I could almost taste it. Then Scruff-Paw caught up, and then Ma, and then White-Ears and myself. Scruff-Paw and Ma leapt onto the animal and bit down on its neck and belly. It thrashed and fell into the dirt and wildflowers. I jumped beside the animal and bit down on its leg. Its muscles twitched, and hot blood spurted into my mouth.

We ate as a family. I had pieces of the innards and the fat between the ribs, and it was very good. When I was done and full, I laid down beside the carcass and closed my eyes. With the warmth of the sun on my face and back, the heaviness of sleep pulled me into the ground.

A shadow flashed across, and I opened my eyes to see Ma

standing over me with her slender, grey chest and deep golden eyes.

"Eat more. You need to grow big and strong," Ma said. She reached down and kissed the top of my head.

"But we are strong," I said, grinning, "or, at least, I am strong." White-Ears was lying down and within range of my legs. I kicked her. She snarled at me.

"You must be stronger," Ma said, ignoring us.

"Why?" White-Ears asked.

"Because winter will be here soon," Ma said. She turned to the dark blue sky and smelled the air, so I did the same. "It's colder now, and winter will be here soon."

The air was light, and there was dew on my nose, and my breath made tiny puffs of clouds. It took longer for me to warm up. But the day was still warm, and by the time the sun was high in the sky, the whole forest had come to life again, and our family spent the morning sunbathing. I loved the sun. The grey patches down my back soaked up the sunshine. It was warm and cozy, and I was comfortable from nose to tail.

The daily thunderstorms had stopped, and without the storms, the elk stopped sheltering in the dense forest. They went up the slopes, and we followed them. We had to leave the lake behind, but it was fine because I had my family, and family was more important than fish.

When the wind was calm, and the skies were grey, we roamed the meadows under the mountain looking for animals to kill and eat. Ma and Pa and Scruff-Paw ran at the front, and White-Ears and I followed closely behind. We stuck to the treeline, and we walked, and we waited.

The further we went, the less the ground smelled like family. After the scent of family faded away, I found a thick tree with smooth sections of bark. It stank like danger, but I was curious, so I moved closer until I could see the deep grooves running lengthwise down the tree trunk. It was murky, pungent, rotten like the marsh. Old, yet it made my fur puff up.

I ran back to Ma. "I found something!" I said. "Come with me. You should smell it."

She trotted behind me as I raced along the forest floor. I filled my lungs with air and ran fast because the rest of the family was still looking for elk, and I didn't want to miss out on an exciting hunt. Branches and leaves crackled beneath my paws, and Ma said, "slow down," but I didn't. When I got to the tree, I made a wide circle around it and sat down, facing the semi-detached strip of bark on the ground.

"Smell it!" I said. "It's weird."

Ma cracked a half-smile and came up and sniffed the tree. I jumped to her and sniffed the tree as well. She lowered her head to look at me and spoke softly, "Do you know what this is?"

"No." My tail flickered.

"It's a bear. They eat the bark and scratch themselves."

"Will the bear hurt us?"

Ma laughed. "No, they're already asleep by now," she said. "We're safe."

She leaned and touched my nose. I closed my eyes and whined and felt her warmth all over my head and neck.

"How about this?" she said, standing tall again, "I'll make the scent go away."

I said, "okay," and I tilted my head to look at her. Ma walked past the tree and back, smelling the surface of the bark until she stopped, turned around, and marked the tree with her scent.

We jogged back to the family. We looked all day, but there was no elk.

Pa took White-Ears and me up to the place where rock met grass. It was a long hike through winding trails, doubling back and forth along the steep slope of the mountain, across the meadow, and up some more. We started in the morning when the sun peeked through the bright clouds, and by the time we got past the tip of the meadow, the sun was already receding into the mountains.

We stood on the big ledge and looked towards the southwest, where the sun hovered behind the clouds. A vast swath of forest stretched towards the sun, and beyond that, far away towards the west, there were mountains like wolf's ears, strutting out of the earth, each capped with a brilliant white peak.

I turned to White-Ears. "Those look like you," I said. A stream of fog came from my mouth and lingered in the cool mountain air.

She pulled away and tilted her head. "How so?"

"The very top where the mountain meets the sky is white, like your ears."

She said nothing for a moment, then she grinned and nudged me, and I had to jump aside to avoid falling down the cliff.

Pa started walking again, straight up the side of the mountain, so we followed. Sharp rocks shuffled under my paws with each step as I followed behind White-Ears. The air was sparse. Sparse and crisp and completely silent. When the sky was dim and many shades of purple, Pa stopped at a large flat patch of rock.

"Smell the air," he said.

"I don't smell anything," I said. I didn't take a whiff because I wanted to keep looking at the valley below. The hills, glowing orange, crested and fell, floated between glimmering mountaintops. I couldn't take my eyes off it, but Pa was insistent. A low growl came from his throat. "Pay attention. This is important," he said.

I snapped my head back, closed my eyes, and took a big whiff. There were many scents, at least three different wildflowers, the faint scent of elk poop, the strong scent of family, the distant freshness of the lake, and something else, a musky something else that reminded me of wet dirt.

"I smell it!" White-Ears said. Her ears perked up, and she jumped towards Pa.

"That is the scent of a rodent burrow," Pa said. "Remember it. You will need it."

I swung my head up and down and tried to isolate the scent. It was faint and earthy and slightly sour. I locked onto it and followed it until my nose touched the ground. There was a hole in front of me, hidden near the edge of the cliff. There was something in here! I stretched my claws and started digging with both paws.

"Don't do that," Pa said and batted my paws away from the hole. "You'll never dig them out."

I stopped and folded my ears back and whined.

"You wait downwind until they come out, then you jump on them. I'll show you," he said. He moved north of the burrow and sat down, facing away from the cliff. We sat behind him and waited as the light of the sun slowly dimmed until it was a glimmer of light behind the mountains. The air was chilly and quiet. I snuggled against White-Ears, but Pa sat attentively with his ears twitching. He didn't move, and he didn't make a single sound.

The ground beneath us rustled, and Pa stood up silently. His eyes glowed in the dark as he waited, and from the hole in the ground, a tiny fuzzy rodent climbed out. The creature stuck its neck out and shrunk back in and out again. Its head darted around. I tilted my head to hear better, and I picked up the scratching of tiny claws on rock. Finally, the rodent climbed out, and its nose twitched, and its body wiggled along the ground.

Pa took aim and leapt into the air, soaring through the cold mist and landing forcefully. Crack! He looked at us and grinned with his mouth open and his tongue hanging out, and for a moment, with the last shimmer of light reflecting off his white fur, he was the brightest object on the mountain.

"That's how you do it. You wait until they come out, and then you jump on them to stun them. Do you understand?" he said. White-Ears and I nodded.

Pa lifted his paws to show us where he landed. Under his claws, the creature was splayed out against the rock, bloodied and still twitching. He bit down and tore the rodent in half. It wasn't much to eat, but we got a chunk each. I ate mine whole, in one bite, bones and all.

Chapter 3

The air was warm and dense, and the clouds hung lower than the tip of the mountain. Grey bands rolled across the sky and left wispy trails one after another. "Snow is coming," Ma said while sniffing the air, then she leapt towards me and nuzzled me with her snout.

Ma, Pa, and Scruff-Paw ran around and played with each other. There was energy in the air, so we joined them, and we bolted behind a patch of trees and chased each other. Later, the winds calmed down, so we moved along the tree line searching for elk, but we found nothing. The newest scent of elk was many days old. So was the deer. So were the hares.

The family split up towards the end of the day, with Ma going east, Pa going up the mountain, and Scruff-Paw going west. They each promised to bring back whatever they could find: berries, rodents, dead and decaying things. I wanted to join, but Ma insisted that we stay put near the tree line, "In case the snow comes with a vengeance."

I tilted my head and let my tongue dangle. I didn't know what she meant, and it didn't matter. Snow sounded exciting.

White-Ears and I played a game around the largest tree we could find, where we took turns chasing each other around the tree until I bit her tail or she bit mine. Then the roles reversed, and we did it again and again until White-Ears was tired.

The adults returned with nothing. We slept together in a pile that night, hungry and huddled together for warmth. When I woke up, it was still dark, and the family was still asleep. The air had taken on a sharp, almost painful chill, and there was snow all over me, on top, on all the sides, inside everywhere my fur parted. I stood up and shook myself, but it wasn't long before the snow covered my back again. I walked over to White-Ears and licked the snow off of her head and laid beside her in the snow and fell asleep.

The next morning was bone-chillingly cold. White-Ears and I woke up shivering. The entire family snuggled and held onto each other for warmth. Everyone was covered in snow. The snow had muted the smells of the forest, and it was dead silent, so all I smelled and heard was family. Despite the grumbling of my belly and the jabbing cold at my toe tips, it was a good, comfortable, and safe morning.

"It won't be so cold soon," Ma said.

"Winter will be over?"

"No," Ma grinned at me, "but you will grow a thick coat to keep yourself warm and happy."

"And me too?" White-Ears said, tail twitching.

"Of course."

When the snow stopped falling and the sun peeked through the dense grey clouds, Pa and Scruff-Paw stood up and walked together up the slope towards the meadow. Ma stayed with us in case we got cold. She taught us how to eat snow for water, and we giggled as the soft, cold flakes turned into water in our mouths. It was sweet, almost smoky, and it tasted very different from the water of the creek or the lake.

Pa sang for the family and told us he found a deer trail. Ma got up and followed his voice south, and I followed Ma, and White-Ears followed me. I hadn't eaten a real meal for many days, and my stomach was just gnawing at me, constantly and non-stop. We meandered down the meadow and through the forest until we were at the lake again, where a shining flat surface of ice replaced the cold blue water. It stretched for as far ahead as I could see, and from one peak to the other, and where the ice met the snowy shore, jagged shards stuck out from the snow and rock.

I tagged behind Ma, and we circled the shore of the lake. Snow squeaked under my paws. It was dry and cold, and I liked it. The sun, low to the south, peeked between two bands of clouds, and a wave of warmth washed over my back. The snow crinkled all around me. Step, squeak, crinkle. Step again.

"I'm hungry," White-Ears said.

"Shhh, don't fret," Ma said without turning around. "I'll find you something to eat."

White-Ears turned to smile at me. "Just me," she whispered, "and not you."

I snapped my teeth at her, and the sound echoed in the air. It was an interesting sound, so I did it again, closing my eyes to hear the ping between trees. It faded slowly.

Pa sang for the family again, so we ran back to the east shore and converged on him. I ran up to Pa and Scruff-Paw and greeted them. Together, we went for another loop, this time through the forests around the lake. I walked in a zig-zag, trying to find the scent again, but there was nothing. We slowed down and then stopped to rest near a cluster of three pines. Pa lifted his leg and marked the middle tree.

Scruff-Paw then left by himself, heading for the lake. I looked at White-Ears, and she nodded, and we followed him. I tugged on his white tail, and he shook me off, so I walked beside him. At the lake, Scruff-Paw carefully stepped onto the ice towards the grey and white rock that jutted out from the ice. My claws clacked against the solid ice. I took a big step, lost my grip, and slipped, falling hard on my shoulder. A burst of pain surged through me, but it wasn't so bad. I stood up, shook the snow off, and told myself to dig in with my claws with each step.

I stood for a moment on the patch of lake where I caught my first fish. It was cold and slippery, and the surface was brilliantly white against the sun. If there were fish down there, they would have frozen to death. I tried digging, but my claws couldn't even dent the thick ice. White-Ears joined me, and we scratched the ice together, but it still wasn't enough.

Ma's song called us to the shore. We both answered with our own songs, and I took off running, and White-Ears came up fast behind me. We raced on the slippery ice, and I slid headfirst into the rocky shore with a thud. There were rocks in my fur. White-Ears nibbled on my head as we walked towards Ma's song. Then, as we weaved through the trees, I caught Ma's scent and followed it to a clearing in the forest.

This was the safe place, and around it was the stump and the great big tree and the deer bones that had since been bleached dry. This was where we grew up, many days ago when I was still small, and the world was still scary. This was a good place. I tilted my head back and sang how I felt. White-Ears joined me, and soon the whole forest echoed the songs of the family.

I ran around the old perimeter, from the great big tree to the stump and back. It wasn't as long of a trip as I remembered, so I did it again, and once again just for fun.

The faint scent of meat caught my nose, and I followed it until, under an overturned tree, there was a chunk of bone. I picked it up and examined it with my teeth and tongue. There was still some flavour, so I brought it back to the clearing, laid it on the ground, and started gnawing on it. White-Ears came over and nuzzled my neck. I growled at her, and she hissed back, but she didn't leave, so I picked up my piece of bone and went to the other side of the stump where I could chew in peace.

The sun ducked behind the thickening clouds, and all around us, the bare trees rustled and shook. In the distance, the wind bellowed. "Storm's coming," Ma said. "Huddle together." She pushed us under the leaning tree and said, "We'll be warm here." She motioned for us to stay put, and White-Ears curled into a ball and closed her eyes.

"What about the rest of the family?" I asked.

"We'll come join you soon," she said.

The snow came down in sheets and the wind howled around us. It swirled, twisting in the air, billowing. Everything was white. The family didn't join us under the tree, but they were safe and close. I smelled and heard them. Close was good enough. I closed my eyes and fell asleep, and I dreamt of frozen fish.

White-Ears invented a new game. We took turns hiding the piece of bone I found. The bone was white and so was the snow, and it smelled like nothing, which made it hard to find, which made it a fun game. White-Ears hid it in the crack behind the stump the first round. It took me the whole morning to check every crevice and overturned log and pile of snow before I found it. I took it to her triumphantly and gloated with my tail held high until she wrestled me to the ground. There was snow everywhere, but I wasn't cold anymore.

When it was my turn, I rolled around in the dirtiest snow pile I could find until I no longer smelled myself. Then I took the bone and ran into the forest, and I threw it into the prickly bushes. White-Ears traced the ground, tail high and nose twitching, and she found it quickly.

"I followed your big fat paw prints," she said with the bone in her mouth. She dropped it in front of me and bent down and wagged her tail. I growled. She picked it up and ran away, yelling, "I win." I closed my eyes while she hid the bone, then I got up and let my nose do its job. It wasn't long before I found it wedged in between two gnarly, crisscrossing pine trees, but it took a few tries before I could dislodge it. White-Ears wasn't very good at hiding either.

Then it was my turn to hide, and I was determined to win this game. I took the bone in my mouth and ran around the clearing. I thought about burying it under a huge pile of snow, but it would have been too obvious. A hole was too hard to dig with the ground mostly frozen, but then I remembered there was a hole that was already dug, so I took the bone and ran for the center of the clearing where the den was.

I stuck my nose in the hole and wiggled my way into the center. It was much smaller than I remembered, and it smelled different too. The familiar feelings were gone, and all that remained was the smell of moist dirt. I took the bone to the very end and wedged it against the soft back wall. I climbed out of the hole and licked the dirt off of my fur, moving my tongue between my toe tips until it tasted like my own saliva. I sat at the entrance and looked at nothing in particular and smiled.

White-Ears came by not long after.

"I hid it," I said, laying down with my head in front of the entrance, looking up but not moving. Her tail started wagging the moment I said it.

White-Ears went off prancing in the clearing. She over-turned every rock and log. She dug through snow piles, and she ran to and from the big trees, clawing and pawing at patches of ground. I laid in front of my hiding spot and watched as White-Ears tired herself out. First, she stopped at each tree. Then, once every wolf-length, and finally, she trotted back and forth aimlessly with her nose brushing against the snow.

She came back with her ears drooped, and she laid down beside me and buried her snout in my neck.

"I'm tired," she said.

"I win."

Chapter 4

The snow glowed and glistened from the sliver of moonlight coming from the horizon, and if I looked closely enough, the snowy hills began to undulate. I stared at the faint stars glittering behind the patchy clouds for a bit, then I closed my eyes, snuggled against Ma, and tried to fall back asleep. Her breath was steady, and she smelled warm.

A gust of wind blew, and I caught a familiar scent that made me twitch with excitement. I jumped up with my head held high. Beside me, White-Ears shuffled against the snow. The smell of meat was faint, so I scanned the air again and smelled it coming from the direction of the lake. It was close, so I jumped against White-Ears and kicked her on the side, not wanting to take my nose off the scent.

"Wake up!" I whispered.

"What? What's going on?" She leapt up, fully alert.

"Smell that," I said.

She scanned the air, and her face lit up, smiling vibrantly. "Should we wake the family?"

I looked around and saw Ma sleeping. A dusting of snow covered her head, and it looked like shiny white specks against her dark fur. I didn't know where the Pa and Scruff-Paw were. "Let them sleep," I said, "we'll bring it back."

We took off in the direction of the smell of meat. It was sharp and tinged with blood and it made the silent night air come to life. We weaved through the trees and vaulted over logs, listening to the snow and branches crunch under our paws. At first, I wasn't paying attention to the surroundings because all I wanted was a chunk of that meat, but when we got to the frozen marsh by the lake, I noticed that the smell was more complex, and there were familiar tones in there, with hints of family. White-Ears ran ahead of me. She stopped beside the shoreline where the rocks met the ice, so I stopped too.

The smell was stronger now, and it permeated everything in the cold air.

"Where is it coming from?" White-Ears said.

"Deeper," I said. I didn't know, but it seemed to be coming from the lake.

We stepped on the ice and took small steps, careful not to slip and fall. White-Ears kept her head down and focused on the smell. Her tail twitched erratically. Around us was a white blanket that glowed in the moonlight, a vast stretch of perfectly flat ice, from one mountain to another. We walked past our fishing boulder, and the smell got stronger still. A part of me wanted to sing my song to call the family, but in the end, I didn't, so I just followed White-Ears. She wasn't in the singing mood either.

Something moved along the north shore, and we both stopped. It was quiet, and the smell of meat was everywhere. A shadow dashed across. Then, another. A low growl! It echoed through the valley like the crack of thunder. Two white wolves were attacking each other. I instinctively lowered my body and folded my ears. White-Ears lowered her tail, and we hid behind the trees and watched the two shapes dashing back and forth, exchanging snarls.

I smelled the air, and it smelled of family, but also meat. The smell of meat was everywhere. I turned to White-Ears and nodded, and we trotted towards whatever was going on. We were both very hungry, and the meat wasn't very far away. It was fifty wolf-lengths at most. We stopped near the shore as the moon was revealed from behind the clouds. The moonlight bathed the lake and we saw Pa and Scruff-Paw on the shore behind the first tree. The growls were loud, and they moved fast.

White-Ears whimpered. "I don't understand," she said. I nuzzled her softly.

I opened my mouth and barked, but the fighting wolves ignored me, so I turned back to White-Ears. "There's food here," I said. I took a few steps closer and heard White-Ears follow behind me. Sure, there's some kind of fight going on, but the food was undeniable, and I wanted it. I looped around a rock and hid and watched the exchange between Pa and Scruff-Paw. About ten wolf-lengths away, there was some kind of small carcass. I lowered my head and took quiet steps. One. Two. One step at a time. White-Ears didn't follow me.

In the distance, there was the rapid fluttering of paws. I turned around and saw it was Ma. She came out of nowhere. She snarled at the fighting duo and leapt for the meat on the ground, snatching it in her jaws and running towards us. White-Ears whimpered loudly, and I stared at Ma with my mouth open, expressionless.

"Follow, quickly," Ma hissed, running past us, so we followed her.

We ran at top speed until we got across the lake onto the south shore. Ma took a few breaths, then dropped the meat on the frozen ground and nudged it towards us. "Eat," she said.

It was a rabbit of some sort. It smelled fresh. The innards had already been eaten, and there wasn't much other than the legs, ribs, and skin. White-Ears and I leaned in and tore into the carcass at the same time. The meat and skin and bones ripped and crunched and cold chunks of blood splattered against my snout. I savoured each crunch of the cold meat, the feeling of it melting in my throat, and the sweet smell of blood.

When we finished, Ma hurried White-Ears and me back to the clearing, and the two of us slept inside the safe place that night. It was damp and cold, and I could not stop myself from trembling. I took the piece of bone I buried and nudged it in front of White-Ears, but she wasn't interested.

⌣

In a few days' time, the adults began playing among themselves again. White-Ears and I played the bone game every day until she lost the bone in a snowstorm, so we switched to a rock, but it was too hard on my teeth, so we gave up.

⌣

It was a bright night. The sky was finally clear, and the air was light, and everything was quiet except for the breathing of my family. White-Ears still slept in the middle, in the pocket of warmth between Ma, Pa, and Scruff-Paw, but I didn't want to wake the family, so I laid down on the edge of the pile.

Time passed. I turned restlessly but I could not fall asleep.

I yawned and stood up, tiptoeing away from Ma before leaning down to stretch. I exhaled, and my breath billowed in front of me. Dissipating. I walked towards the lake, past the silent forest, and past the frozen marsh until I came across the shore. I jumped over the pile of snow and rock and felt my claws slip against the perfectly smooth ice.

A tickle of wind brushed against my face, and the calm moon glimmered overhead. I walked down the ice aimlessly, feeling my paws against the unforgiving surface. I stood in the middle of the lake, facing south, watching a cloud drift by. The air smelled different here, and it made my fur stand on its own. It got darker. The snow, the trees, even the mountaintops were all darker, and even though it unsettled me, I sat down anyway and stared into the rippling blackness until it faded away into the distant hills and everything blended together.

The moon flickered, and the wind blew, and a tremble crept down my back. I didn't want to be here anymore, so I turned quickly and ran, bolting down the ice as fast as I could. The shore grew from a dotted patch to a fully realized forest. Something was stuck out of the ice. I didn't notice it in time, and I tripped, and it sent me flying through the air. I landed on the cold, hard ice with a thud.

I shook my head and blinked rapidly until the pain faded away.

I approached it cautiously, taking small steps and sniffing the ground. It didn't smell like anything, yet it looked familiar even under the light dusting of snow. It was bigger and longer than my paws and stuck out of the ice at an angle, with a rounded flat top like that of a thin tree stump. I licked the snow off of it and watched my saliva soak into the ice. Hoof! It was a hoof, and that meant there was something edible attached to it, or at least I could chew on the hoof and get the taste of something other than snow and dried berries.

I bit down on the base of the hoof, just above the ice, and felt it crunch between my jaws. My tail was going wild, and my body shook, and I pulled on it some more. Then I tilted my head and sang as loudly as I could, and I didn't stop singing until my throat was dry.

Not long after, in the moonlit distance, a few bright dots zipped along the shore, getting bigger with each heartbeat. Pa was first, followed by Ma, Scruff-Paw, and White-Ears. As they got closer, I saw that their mouths were open with excitement. I wagged my tail in response and sang some more, and then I ran to greet the family.

"You have something?" White-Ears tackled me to the ice, and we slid together.

"It's meat," I said as I licked her face.

I took them to the frozen hoof. It stuck out of the ice motionlessly, and beside it was a tiny, hoof-shaped shadow on the white ice. "There," I pointed with my snout, "must be a whole elk down there."

Pa jumped on the hoof, bit it, and tried to pull it out, but it didn't budge. "This could feed the whole family. Nice job," Scruff-Paw said, nuzzling my face.

"We have to get it out first," Pa said.

"It will still be here in the morning," Ma said, "I'm tired, and the kids are tired."

We started digging early. I tried very hard, but the ice was nearly impossible for my claws. Digging made me tired, so I laid down on the ice and started to lick the base of the exposed hoof and leg. Then, in a flash of inspiration, I realized my teeth were better tools, so I chewed the ice instead. It was hard and crunchy and made me wince with every bite.

It didn't take long before my teeth were cold and raw. I needed a break from the pain, so decided to go for a quick walk from the east shore to the west. When I came back, everyone was trying to bite the ice, and it was working. The hole around the hoof slowly became bigger and bigger until the tip of the leg was exposed.

In the afternoon, Pa yanked on the leg with all his strength, and it loosened with a loud crack. The sound startled me, and I jumped from the ice and landed on my butt. It hurt, but it didn't matter. I ran towards Pa, and the whole family converged on him at the same time, and we greeted each other with licks.

Beside him, half of the carcass jutted from the ice. Pa was already gnawing on the base of the leg, and I heard the mashing of frozen flesh in his teeth. Ma leaned in and delicately tugged at the opposite end of the exposed, frozen animal. It barely moved at all. Pa half-snarled at her, and she hissed back. She leaned in further, and Pa didn't say anything, so the family huddled together and feasted on the chunk of frozen meat.

The sweet, tangy taste of meat flooded my senses as it melted with each bite. I ate as much as I could. It didn't matter to me that the meat was frozen solid. It didn't matter that I could only get small chunks. This was the first proper meal in many days, and nothing could have made me happier.

⌂

With my snout resting against the ice, I opened my eyes and saw the mountains towering straight up. The icy lake stretched on forever, and both shores were very far away. I didn't want to get up, so I stared straight down the length of the frozen lake until the warm light of the sun peeked over the mountains, but even then, barely a hint of sun filtered through the clouds and the tall peaks. Wind blew and snow swirled on the flat ice stretched until it became one with the sky. I blinked twice and shook my head, trying to clear up the haze, but it didn't help at all.

By the time White-Ears woke up, it had started snowing again. I heard her pawsteps shuffling and felt her warm and coarse fur beside me.

"Hey," I muttered, not bothering to lift my head.

"Hey yourself," she said.

I wiggled my butt, bouncing into her leg. White-Ears spoke a low growl from deep in her throat, but she still didn't move. Her belly grumbled.

"Feeling full?"

"A bit too much," she said, "the meat wasn't very fresh."

"Still better than nothing," I said. I paused for a moment before I whiplashed my body around and bit her nose. She yelped. I jumped back on the ice, sliding as I did so, and bowed with both my paws outstretched. White-Ears jumped up and shook the snow off her patchy grey fur and then ran towards me. I sprinted the other way, and with each step, I felt the ice skid under my claws.

I ran towards the thin forest under the towering mountain to the west. White-Ears trailed not far behind, and her pawsteps shook the ice. She had always been slower than me, but she was fast on the ice. I took a sharp turn and kicked up a cloud of snow and ice crystals with my hind legs. White-Ears slowed down but did not stop.

She caught up to me just as I felt the first rocks under my paws. I heard her whooshing through the air before I felt the wind knocked out of me. A great grey mass slammed into my back, and we tumbled on the ground, rolling on the thick snow. I must have taken four or five rolls because by the time we stopped, I had no idea which way was up.

But White-Ears did. She sat on top of me and took great joy in taking my entire snout in her mouth. I choked when I tried to growl, and it came out as a cough. She won this time.

White-Ears and I spent the morning near the den trying to find the bone. Then the snow returned, and as the sky lightened, the air started whistling. It took on on a distinctive sharpness as the day went on, and the smell made my fur stand on its end.

When we meandered back to the frozen carcass, I saw Pa tugging at the exposed bones. Then, with a loud bang, the rack of bones detached and flew down the ice, clacking and skidding. I came up to the carcass and saw the meat trapped under an impenetrable layer of clear ice. Pa circled it anxiously. I walked up to Pa to greet him, but he hissed at me, and I backed away. He left soon after, and I made White-Ears reach into the ice with her narrow snout, but there wasn't anything she could do.

I laid down, away from the hole in the ice, and watched the snowflakes drift past my nose.

A grey dot appeared over the ice, and it slowly grew until I could make out the white circles around Ma's eyes. Then a white dot. It was impossible to see who it was, but a gust of wind told me what I needed to know. Ma circled the pile of bones on the ice. Scruff-Paw came behind, walked around the carcass, and nuzzled Ma on her side, but she turned her head and snarled. Scruff-Paw backed away slowly and laid down beside the carcass. Ma did the same, except on the opposite end.

I walked up to Ma and laid down beside her. "What's wrong?" I whispered.

Ma shook her head and said, "Everything will be fine. Go find your sister." I breathed her scent and then stood up and shook the snow off. I walked over to Scruff-Paw, who grumbled and didn't acknowledge me.

I left them alone. Some of the leftover bones were clean and ice-cold and broken in many places. I took the largest bone I could find and went around the forested shore to find White-Ears. Her scent was fresh, and so were her pawprints, so it wasn't hard to find her. I saw her from far away. She was sitting and staring up at a tree near the marsh.

The bone in my mouth had a ball joint on the end. I was determined to whack White-Ears over the head with it.

I took a deep breath and carefully planted my right paw on the snow. It was deeper than I thought, and I stumbled. Her ears twitched, but she didn't turn around. The wind was blowing towards me, so she couldn't smell me. This was the perfect ambush. I stood up carefully and took another step and another. There was the slightest crunch of frozen old leaves with each step, but White-Ears took no notice.

When I felt like I had snuck close enough, I leapt into the air with the bone in my mouth, yelling my battle cry, whooshing through the trees. White-Ears turned around, her mouth opened, and her eyes wide. She started moving to the side. It was too late! I couldn't change directions. My eyes widened, and I watched as she dodged me. I slammed into the nearby tree, bone first. It sent a shock through my jaw, and I winced and dropped the bone.

I closed my eyes and shook the snow off of my back. White-Ears looked at me and then the bone on the ground. She chortled and then started laughing at me, rolling on the snow and laughing. I told her to stop, but she wouldn't, so I bared my teeth on her neck. But I didn't bite her. I headbutted her instead, and then we both sprawled out on the snow, staring at the grey clouds overhead.

I left the bone and started walking back to my family. I told White-Ears we were perfectly competent hunters, and the adults would need our help when we found another herd of elk. She shrugged and followed me.

On the ice, Ma and Pa were playing with each other. From a distance, I saw Pa jump on her and heard the sound of jaws clicking, barking, and yelling. I tilted my head back and sang a song. White-Ears joined in, but Ma and Pa ignored us. I kept going anyway. It felt good. After a few moments, I heard Scruff-Paw join from nearby. And then Ma finally joined the chorus, and Pa followed reluctantly. Our voices filled the valley and the lake, and it was a beautiful song of family and love. I sang until I got tired and then sang some more until White-Ears told me to shut up.

⌂

I snuggled beside White-Ears. It was still early in the night, but I was tired and hungry and there really wasn't anything to do but sleep. But I couldn't. Distant snarls filtered through the trees, and my ears perked up to listen. Pa's voice was faint but recognizable. I pushed White-Ears on her neck until she woke up. "Come on," I said. "Something is wrong."

We trotted towards the direction of the snarls. It was across the lake, across the vast frozen expanse, and with each step, it became louder. Scruff-Paw was snarling. Ma was barking, and Pa was angry, and I could feel his anger before I saw any of them.

I didn't want to get closer, so I sat and watched as the three shapes danced in the dark. I didn't know what to say to them. I rested my head on White-Ears, and we watched our family fight. They got closer and quieter, and I found the courage to say something, so I whispered, "Stop fighting, please."

The adults ignored me.

A surge of warmth washed over me, and suddenly I found my loud voice, and I yelled, "Stop it!" And there was nothing. "Stop it, stop it!" I said, "We're a family. Stop fighting!" And moments later, as quickly as it began, the growling stopped. Ma and Pa and Scruff-Paw scattered in different directions, and none of them even acknowledged me.

I told White-Ears everything was going to be fine. We walked back to the safe place together, and neither of us said anything. It was late. Exhausted and dizzy, I laid down on the snow and closed my eyes and went to sleep.

Chapter 5

In the morning, the air was unpleasant and smelled of anger and blood mixed with the sour odour of the grey snow. The sun beamed down on the clearing. This was the first time I had seen the sun in many days, but its rays were cold and carried the same smell as the snow. I snapped my head right to left. Ma and Pa were talking at the other end of the clearing near the stump. White-Ears was still asleep. I barked low and quietly to wake her up.

"What?" White-Ears woke up with her usual twitch.

"I don't know," I said, "do you smell that?"

White-Ears nodded and stood up, shaking the snow off herself. She walked towards Ma and Pa, and I followed. When I came closer, I saw that Pa had a bloody gash on his back leg just above the thigh. It didn't look too deep and the bleeding had already stopped and dried. I came up to him and tried to lick his wound, but he batted me away with a paw and a sharp growl.

"What happened?" I asked. Ma had sat down across from me. She looked tiny beside Pa's huge shoulders.

"Your brother left. It's just your father and myself now," she said. I tilted my head to look at her, then sat down beside her. White-Ears looked at the both of us with her tail flat against herself.

"Where did he go?" asked White-Ears.

"Away. Across the lake. I don't know."

"Is he coming back?"

"No, he's not part of our family anymore."

I frowned and didn't say anything. I wasn't sure what to say. I stood up and walked up to Ma and licked her snout. She nuzzled me back. "Sometimes families split up," she said. "One day, you will leave too, and that's fine."

Pa stood up and pawed the stump before climbing up and sitting down. The snow on its cap was already matted and dirty. He sat facing us and spoke softly. "We'll head west as soon as I get better," he said. He tilted his head and sang a song, and his voice crackled, and there was a persistent quavering in the high notes. I joined his song, and so did Ma and White-Ears. I would have liked to think that our voices made the song happy.

We left, together, as a family, to look for food. We followed Ma around the dense forests just north of the den. We took a big loop up the mountain slope until I could see the lake from the gaps in the trees. Pa called for us to take a break. I needed a break, and so did White-Ears, who flopped onto the ground with no resistance whatsoever. I sat beside Pa. He ate some snow and looked at the lake before turning away.

"What's there for him on the other side of the lake?" I asked.

"I don't know," he said. He glanced at the lake once again. The wind blew in a way to lift the snow from the lake's frozen surface and deposited it some distance away. Clouds zoomed past the tip of the closest mountain peak, and for a moment, the sun's rays pierced through it, showering my eyes with sunlight.

"Do you miss him?"

"Not right now. Right now, I'm angry at him, but I know I will miss him in time."

We returned to the den in the afternoon. It was a long trek down from the mountain. We stopped and sniffed every crevice and exposed log, but there wasn't anything to eat, not even dried berries. White-Ears and I took off for the shore. I had a feeling that maybe I could find some unlucky fish frozen in the ice.

"Are we going to look for him?" White-Ears asked me as we crossed the frozen marsh.

"Oh," I hesitated, "no. I just thought maybe we could find some fish."

"Fish in winter? That's silly."

"I suppose," I said. "But we still have to try, right? I don't like being hungry."

"Do you think that's why he left? There's no food anymore?"

"I'm sure it is. Maybe he'll come back with something."

"Maybe," she said. We slid on the smooth ice and clawed at it for a few moments before giving up and heading back.

We came back before sunset to the sound of Ma screaming. They were both standing up, Pa was on top of her, and he bit her neck while she thrashed around. He mounted her and moved his body, and she made unfamiliar sounds. It didn't last too long. They stayed beside each other for a bit after.

They called it mating. I didn't know what it was, but something about the air made me all excited. Nervous, maybe, or even frustrated. I couldn't help but run in circles and sing and bark, and then after they were done, I played a game of tag with White-Ears.

Chapter 6

Pa woke us up in the middle of the night. It was very late. An acidic sharpness dug its way through my nose and into my brain and made it hard to breathe. Grey flakes drifted from the sky. I turned to look at Pa, who stared in the direction of the lake. A warm glow emanated from the distance, just barely flickering in the darkness.

Ma stood up and rubbed her snout against White-Ears's neck.

"We have to go," Pa said.

"Where are we going?"

"Far away. Past the meadow and the mountains to the west," he said. He paused and took a deep breath, and then said, "We have to go now."

"I don't want to leave. Why do we have to leave?" I said. I looked around at the safe place. It looked so much smaller than I had remembered it. The stump was merely a few wolf-lengths away and looked like a pile of snow in the darkness. The hole wasn't even there anymore. It was buried a long time ago by the snow.

"It's not safe here anymore," Ma said. "Come on, children, we'll leave and find a better place with more food."

"I don't want to leave," I repeated.

Ma bared her teeth at me, but I stood tall and didn't lower my head. A growl came out of her throat, but she stopped halfway and shook her head.

"What about Brother?" I relented. "If it's not safe for us, then it's not safe for him either." For a moment, I felt the wind brush against my back, and I looked around, expecting to see Scruff-Paw, but he wasn't there. When I turned back, Ma was right in front of me. She pressed her nose against my cheek, her warmth radiating from her face, and her fur was coarse and prickly.

"Shhh," she said. "We have to go, and I have to keep you safe."

She turned around to leave, and Pa followed. White-Ears looked at me and then at our parents, and we followed behind them. Snow crunched under my steps, and with each step, I felt the trees collapse in, all around me, getting closer and closer. I kept turning around, once every few steps, watching the stump disappear behind the trees until it was gone, and I didn't turn around again.

The air glowed behind us, and it made the night as bright as the day. We took our path through the forest towards the meadow where I learned how to hunt. Ma took the lead. Pa had a limp, so he walked in the middle, then it was White-Ears, and finally me. Ma slowed down just enough for Pa to catch up, but we were still in a hurry. It wasn't that we were fast. It's just that I found it hard to keep my eyes open. It was the middle of the night, and the acidity lingered in the air.

To pass the time, I tagged behind White-Ears and nipped at her tail and hopped back every time she turned around. She didn't chase me, and I got bored pretty quickly. I picked up my pace and caught up to her and walked beside her.

"Where do you think we're going?" I asked her.

"Somewhere with food, I hope," she said.

"We've never been past the meadow."

"It looked nice from the mountaintop."

"I thought it looked the same as everywhere else," I said, "trees and mountains."

White-Ears turned to headbutt me. "Trees and mountains are nice."

By the time we reached the meadow, the snow had stopped, and the crescent moon was peeking through the clouds. We hovered at the treeline until Ma was satisfied that there wasn't anything waiting to ambush us. We went up the same trail that the elk used, around the lichen-covered boulder and then along the rocky shore of the creek. The moon provided us with enough light and the night was bright.

I was very tired now, my body was tense, and my tail raised and lowered on its own, and there was soreness creeping up my paws and into my body. The smell of hogweed had wafted in the air, and we were at the very top of the meadow. It wasn't as sour up here as it was near the lake. The eerie glow had disappeared behind us, and the yucky snow had stopped, but we kept going, silently, walking in a single-file with Ma at the front.

We rounded the other side of the mountain, and we came down a steep and gravel-filled path, past the knotted trees that lined the base of the mountain and into the valley below. White-Ears helped Pa come down by pushing against his injured side, but I wasn't sure if she actually helped.

"We'll stay here until the morning," Pa said. I nodded and wagged my tail once. Ma had darted away to scope out the area. I knew she would be back soon, so I found a soft patch of snow and went to sleep.

We left early the next morning. It was a new day. A new day with a bright, warm, blue sky and crisp sunlight that filtered through the gaps in the trees. The trees stood tall and narrow, and their smell masked the acidic scent still lingering in the air. Occasionally the wind knocked large pieces of snow from the tip of the trees. These pieces crashed into the ground with a dull thud.

We followed a wide trail that smelled faintly of elk. There were many strange smells in the valley, and Ma and Pa took it slow today, so I found myself digging under almost every tree and bush. My claws made quick work of the light dusting of snow and the soft earth below. There wasn't anything to find underground. Above ground, I rolled on many things, from a bed of exposed lichen to old bear poop, and I carried those scents to White-Ears.

She decided to join me in the scent rolling, so I had to fight her for the strongest smells. But we didn't really fight. I barely danced around her before I felt too hungry to continue. I thought that if I bit into her shoulder, I might have actually eaten her. Ma and Pa would not have been happy if I had eaten my sister.

We stopped at a creek around midday for a break. It was barely flowing because of the ice and snow. The cold water tasted much better than whatever old snow nearby, and I drank two huge gulps of it. It was too much, and I immediately felt a sharp pain against my forehead. I closed my eyes and fell face-first against the snow, and the pain slowly dissipated with the cloud of snow around me. Lying down on my side, I kicked some snow into the air and watched it fall into the creek and disappear. My tail wagged on its own.

"I'm hungry," White-Ears mumbled while chewing on a branch.

"Eat snow," I said, sitting up.

"I'll eat you."

"You can't even catch me." I shook my head and laid back down with snow against my chin. The snow coated my whiskers. It was a strange but pleasant feeling.

"There will be food soon," Ma said. I hadn't noticed that she was standing beside me. I turned to look at her. She stood tall, grey, and thin. Her ears drooped slightly more than they usually did. Her gaze was warm, but her face betrayed her tiredness. Or maybe it was weariness. Maybe it was just age.

"Where are we even going?" White-Ears asked, this time coming from behind me. I sat up again and saw her paws in the cold water.

"Somewhere where the two of you will have plenty to eat," Ma said. She paused before continuing, "I never talked about the ocean, did I?" I looked at her blankly. White-Ears stepped out of the creek and shook her body, even though only her paws were wet.

"No, I guess not. Let's get going. I'll tell you on the way."

I got up, and we followed the creek further west, winding through the dense forest with narrow trees. Pa's limp looked much better today. I walked beside him while Ma and White-Ears trailblazed ahead. "When I was little, I lived beside the ocean. It was a land of plenty, and the weather never got cold. It was warm all the time!" Ma's tail swung side to side, and there was a spring in her step. I looked over at Pa, who was still a head taller than me. He smiled thinly.

"There was always meat near the ocean. If not meat, then we

caught fish, or clams, or whatever the ocean would provide."

"If there's so much food, why did you leave?" White-Ears asked.

There was a long, drawn-out moment of silence, and all I could hear was the sound of our paws against the snow. For a moment, Ma looked deep in thought, but then she shook her head and kept walking.

"How far away is the ocean?" I asked.

"Too far," Pa said quietly. I turned to look at him, but he just walked ahead.

"Many seasons," Ma said.

"I don't want to walk for many seasons," White-Ears grumbled.

"We won't have to," Pa said. "As soon as we find a place with food, we'll settle down. Your mother is just nostalgic about the ocean."

"Were you there too?"

"No. I met your mother inland."

The conversation faltered and faded as the sun began to set. There was nothing but the smell of family and trees in the air. No deer, no elk, no rabbit or beaver or anything big enough to be worth eating. I would settle for a squirrel. Or maybe a particularly softened piece of tree. Or White-Ears.

We stopped for the night when the sun cast long shadows on the mountains. I jogged around the woods, looking for anything at all. A faint smell called me to a log, and from underneath, I dug out a dried, foul-smelling skin with some meat attached to it. I took it back to the family instead of eating all of it myself. It didn't help the hunger at all.

"Do you smell that?" I asked White-Ears. She stared absent-mindedly into the distance.

"What?"

"I'm not sure," I said. I dug my nose against the surface of the tree and inhaled. It smelled both familiar and foreign at the same time. "Come here and smell this," I pointed, and she did. She didn't know what it was either. We ran to Pa and asked him to come over and smell the tree. He narrowed his eyes at us and lowered his head towards the tree.

"What is it?" I asked.

He looked at us. I leaned in to lick his snout. "It's strangers. Wolves. The scent is very faint, though."

"I don't like it," I said. I folded my ears back and leaned away.

"You're right not to," Pa said. "Strangers are dangerous. We should stay away from these scent trails."

"Have you ever met a stranger?" I asked.

"Yes. Once in a while."

"Strangers can't be all bad. Mother was a stranger to you at some point, right?"

"That was different. Love is different. It's difficult, but you'll understand when you're older."

"Stay away from strangers unless you love them. Got it." I laughed and wagged my tail involuntarily. Pa looked at me with a strange look and then half-smiled, and then we left the tree alone.

Later the next day, the trees thinned out. The dense forest of bare tree trunks became clumps of smaller trees with fatter canopies. We started heading uphill again. Pa's limp had returned. He kept scratching at it.

"Does it hurt?" I asked.

"I'm fine," he said. He strained to go up, and when I came to

49

help him, he pushed me away.

On the plus side, we found something to eat. It was a newly dead bird, some kind of owl. It looked like it fell out of the sky and smelled like the air from a few days ago back at the lake and the den. It tasted like it smelled, but it also tasted extremely good. We split it among the four of us. I got the head and a part of the breast, and I ate the whole thing. Feathers could be filling, right?

After the meal, we stayed to look for more fallen birds. "Where there's one, there's more," Pa said. This painted a wide open-mouthed smile on my face. I spent most of the energy from the owl meat running around the hillside. There wasn't anything, though, and by the time I got back, I was hungry again. We left without food, and we had to keep going, up the hillside and over the ridge. I could see over the treetops in the distance now. The snow-covered tips curved over a gently sloping hill and beyond it, mountain peaks in the distance. I wondered what the ocean would look like. It was hard to imagine a lake in the middle of the mountain bigger than the one beside the childhood den. Maybe it was at the top of the mountain and filled an entire valley, but whatever the case, I was ready to catch as many fish as I could.

☁

The mountains slowly floated by, and so did each tree, rock, and gully in the snow. The valley ended against a pile of huge rocks. We had to go around and up, to the northwest. We travelled along the rocks until we were high enough that the trees turned into bushes, and the rocks had thick, blue ice between them. Ma jumped from rock to rock until she found solid ice. We followed her.

The air was thin. The ice was brilliantly white and sparkled under the sun. To each side of us, there were snow-capped peaks that towered high and mighty. We followed Ma across the icy field. I slipped and slid until we got to solid ground on the other side, where we stopped at the place where ice became rock.

A vast, open landscape greeted me when I turned around. I realized that we had crossed the entire valley, and we were now on the opposite side, the side of the tall white mountains. I squinted in the direction we came from. I thought I could see the meadow where Pa taught me how to hunt for rodents, but I wasn't sure. The sky was hazy.

Past the edge of the ice, the ground was loose dirt and tiny rocks that stuck themselves between my toes. I had to stop and lick them off. The rocks tasted like nothing. I shook myself and jumped ahead to where Pa was. We walked side-by-side.

I was breathing heavily by the time we reached the top of the ridge. Pa may have had a limp the whole time, but his stamina was incredible. He barely huffed at all. I collapsed against White-Ears as soon as we got to the top, and I closed my eyes for a second to catch my breath.

When I opened my eyes again, a meadow revealed itself to me. It was flat and huge and stretched from one peak to the other. The meadow smelled of snow and old flowers and the dens and droppings of small animals. On either side towered brilliant white peaks that jutted out of the meadow like wolf's ears. I turned and licked White-Ears, and she licked me back.

"Remember the peaks that looked like your ears?" I said.

"No," she said.

"Well, these are the ones, I think. Look!"

"I'll take your word for it. I don't really know what I look like anyway."

I got up from my flat mode and dusted myself off. Ma had already jogged in a huge circle, but she barely got closer to the opposite edge of the meadow. She tilted her head and sang her song, so I joined her, and so did White-Ears and Pa.

"I like it here," Ma said, "let's stay the night here, and we can keep going tomorrow morning."

It was late, and there was barely a hint of blue light to the west. The stars twinkled in the east. I ran from one end of the meadow to the other, and I was at least a wolf-length faster than White-Ears. She didn't have a chance, as usual.

I laid down to rest and cool down. There was a rustling sound. It was a faint crunch of a tiny limb against a tiny rock, and it sounded close. Maybe fifty wolf-lengths away, maybe a bit more. I felt my ears perk up, and I slowly tilted my head in the direction of the sound. There was enough light to see. Just barely. Just a little bit.

A white-coloured blob. I stared at it with intense focus, not even blinking once. I wanted to see where it was looking, where it was going to go—if it was an animal at all. Then it moved a little bit, and I knew it was food. I sprung up and kicked my hind legs back as hard as I could, pushing myself forward and giving me a bit of a head start. This startled White-Ears, but she immediately realized what I was doing and ran after me. I got up to full speed immediately. The shape tensed up and darted to the left, towards the parts of the meadow covered in snow. I swung my tail and turned with all four

52

limbs. I was closing in. A gust of wind told me that it was a hare.

It turned again, kicking up snow and dust. I anticipated the turn and shifted my body and lifted my tail. It worked. There were less than five wolf-lengths between the hare and me. White-Ears breathed behind me, and I heard her paws as clearly as the hare's panicking footsteps. Two wolf-lengths now. It slowed down for a split moment and then made a sharp turn to the right. I skidded on my front paws, and I nearly fell over. In the time it took for me to balance myself, the hare was over ten wolf-lengths away again. I ran after it. As I got closer, it turned again.

I snarled at it. There was the familiar taste of blood in my throat from running.

The distance wasn't closing. I was tired. If it weren't for the damned twists and turns, we'd be having meat right now. Heaving, I slowed down and watched the hare make another sharp turn. It was already fading into the darkness. I felt a surge of anger in my body. I hated the hare for outrunning me.

A low and grey shape whizzed past me. It was Ma. She was fast and agile. And she anticipated the hare's turn. Behind her, White-Ears. I ran after Ma. Maybe I could do something to help her. But of course, she didn't need any help. She quickly closed the distance and jumped on the hare just as it was about to change direction. The animal squealed under her jaws, but only for a moment. When I caught up, Ma had already torn it open. Her snout was stained with fresh blood.

We danced around the carcass and waited for Pa to jog over with his limp. Then, once the family was all there, we feasted, and for a moment, life was perfect. Ma was right. I liked this meadow too.

➢

Ma found a frozen hare in the snowbank towards the south-west side of the meadow. Under the mountain's shadow, there was snow that came all the way up to my chest. The meadow itself sloped down gently until there were bushes, and then trees, and then past a row of boulders, there was an entire forest waiting to be explored. It smelled pristine on this side of the mountain. The snow was good. The sun. And of course, the food. These hares tasted as good frozen as they did fresh.

We rested after eating. I sprawled out on the snow in the bright sunlight and played with Pa's tail as he slept.

"We should stay here for now," Ma said, and we all agreed. This was a safe and good place.

At night, I heard the faint songs of strangers. Pa assured us that they were very, very far away and they would not be able to hurt us. I told him that I could hold my ground against a couple strangers, so he tackled me to the ground.

Fair enough. Pa was stronger than he looked.

➢

It had been a few days since the family settled down in the meadow. White-Ears and I went exploring, all along the cliff edge, past the thick snowbanks on either side of the meadow and then down into the forest. It wasn't a thick forest. The trees were tiny and looked different, rougher, and less straight than the ones we had passed to get here.

At the foot of the meadow, to the southwest, we found a

very nice flat rock. It faced the sunlight, and there was no snow on top. It was warm and big enough to fit the two of us. White-Ears and I sat on the rock, warming our bottoms and watching the clouds pass by.

To the west, the mountains seemed to extend infinitely far. The peaks close by had snow-covered tops that pierced through the wispy clouds. Beyond that, it was far away and difficult to see, but those mountains looked less sharp. There were plains of rock and snow and huge slabs of ice resting in the valleys. Behind us, the meadow sloped gently up until it flattened out.

"Do you think winter is over?" I said without lifting my head.

"Feels like it. It's hot during the day."

White-Ears was right about the heat. My fur was thick, and the midday was getting too hot for me to be standing in the open.

"I can't wait for the summer," I said." I'm going to catch a lot of fish when the ice melts."

"I'm going to catch more."

"You didn't catch a single one last summer." I opened my mouth and stuck my tongue out. White-Ears nudged me with her nose.

"We were kids, and you're the older child. Now I'm better than you."

"Liar," I said, "I can get to the top before you."

I stretched and waited for White-Ears's response, but instead of saying anything, she leapt up and off the rock and started running.

"Hey!" I yelled and raced after her. "Not fair!"

We got to the top at the same time. Maybe she was a little bit faster, but it was because of her head start, and I wasn't going to count it as a win.

Chapter 7

I explored the forest by myself, and with White-Ears, and sometimes with Ma and Pa. With my nose against the ground, I meandered along the cliff-side to the northwest, down the gentle slope of the meadow and as far as the frozen creek to the south. I didn't like how the air smelled beyond the creek. Ma told us to always listen to our instincts, and my instinct told me that it was dangerous over there. Once, I heard faint sounds on the other side of the creek, so I stood and waited for something to show up. If it was food, I would go after it despite my discomfort.

Nothing ever showed up, but I spent nearly a day pacing the length of the creek anyway, which seemed to meander and stretch forever. I never got to the end, and I was beginning to suspect that it did not end.

In the meadow, I had never seen so many hares in my entire life. Pa taught us the proper way to anticipate a hare's turn. It worked better with two wolves. If you turn to one side, it tricks the hare into turning to the same side. If there are wolves on both sides, one wolf can fake a rush, and the other wolf can grab the hare. It was quite simple, really. The only thing was that we had to work quickly. Since hares ran faster than us, they would just run away if we didn't ambush them.

White-Ears and I practiced on our own. We corralled a hare against the northern cliffs where there was less snow and only one way to turn. White-Ears faked it out with a leap, and I managed to grab onto its head with my jaws as it turned. I shuffled until I clamped on the base of the skull and mashed it against my teeth. Blood spurted and bones creaked together, and the animal twitched one last time before falling limp. Nothing tastes as good as an animal that I killed myself.

A small hare wasn't much to eat between the two of us, but Ma and Pa were away on a hunt, so I had fewer wolves to share it with. The liver was still my favourite part of meat. I was surprised how good the stomach was, even though it was filled with partly digested grass.

It was a sunny day again, and it had been sunny for many, many days in a row. There were clouds to the west and the north, but the sky was blue and my entire body was warm for the moment. Earlier, I woke up with a headache. I drank many gulps of fresh snow and hoped that it would go away, but it lingered. A dull pain pounded at the back of my head, just under my ears.

I thought I would quench my head in a pile of snow, so I stuck my face in there and waited. I stood there until the snow started to soften around me, but the pain was still there.

White-Ears tagged along behind me as I sniffed the south side for a bigger and fresher pile of snow. I could tell that she had nothing else to do. Ma and Pa were still asleep, and there was nothing to eat. I turned and headed down the meadow slope. White-Ears followed.

Suddenly, she ran past me and skidded to a stop directly in front, bowing with her paws stretched, and her tail waved side-to-side. She was full of smiles, and from her open mouth, she uttered a high whine. It was shrill and very annoying.

"No, not now," I said. I closed my eyes and just stood there. When I opened my eyes, White-Ears was still there.

"Come on! I'm bored," she said. "We can go do something."

"My head hurts."

"Play with me, and I'll make your pain go away."

I snarled at her. I didn't know what else to say. Her sharp voice shot through my head and reddened my vision. The smile instantly faded from her face. She got up from the ground and growled back at me.

"Fine," White-Ears said, "go be moody."

I growled again, turned, and walked towards the mountain. I heard White-Ears walk away behind me, and I kept walking with my head held high until her pawsteps disappeared.

I travelled along the north side of the meadow and forest. It was cloudy now, and the air smelled moist. On the west side of the mountain, a giant crack ran from the sky to the ground. Short and intense bursts of wind came from there. When the wind gusted, the crack whistled ever so slightly.

The dull pressure pushed against the base of my ears, and I kept thinking about White-Ears. How could she not have realized how annoying she was? I didn't want to play with her. She shouldn't have kept bugging me! I snapped my jaws together and gritted my teeth, shaking my head.

Near the tree line, I caught a whiff of something in the air. I wasn't sure that it was real, so I lowered my head and scanned the ground for the scent but came up empty. There was nothing but the smell of lichen and grass and…and something else. Yes, definitely something else. It was faint but fresh. I looked up. Shadows of clouds raced past me, and all around me, patches of sunlight disappeared as quickly as they appeared. Then, off to my right, hidden behind rocks and snow, something moved. It was red and maybe a bit yellow, and it had a black-tipped tail. I lowered my head again. I didn't think it noticed me. I was downwind of this creature and far enough to blend in with the snow.

I took a few steps closer. My steps crunched the snow, but the noise of the wind gave me cover. Oblivious to my advance, the creature leapt into the air and landed with its front paws in the snow. It wiggled around before pulling away from the pile of snow. Nothing. It was hunting for rodents without success. The creature had a narrow snout and a black nose and smelled of dirt and sweat and meat. I wanted to eat it. I wanted to dig my teeth into its neck and feel the life force leave its body.

It jumped and landed once more. I pressed myself against the ground and snuck from one bush to the other, circling around the animal, making sure to stay downwind of it. When I was close enough to see its whiskers, I ran for it. Full speed. I took off against a gust of wind that swirled the snow, paws glancing off the snow, front-back-front.

I was a fast runner, and the feeling of wind rushing past my face dulled the pain.

The animal heard me. It turned around and fled the other way, with its black-tipped tail dancing in the air. It was surprisingly nimble. As it flew across the snowy meadow, it tucked itself behind every tree, round and round, using the gnarly tree trunks as shelter. I followed closely. I took in its scent and made a note of it, just in case I had to find it again.

I chased the creature from the treeline down to where the

forest started to thicken and the ground became littered with giant boulders. I worried that I would lose it behind a rock. Maybe it had a den somewhere, and it would disappear into the ground where I couldn't reach it. Instead, the creature swung right and ran past me. I lunged at it, but it was still too far away.

Back up the hill again. This time, I followed it along the cliff-side to the north, but there was snow blowing in my face. I shook it off mid-gallop. I wasn't going to let a little bit of snow get in between me and my dinner, and despite the snow, I could still see its body—a small and active lump of fur not too far in the distance. It was too brightly coloured and stood out against the white ground and the drifting, shifting grey mass that was the snow and rock. As it ran, it turned around to glance at me as if it was taunting me.

I had to get it.

Snow billowed all around me. It got into my eyes so I squinted and kept running. It covered the scent and sounds of the meadow. I was chasing blind. The creature turned again, and it jumped on a rock next to the cliff face.

I hesitated. The thought of climbing onto the cliff face made my leg fur stand, and I felt a shudder from my neck down my spine. It hovered on this rock, patted its paws down, and looked at me. Taunting me. I stopped. We made eye contact. Its beady black eyes darted back and forth, its large, black-tipped ears quivered, and the bright orange coat of fur poofed up. It was about ten wolf-lengths away. If it wasn't on the ledge, I was confident that I could get it.

The standoff lasted only a moment before it started running up the ledge. It must have followed a path that I had never seen before.

I jumped. My claws clashed against the cold rock. I planted my paws down on the snowy surface but as I pushed forward, the ground gave out under my hind paws. For a moment, the feeling of freefall gripped me, and I braced for the impact, but then it was okay. Breathe. I heaved in and out and gripped my claws until they marked the rock beneath. Everything was fine. I managed to balance myself on the ledge by swinging my tail and I wasn't going to fall off.

In front of me was a narrow, rocky ledge that led up the mountain. It seemed wide and passable, but I couldn't see well because of the blowing snow. The creature ran ahead. I took careful steps until I was comfortable with the height, then I jogged, then, once the jitters had calmed down, I ran after it, pressing my body against the rock cliff and holding my tail up for balance. Breathing lightly. In. Out.

Far ahead, the creature turned right and disappeared. I followed it closely, around the ice-covered cliff face and up, away from the ledge. The ground kept going up until it curved up and opened to a gentle slope. I gasped silently and shook my head. I had no idea this field was even here. It wasn't visible from the meadow. Even here, the slope was barely visible against the blowing snow and the darkening skies.

The creature ran up the slope in a straight line. It turned left and slithered around a rock, so I ran to the same rock. I couldn't smell anything in this chaotic wind, and now I couldn't see anything either. Everything was grey and white. The snow was blowing hard, hard enough to push against me and dig into my thick winter fur. When the wind gusted, it sent chills down my back to the tip of my tail.

I kept going.

The slope levelled out, and then it was a flat and barren field.

I was high up above the meadow, and the air felt thin. The creature disappeared into the wall of blowing snow, but its tracks were still there. It had tiny little pawprints that lined up in a straight and unbroken chain. I bent down to smell the tracks, but when I looked up again, the line of pawprints was gone. The ground was an unblemished white. The wind howled in the air. Snow whizzed in every direction.

I lowered my head and took in the scent again. It smelled like nothing at all. A violent tremble crept through my body, and suddenly, I just wanted to lie down. But the wind wouldn't let me. I looked down and saw the snow swirl around my legs. I looked up again and saw nothing but a dull white, all around me, billowing and howling. I was completely blind. Deaf. Couldn't smell anything. The void of snow closed in until there was nothing except whiteness, and I...

I could feel my heartbeat speed up, so I took a deep breath. In. Out. Feeling my chest rise and fall, snow cutting into every inch of my fur. In. Out. I made a circle on the ground, and my pawprints disappeared instantly. This was bad. I didn't like it. I had to get back to Ma and Pa, so I turned around to face the blinding whiteness. I just needed to retrace my steps until I could see the rock and then go down the slope until I got to the cliff-side. It was no problem. No problem at all.

I walked, and walked, and walked, with my eyes narrowed and ears folded back. There was no rock. There were no rocks anywhere, just a flat, endless plain of white snow. I turned again and saw nothing on the ground. My heart skipped a beat and then began to pound against my chest. I could wait it out. These snowstorms never lasted for too long, and once it was over, I could start heading back.

Maybe Ma caught something fresh to eat. I was hungry. I

spun once on the spot and laid down and used my tail to cover my nose. I just needed to wait out the storm. I just needed to wait out the storm.

It was much darker when I opened my eyes, but the same blanket of whiteness was everywhere, and the wind blew even harder than before. I wasn't sure how much time had passed. When I turned my head, I noticed that there was a thick layer of snow on my body. I shook it off and stood up. It was cold too, much colder than it was before. Each gust of wind sent shivers down my back all the way down to my tail. Some of the snow must have melted and soaked into my winter coat. I shook myself violently, and it helped a bit.

I tilted my head back and sang for the family. I tried hard to lower my pitch. Lower pitches travel farther, Ma told me. I needed this song to travel as far as possible. Maybe if I heard their voices, I would know where to go. I sang until I ran out of air and then sang some more until I felt my throat tighten up. Now I had to wait, and I waited.

Time passed and snow accumulated on my nose. There was nothing but the shrill howl of the wind and the irregular thumping of my heart. Boom. Boom. Boom. Like the earth itself was shaking. I couldn't wait anymore. I didn't know where I was or how long this snowstorm would last, and with each passing moment, it got darker. If I stayed here, I would end up buried in snow like the frozen hares. I shook my head again and stood up and walked in a random direction. It didn't matter. If I went far enough, I was bound to find something.

With each step, I was more convinced that there wasn't anything except an endless grey void. Then I felt the ground shift underneath me. It was softer, less firm. I stepped back, and forward, and back again. I barked into the void, and there was almost an echo. Forward. Forward again. With the third step, the snow loosened, and I saw it tumble down into the chasm below. I was standing on the edge of a cliff.

I sang for the family, and a plume of hot, moist air streamed out of my mouth and turned into ice in front of me. "Jump. It's better than freezing to death," a voice whispered in the depths of my head. I wasn't going to jump. I just needed to wait out the storm. It won't be too long now. I just had to stay warm and wait it out. "You're going to end up like all the stupid animals that got lost," it said.

"No, no way," I whispered.

"Nobody is coming." "You're going to get buried in snow." I shook my head and buried my nose against my leg. "Should have played with White-Ears instead, and now you'll never see her again."

I heard them before I saw them. I heard Ma's low barks in quick succession. One. Two. Three. They called me. I answered with a song. White-Ears replied with a song. I ran in the direction of the voices, blind and barking. I crashed into them, and they embraced me. I licked them in the face and nuzzled each of their necks. Ma and Pa's familiar smell relaxed my tense shoulders. Their faces made my tail swing wildly from side to side. I jumped on White-Ears's back and knocked her over, and we both fell in the snow.

"We have to get out of here," Pa said, "it's not safe up here."

I lowered my head under his neck and licked his face and whined. "I'm sorry," I said. He pulled away and started walking.

"Can't we go back the way we came from?" White-Ears

asked.

"No, it's too slippery to go down," Ma said. "The snow will freeze on the rock as it gets colder."

Pa told us to follow him carefully. I walked behind Pa, my nose right up to his tail. White-Ears followed me, and Ma came last. Pa was careful. He stopped to smell the air once every few steps, moving his head up and down and scanning the ground. I couldn't smell anything in the snow, and I didn't know what he was looking for.

It took a long time to cross the mountain, or so I thought, but I couldn't see much, and the snow and darkness screwed with my sense of time. Maybe it was the middle of the night. I wasn't tired, just scared. Snow came up to my chest, and with each step, I felt myself sinking endlessly. I kept looking, squinting, for the large rock that I saw during the day. Pa seemed to know where he was going, but I still hated not knowing where I was.

White-Ears sneezed. She was right behind me and sneezed into my tail, so I smacked her in the nose with it. She snapped at my tail. I hissed back. One of these days, she's going to bite it off! I laughed at that thought and then shook my body again. The snow was beginning to melt against my fur. The air was warmer, which meant that we weren't so high up anymore.

Pa stopped. I ran around to get beside him. He nodded at me and then said, "There is a very narrow path ahead that leads west. We'll have to go down slowly. It will be slippery and dangerous."

"Will you be okay?" I asked.

"Going down is easy. Follow my lead."

I let Pa take the lead, and I followed behind him. The snow was thinning out, and I could see a few wolf-lengths in each direction. The ground was still covered in thick, moist snow. The faint edge of the snow blended in with the grey skies, and I thought I saw the tips of trees far below. Pa brushed the snow aside with his paws and snout, and then he took a step.

He was careful to plant his steps deep into the snow, so I did the same. My claws gripped the slushy ice underneath. It became steeper with each step, and Pa deliberately slowed down. "Step here," he said as he gestured.

I missed a step, and the snow under my left paw turned into cold, slippery rock. I gasped and sat down, then, shuffling my butt, I got up again and followed Pa. It was very steep, and I constantly felt like I was falling. Then, ever so slowly, the trail became flatter until the tips of pine trees dangled in front of me. I shook again, splattering slushy snow all over the ground and the rocks that lined the trail. It was brighter near the forest, with less snow and less haze.

As I stepped onto the solid, soft-needled forest, a jolt of excitement shot through me. I ran ahead to Pa and nuzzled him, and then I doubled back to White-Ears and Ma and greeted them both. Ma licked me back with an open smile.

I turned to the sky and sang my song.

"Shut up!" Pa barked.

I turned to look at him. "Strangers nearby," he said. "Don't sing."

I inhaled and felt my entire body shudder before I realized the reason: the ground smelled like wolves. Strong, powerful scents, familiar and disgusting at the same time. I lowered myself involuntarily, folding my tail against my butt and my hind legs.

Ma ran to Pa with her tail high in the air. They converged a few trees away, and together, they examined the bases of the trees and boulders around us. White-Ears and I followed carefully. Their steps were deliberate, methodical, and very quiet, and when they were done smelling the trees, Pa turned around and led us back to the edge of the forest.

"It's not safe here," he said.

"Strangers are close by," Ma said. "We should go back up."

I folded my tail against my belly and sat down. I felt the jitters through my whole body, but it was probably just hunger: I hadn't eaten for the whole day.

"Stay here," Pa said as he turned and jumped onto the narrow mountain trail. "Let me see if it's safe."

We huddled together and waited for him to come back. The white of his fur blended with the stone and sky until he disappeared into the hazy snow. The wind whistled to the tune of White-Ears's breathing, up and down, in and out. I closed my eyes and buried my face in her neck.

Moments later, rocks and snow tumbled down the path. Pa slid down on his butt, skidding, covered in wet snow and dirt.

"Too slippery," he said. "We can't go up. We can't stay here. We have to go through."

Chapter 8

"Remember," Ma said, "fast and quiet. We can get through this territory before the sun comes up."

I lowered my head and nodded quietly. A lump sat in my chest, and it felt like I had swallowed a bone. Everywhere was dark and chilly, and the dampness soaked into my fur, sinking into my flesh, lingering, colder with every step. Step and step. Shivering. I couldn't shake the smell of strangers from my nose, and it was nauseating, so I rubbed my snout in the wet earth below the snow. But it didn't help.

We walked a straight line with Pa at the front. Everyone held themselves close to the forest floor, and we walked through the dense undergrowth instead of along a path. My ears flickered against the protruding branches. I lowered myself even further until my chest was brushing against the snow. The wind occasionally shook the trees and made wet snow splatter onto the bushes. The first dollop of snow startled me, and I backed into White-Ears. Neither of us made a sound. We kept going.

The wind howled less and less until it was barely a whisper. Although the snow kept falling, it was suddenly quiet every-where. I stopped for a moment and scanned the forest. Trees scattered in every direction. Pa was tense, and Ma walked with her tail low and tucked. But I wasn't worried. We moved fast, at nearly a jogging pace, and I was sure that we would pass through this forest in no time at all.

Later, when the snow stopped, moonlight filtered through the treetops and cast long shadows on the undisturbed snow below.

"Should we head back?" I whispered.

"No point now," Pa said. "We're almost through."

"We're not heading back," Ma said. She paused to smell the air before continuing. "We'll keep going west."

"To the ocean?" I asked.

"To the ocean. There will be plenty of food there."

My fur had dried, and the jitters had worn off, and I slowly peeled myself away from the ground, and we kept going. The forest was long and wide and it never ended. Just when I thought I saw an edge, another line of trees appeared in the darkness. The night was brighter, and the shadows shortened until the half-moon was right above us, and the shadows of the trees hugged their roots.

The trees became more sparse. I could see through the trunks now, and on either side of me, it looked like the trees disappeared into the darkness after a hundred wolf-lengths. Maybe two hundred. I stepped on a branch, and it cracked, which echoed back and forth between the cliff walls on both sides. The echo lingered for a very long time. It felt as if the cliffs were closing in on us.

"Quiet," Pa said.

He stopped and tilted his head. His ears twitched. The forest rustled silently and I found it very hard to breathe. Every breath I took was too deep and too loud. I turned my head in the air and stared into the darkness.

The wind changed directions, and slowly, the air was filled

with the smell of strangers. Everywhere. In all directions. I yelped and a tremble went down my back and the hair on my neck stood up. I had never been so close to strangers before. I closed my eyes for a moment, and when I opened them again, the trees started pulling away from me, and the silence of the forest emitted a sharp ringing noise.

Pa's snout flicked up, and he gestured for us to follow. I glanced at him, and he looked like he was saying something, but I couldn't hear him. His mouth opened and closed. The ringing drowned out everything. Dumbfounded, I tilted my head and narrowed my eyes until I met his green, glowing eyes for just a moment. Just a brief moment.

"Hurry!" Pa's voice cut through the ringing, and I snapped out of it. Ma looped around behind White-Ears with her fur puffed and her body low to the ground. I shook myself and ran towards Pa, and I heard White-Ears follow.

The snow was coming up to my chest, and every few steps, I jumped to get out of it. White-Ears was panting rapidly, and so was I. My steps were heavy. My lungs burned. My legs trembled, but I knew we had to keep going, so I ran as fast as I could.

Pa turned sharply. A massive tree expanded in front of me, and I turned to avoid it. I flew through the air and felt compacted, icy snow below my paws. It was a trail. I shook my head and looked around and everything was dark and damp. There were paw prints on the ground, sunken into the snow, glimmering from the faint moonlight. It smelled of strangers.

Pa stopped. His fur expanded in front of me, and he held his tail in the air.

"Kids, get behind me," he said. He turned to Ma and kissed her on the cheek, and in a low and solemn voice, whispered,

"We have to keep them safe." Ma didn't say anything. She looked behind us with her tail held high. She was almost as big as Pa, and she had his body posture. A long shiver travelled down my back and stayed there. I leaned in against White-Ears and nuzzled her face.

Pa turned to us. "If I tell you to run, you run, and you don't stop until you are safe, understood?"

"What is going on?"

"We're going to be attacked, and I need you to listen to me."

"I can help," I said with my head held high. The ringing had stopped, and I wasn't small anymore. "We can defend the family together."

"Don't be stupid," Pa said.

White-Ears giggled.

"You too," he said, "don't be stupid. Your mother and I will hold them off while you run. Go up the mountain and find somewhere safe. We'll find you later."

I nodded. In the corner of my eye, I saw a flash of green and yellow.

⌒

There were eight, maybe ten pairs of eyes scattered on each side of us. The black cliffs towered over the other sides. It was the strangers, and their eyes glowed brightly in the crisp winter night. Ma and Pa were quiet, and I didn't dare to breathe except in short, shallow breaths. I shrank into the snow and waited.

The eyes became brighter and sharper until their faces gleamed. Their black noses shined against the moonlight. I felt like running away. A part of me screamed danger, the other part told me they were just wolves, and I knew wolves were friendly. Ma, Pa, and Scruff-Paw were friendly. Maybe if Scruff-Paw was here, we could hold them off. His presence made us a more powerful family.

Pa moved towards the dim faces and eyes in front of us. He barked once. In the quiet night, it echoed between the walls until it died out.

"We mean no harm," he said. He paused and waited for a response, but the eyes stared back unblinkingly. They were no more than a hundred wolf-lengths away. I could hear the huffing of their exhales.

"We will pass through here and never bother you again," Pa said.

The strangers closed in. Ma leaned against me and kissed me on the chin. "Go," she whispered. "Go now."

Snarls echoed in the darkness, and the strangers started running towards us from both sides. The air was filled with the scent of wolves. Ma leaned away now and snarled at them. Her back was arched, and she moved closer to Pa until she was behind him, facing the other way.

I blinked. I couldn't breathe. My entire body vibrated, and I was frozen in place. I could stay and fight. I just needed a moment to catch my breath, and I could fight. Slowly, I opened my mouth and bared my teeth, waiting for the growl that never came.

Pa was face to face with a grey and yellow wolf of his equal size. The stranger, a female, was growling, and her teeth snapped. Pa had his tail high. He sidestepped the stranger as she charged him. Then he leaned in and brought his jaws together on the stranger's shoulder, and she turned her head and screamed.

"Go!" Pa yelled at us. His voice shattered the ice and snow that held me to the ground, and I leapt away, and White-Ears followed closely behind. We ran. Snow flew from my paws, and trees whizzed past, and all I could hear was snarling and screaming.

Less than ten steps in, I stopped and turned around to look. It wasn't right. I shouldn't have stopped, but the gut-wrenching screams and whimpers gave me no choice. I saw Ma being swarmed by two strangers. Pa had broken from his attacker and charged at the black wolf that was attacking Ma. Thunderous, explosive anger swelled in me, and suddenly I wasn't afraid anymore.

I turned and ran back. I wore a full mouth snarl, and I could feel the spit spraying from my throat and the thump-thumping of my heart.

"Wait! Wait for me!" White-Ears said. Her pawsteps followed me. I lowered my head and hissed at the wolf that had Ma pinned on the ground. I ran and plowed through him. He yelped in surprise and doubled over, rolling on his side and slamming against the nearest tree.

I made eye contact with Ma. Her eyes were furious. Three strangers surrounded me. I faced them, snarling, with my ears folded back and tail held high. White-Ears was behind me.

"Go!" Ma said between growls. "Don't stop until you're safe. We'll find you after."

A stranger lunged at me. He had a white patch on his chest, and his face was filled with rage. I ducked aside, and before I turned around, I heard a horrible scream. White-Ears! The stranger had my sister's rump in his jaws, and the smell of blood stung my nose. My vision tunnelled, and I saw nothing but the stranger's exposed neck, and I lunged for it. I felt something crack under my jaws. The stranger squeaked pathetically and released his grip. White-Ears stumbled back, and her leg started oozing blood. I tossed the stranger aside, and he crumpled to the ground, whimpering.

I nudged White-Ears, and she started running. Limping, but running. I turned to the two other strangers and let out a menacing snarl. They froze in place, and I roared once again. I tried to put as much space between White-Ears and the stranger wolves. But when the third one staggered up from the ground, I ran after White-Ears. I had to run. White-Ears needed me, and I couldn't have stayed any longer.

There were drops of blood on the snow, patches of dark against the glimmering moon-lit snow. I took big steps and big breaths until I caught up with White-Ears. The entire right side of her body was blood-stained, and the entire forest smelled of blood.

"Up the mountain," I said. She didn't reply. She kept running. I stayed close behind her. The three wolves that chased us were still some distance away, but they got louder and closer with each step. "Left," I said. There was a gap in the rocky walls of the valley, and White-Ears saw what I meant. She turned, and I followed, and so did the strangers.

She dripped blood as she leapt up the steep slope. She yelped in pain with each step, and her leg twitched. I stuck close to her, ready to catch her if she fell, but she was tougher than that. White-Ears was the toughest wolf I knew.

Over the hump, she sat down and licked her leg. There was still the smell of blood everywhere, and the sounds of the stranger wolves filled my ears, and I wasn't sure whether they were right behind me. Even if they gave up, it wasn't a risk I was ready to take. Maybe there were more of them out here.

Ma told us to go up the mountain and hide.

"We have to keep going," I said.

"I know," she said. She panted and looked like she was about to pass out. We kept going. Up, around, winding around. It was still dark, but the sky lightened up over time, and the sounds of the snarls and growls faded into the background. In time, all I heard was my own heartbeat and White-Ears's shallow panting.

We were up high in the mountains. I pushed her to keep going, but she was limping more now. "Stop," White-Ears said as she sat down, panting loudly, "I-I need a break."

I sat down too. I couldn't calm my heartbeat, and there was a loud ringing in my ear that obscured the sounds of the mountain. Were the strangers chasing us? I kept hearing pawsteps, and I kept turning around, but there was never anybody there.

We sat for a bit. I waited for the ringing sound to dissipate, and then, when I was sure there wasn't anyone chasing us, I turned to White-Ears. "Are you okay?"

"It hurts," she breathed.

"I know," I said. "You need rest. Come on."

We walked along the foot of a wide ridge that jutted into the sky, away from the trees and the valley below. To my right was a trail of pawprints and occasional drops of blood. It was quiet now, and the smell of strangers only lingered on my snout and White-Ears's body. I looked left, and then right, then back left again. There was a part of the ridge that dipped into the rock face. It looked like a shallow cave, and a path of thick snow led up to it. It would be a safe place to sleep for the night.

I nudged White-Ears. She had sat down and closed her eyes. "Come on, let's get to shelter, and then you can sleep," I whispered. She wobbled as she walked, so I put myself between White-Ears and the steep cliff below, and we walked one step at a time along the narrow path. "That's it, almost there now," I said. "Be strong for me." And she was.

When we got to the cave, and my paws touched the cold earth, White-Ears collapsed on the snowless ground, kicking up dirt and passing out. I licked her wound clean and laid down beside her, nuzzling her neck. Outside, the snow started again, and in no time at all, it covered the entire world in a suffocating cloud of whiteness.

Chapter 9

White-Ears wouldn't stop bleeding. Bright blotches of blood oozed out of her wounds, and I licked it clean. All of it. This went on for a very long time, and for the entire night, I stayed awake tending to her wound. By morning her bleeding stopped, and I turned to face the entrance of the cave. The snow whistled outside, and it was white, dull, and endlessly white.

She was fast asleep. I closed my eyes and tried to sleep, but I always jolted awake just before the tiredness overtook me. My heart raced, and I found it hard to breathe. I would get up, walk to the edge of the cave, look into the snowstorm, come back and lick White-Ears's wound clean, and try to sleep. And I would jolt awake again.

I wanted to bite something. To feel my teeth crunch around the bones of something and hear it scream and taste the blood. I wanted to sing for Ma and Pa, but I didn't need to. They would find us. We would go to the ocean together, and I would catch lots of fish.

My restless sleep was filled with sounds of snarling and feelings of the ground trembling. I woke up to White-Ears curled up in a ball. She shivered constantly, and she wouldn't stop. I put my body around hers and tried to warm her up. I nuzzled her face and breathed into her neck, and she remained asleep with short, shallow breaths. Her heart was beating fast too, but so was mine. It was okay. We just needed to rest.

It was later and it was dark again. White-Ears woke me up, but before that, I had dreamt of the valley. I dreamt that Ma was being swarmed by dozens of strangers, and all of a sudden, they were all around me, on top of me, they pinned me to the ground and bared their teeth and…White-Ears could barely stand up.

"You don't look too good," I whispered.

"I've been better." She gave me her signature open-mouthed grin.

"You slept the whole day."

"Yep." White-Ears curved around and licked her wound. It wasn't bleeding anymore. She shivered again and sat back down. "We should sing for them."

I looked outside. The snow fell in huge flakes, drifting and wobbling, whistling. I fixated on a single snowflake and watched it trace a path all the way down, past the edge of the cave until I could no longer see it.

"I don't think we should," I said.

"I miss them," White-Ears said.

"Me too, but it's too dangerous. The strangers are still nearby." I sat back down and buried my snout in her ribs.

"What if they don't find us?"

"They will," I said. "I know they will, and if they don't, we will find them. You left quite a trail of blood. Their noses are better than ours. Let's get some sleep."

"Sure," White-Ears whined. I motioned for her to get up, and she did. She limped to the back wall of the shallow cave, and I snuggled against her, protecting her from the elements.

She shivered the whole night.

◒

White-Ears was still asleep when I woke up. She shivered, and her fur was hot. I nuzzled her face, and she mumbled something. Her nose was dry, so I licked it and gave it some moisture until it glistened once again. Then I left her alone.

The snow had stopped overnight. The cave's entrance overlooked a fresh blanket of snow that sloped down to the valley below. White clouds with grey underbellies drifted hurriedly across the sky from west to east, and in between, the early morning sun peeked through, a few moments at a time.

It had been more than a day since I lost them. I had to go find Ma and Pa. I would find them in a nearby forest and bring them to the cave, and Ma would help White-Ears get better.

I stepped out and took a deep breath of fresh air. We were too high up, and the air was devoid of any scents. I carefully walked along the narrow path until I came across the gentle slope of the ridge. Mountains undulated forever into the distance, and the fresh snow covered the trees between all the peaks. Above me, the sun beamed down on my back, and I was warm, and for a second, I felt good. I closed my eyes, absorbing the sunlight and thinking about nothing at all.

The winding path hugged the bare mountainside from the cave all the way down. Our scents had faded, and our pawprints were gone, but there was only one path down, and there was no doubt this was the right path. With the final turn, I found myself at the top of the cliffs directly above where my family was ambushed. I peeked down. There was nothing but trees and snow down there. The trees were sparse and tall, and the ground was a pristine, untouched layer of snow.

I didn't want to go down there, so I sat at the ledge and watched and waited, and when the sun had started to fade behind the peaks to the west, I went back to White-Ears.

She was awake. She tried to stand up when she saw me but she couldn't. I laid down beside White-Ears, and we both stared out of the cave's entrance.

"You didn't find them."

"No," I said. "But it's okay. They will find us."

"We should go. The longer we stay here, the more our scent trail will fade."

I leaned into her and groomed her face with my teeth. There was a knot in her fur where she slept against the rocky ground. I pulled on it, but it wouldn't come apart. I didn't pull too hard. White-Ears was warm, and her heartbeat was fast.

"You're in no position to go anywhere," I finally said.

"I'm fine. See, it's already healing." She licked her wound.

"Did you get up at all today?"

"What does that have to do with anything?"

"You can't even stand up without shivering." I sighed through my teeth. "How do you expect to find them at night?"

"We can't just stay here. They could be heading to the ocean right now."

"She said they would find us."

White-Ears grumbled under her breath, curled into a ball, and closed her eyes. "Will you tell me a story?" she said with her nose under her tail.

"Sure," I said, closing my eyes and leaning against her. "There

81

was once a brother and sister who went fishing in the ocean, and they saw the biggest, most delicious fish in the ocean. It was the size of a wolf. They knew they had to get it…" Before I finished, she fell asleep, and I felt no need to continue.

Later, White-Ears started mumbling while asleep. She talked about running away. Then, she talked about food, Ma and Pa, and the ocean. I was very tired, so I ignored her and I fell asleep anyway.

Groggily, in the middle of the night, I woke up to the back of my neck being tugged by a savage creature, so I turned around and snarled before I realized it was White-Ears. I slumped over and tried to go back to sleep.

"Wake up, we have to go find them," she said. Her breath was hurried and shallow, and she paused between words.

"What-what's going on?" I rolled off my back and stood up. She didn't let go of my neck fur. She kept tugging, dragging me to the entrance, trying to pull me. Outside, the stars shimmered against the night sky.

"Wait," I growled. I tried to shake her off. "Let me go." Her jaws relaxed, and I pulled free. "What is going on?" I said.

"We-we have to go find them. We have to. They're nearby." White-Ears took a step towards the entrance. I jumped in front of her to block. Her eyes were blood red, and her gaze was hazy. She stared through me as if she didn't see me at all.

"You need rest," I said.

"No, no, you can't stop me. I'm going to find them."

"Rest," I said. I rubbed her face with my nose, and she pulled away from me. She was burning hot, and she trembled.

"No, no, no. I'm going to find them! I'm going, and you can't stop me!"

I stood in front of her, and I didn't move. She lunged at me

82

and bit my neck. It wasn't hard or painful, so I kept still and stood my ground.

"Why won't you just-just—"

White-Ears backed away. Her ears lowered, and she hissed at me and backed into the cave. Her hiss turned into a low, sustained growl, and her fur expanded. "It's *you*! You don't want me to see them," she said through bared teeth.

I shook my head. The cave began to spin until I realized I had been holding my breath. "It's not me. Why would you think that?" I said. I took a few steps towards her until I was face to face with her.

"If it wasn't for you, we'd be at the ocean by now." White-Ears hissed. "You-you don't want me to—"

She leaned against the back wall of the cave and fell over, and then she laid there motionless, breathing quick breaths and blinking at me, her eyes unfocused.

"We'll go tomorrow," I said. I nuzzled her neck and laid down. "We'll go tomorrow."

I left the cave at the earliest light. White-Ears was delirious all night, and she mumbled and growled and snarled. Before leaving, I brought clumps of snow into the cave and set it in front of her for her to drink. I left a dewclaw-high pile of snow that nearly touched her nose. She didn't seem to notice it.

It was a cold day with a searing blue sky. I couldn't look at the snowy ground for longer than a glance before having to squint, but this wasn't going to stop me. I had to find food for White-Ears. Ma once told me that food and water and sleep will cure even the worst of sicknesses. I needed White-Ears to feel better so we could start looking for Ma and Pa.

Above the cave, I found a slope with good grip and dug my claws into the snow and climbed the ridge. The forests below sparkled in the sunlight. Once in a while, there was a chirp or squawk of a bird down below in the depth of the snow, and then everything fell silent again. The smells of the ridge lingered long enough for me to make something out of it. There was faint metallic blood from a few nights ago. And there was moss. Lichen. Frozen rodents. Maybe. A frozen hare was exactly the thing we needed.

The ridge flattened out at the top. I had to jump the last ten or so wolf-lengths just to make it over the thick snow. Over the ridge, I stood at the edge of a plateau with stubby trees scattered in between boulders and snowdrifts. I lowered my head and scanned the ground in a circle, fanning outwards just like Pa taught me to. If there was anything to eat here, I would find it.

A bird squawked high above me. I looked up and had to squint against the morning sun. The large black shadow hovered above my plateau with its wings outstretched, flapping twice before disappearing to the west. I ignored it and kept searching under the snow. The wind rustled the branches of a tree, and I thought I heard something move. I leapt and landed on a soft patch, squishing it under my paws, but once I dug it out, it turned out to be a large pile of rotting grass. I tried eating it anyway. It was terrible.

Under the warm glow of the sun, I walked to the other end of the plateau and away from the cave. There was a shallow slope that gradually became filled with trees. It was not until the early afternoon before I canvassed the entire plateau. There was nothing here. As far as I knew, there was nothing alive on this barren mountaintop.

The flutter of wings and falling snow made me look up again. A bird landed on a treetop above me. It was a shiny black raven with a large beak and sharp, intelligent eyes.

"Cah! Cah!" it said. This was a good bird because it was supposed to point me towards food. I tilted my head and folded my ears and squinted. It ruffled its feathers and looked down at me. I sat down under the tree.

"Show me the food," I said through a bark.

"Cah!"

Of course, it didn't understand me. I stood up, shook the snow off of my butt fur, and kept going. A branch cracked. The raven was in the air again. I looked behind each tree and under every crevice, but I could not find a single dried berry. It came back again and landed twenty wolf-lengths in front of me on a log. The flutter of its wings made an imprint on the snow, and it stood there and cah-ed at me with its neck feathers puffed out.

"What do you want?" I said.

The raven sat still. It just tilted its head and looked at me, so I did the same. My tail wagged slowly as I took a step closer.

"Cah!"

"That's it?"

My stomach was knotting itself in hunger, and I had to find some food for White-Ears before the night. She needed to eat and get better so we could look for Ma and Pa tomorrow, but this stupid bird was scaring away all the field mice and hares.

"Cah, cah, cah." It flapped its wings and hopped on a branch. It flew in the air before landing again.

I took another step closer. This bird was too stupid to fly away, which meant I didn't need to find any hares or mice at all. Food was right in front of me. It was the size of my head, and it was friendly enough for me to approach it. I wagged my tail intentionally and made sure to flick my ears. "Cah to you back," I said, opening my mouth and letting my tongue dangle out. I took a few steps closer.

The raven flapped its wings, its eyes darting back and forth. I met its gaze, and for a moment, I was afraid it was going to see right through me. My tail faltered, and I stood still, but it just tilted its head and squawked. I took another step closer. And another, until I was no more than a wolf-length away from the raven. The bird was black and shiny and huge and smelled faintly of blood and meat.

It turned its head north, and I had my chance. I opened my eyes wide and dug my hind legs into the snow on the last wag of my tail and launched myself off the ground with open jaws. The raven barely reacted. The smell of the bird hit me at the same time I grabbed it between my jaws. It cah-ed and tried to twist away, but it was too late. I bit down, and the crunching sound of bone filled the air.

I ran back to the plateau and jumped down and nearly slipped on ice before reaching the cave. White-Ears was still sleeping, so I dropped the carcass in front of her. She stirred. The smell of warm meat filled the cave, and she slowly opened her eyes.

"Eat," I said.

"Thank you," White-Ears said. She grinned at me through her tired eyes and, without lifting her head off the ground, reached and grabbed the carcass and dug into it. She ate most of it. I licked her blood-covered mouth and nuzzled her neck. "You focus on getting better. We'll head out tomorrow and find them."

After she fell asleep again, I ate the remaining parts of the raven until there was nothing but the mangled head with the shiny black beak. It wasn't edible. I didn't want to keep looking at it, so I got up and walked to the corner of the cave where the ground was soft. There, I dug a hole and placed the beak at the bottom and buried it.

White-Ears's heartbeat slowed down and her breathing was deeper. The wound over her leg had developed a white film over it, and when I licked it, it didn't taste like anything. I licked it anyway to help her get better.

She woke up early in the night and walked around the cave. I only knew this because she told me after, deep into the night, when both of us were awake. But she was feeling better, she said, she felt well enough to move. We sat at the entrance to the cave and looked at the starry night. The night was silent, and so was the forest below.

"We should sing for them," White-Ears said. I nodded. It was time. I tilted my head back and sang the first note, and White-Ears joined my song. We sang of family and of hope and of how much we missed Ma and Pa. Our song trailed off with a whimper, and there was silence.

Then, not too far away, a single voice responded in the darkness. Then another, then another. It was the voices of the strangers. I stopped cold. Their songs sent a shiver down my back, and I instinctively leaned against White-Ears. We backed up until we had our backs to the cave wall, and we waited until the song ended. We were quiet for a long time after.

"We have to go," I whispered.

"Go where?"

"Northwest. Beyond the ridge is the forest where I caught the bird. We can keep going from there."

"What about our parents?"

"They will find us. Or we will find them," I said. I believed it. I wouldn't have said it if I didn't believe it. White-Ears buried her nose in my fur. "It's not safe here," I added.

We left in the dark. White-Ears wasn't strong enough to jump through the last of the deep snow, so I had to pull her up to the plateau. She limped, and she took breaks every dozen steps. We rested behind boulders and under trees. We pressed on a few steps at a time. Throughout the night, we walked aimlessly, but the further we went, the safer we were, and just as the sun peeked out from the west, we found shelter in the thick part of the forest. A deep red glow lingered in the sky.

Her fever came back. It wasn't snowing anymore, so we slept in the open. She slept between me and a thick overturned tree trunk. Sleeping there made her feel safe.

Whatever food I found—which were mostly mice—I gave to White-Ears. Food made her more lucid and less feverish. I tried my best, but I wasn't the best hunter, and prey was scarce, and often the snow was too deep for me to run.

When it got colder again, I dug under the tree trunk until my claws throbbed raw and smelled of blood. The ground was hard, but it wasn't impenetrable, and it got easier the deeper I went. It took a whole day. By nightfall, I had dug a den that was just wide enough for the both of us. We slept side-by-side in the den, using the log as cover from the drifting snow and the wind. White-Ears was barely breathing. Sometimes it was hard to hear her shallow breaths. I licked her nose to keep it wet and brought her snow, but there wasn't anything else I could do.

The sun disappeared behind the grey, formless clouds, and the wind picked up from the west. Along with the wind was the wispy scent of blood and meat. It has been days since I last smelled food. I ran northwest towards the source of the smell. The forest was thick and dense, and I ducked under the bushes and trees as I weaved my way across the forest floor.

It was easy to get lost here. I made sure to remember the way back because if there was a snowstorm, I could use landmarks to find my way back to White-Ears. I turned west at the lichen-covered rock with a flat surface, down a dry riverbed, right at the leaning tree, left at the rock, down the frozen creek until it ended, and then the deer trail.

The scent became stronger the further I went. Even when the wind changed direction, it still lingered in the air. I was close.

There was another smell in the air too. It was sweet, musky, with a hint of meadow lichen and frozen ground. It was the smell of a young female, a stranger, and she was alone. The sound of teeth against bone rang in my ears as I scanned ahead. I spread my toes out and gingerly stepped towards the sound, careful to avoid any branches or unstable logs.

Crunch. Crunch. Crunch. The girl stood with her head lowered and her snout bloodied, digging at the carcass on the ground. She was still far away, far enough and upwind so that I would not be noticed. The carcass looked to be half-eaten and still fresh enough to be warm. All the good parts were gone, but there was still plenty of meat between the bones and behind the skin and fur.

I got closer, close enough to see each of her whiskers, and still, she never noticed me. She had narrow shoulders with grey and yellow patches, skinny legs which were mostly fur, and a tail that looked like someone had taken a chunk out of it.

I could take her on.

She bit down on another rib bone, cracked it in half, and tore a piece of meat from the carcass, tilting her head up to swallow it whole. The meat slid down her throat, and she shuddered in pleasure, her tail swaying wildly. I stood straight and stared at her. A growl was coming out of my throat, and I had to swallow it to keep quiet.

Then, she paused and looked up. We made eye contact. It was a flash of golden yellow, like the midday sun, and burned itself into the back of my mind just the same. I lowered my head, and the growl finally came out. I bared my teeth and puffed my neck and tried to make myself look big.

The girl jumped back, tilting her head and inhaling my scent. She folded her ears back and spoke softly, "I didn't see you."

"Back off," I said, and my voice whistled past my teeth. "Back off and leave the kill."

"This is mine."

"Just leave," I snarled. I raised my tail high and took a step towards her.

"If you're hungry, you can come take a bite," she said. She stood her ground, and her ears straightened again. Her snout was dark, but the area around her eyes was white, and so was the inside of her ears and under her belly. I had never looked at a stranger so closely before. She stood confidently, and it made me feel very small. But it was just a feeling. I knew I was bigger and stronger than this stranger. I growled again and bared my teeth and showed off my impressive fangs. I needed to show her that I was more than capable of taking the carcass from her.

She backed away, and I took a step forward. "Eat your fill. You look hungry," she said. She narrowed her eyes but didn't snarl at me. "I'll wait."

"I'm taking the whole thing," I said.

"No, you're not. Don't mistake my kindness for weakness," she hissed. The girl's voice made me shudder, and for a second, my tail lost its buoyancy. But I raised it again. My thoughts drifted to White-Ears, and I knew she needed all of this meat to survive the winter. There wasn't much to think about. If I didn't get the entire carcass, White-Ears would die.

I didn't have a choice. I charged at the stranger with the notched tail and rammed into her left shoulder, which knocked her into a snowdrift. She twisted her body and came around and snapped her jaws at my neck. She was dangerously close.

I leapt back. We looked at each other again, this time less than a wolf-length apart. Her neck fur was ruffled, and her eyes stabbed the air like fangs. I lunged again, my nose filling with her scent. Gracefully, as if she was floating above the snow, she dodged my attack and stepped aside. We snarled and snapped at each other, and then we were far apart again.

She made a move for the carcass, but I was ready. I knocked her off balance, and as she fell, I wrapped my jaws around her neck. I clamped down. It wasn't hard enough to puncture fur and flesh. She tensed up and we made eye contact once again, my right eye stared into her shocked face. I held my jaw in place.

The girl whimpered and I let go and she ran with her tail swaying. The furless patch dangled back and forth. Was it a scar? It must have been. She must have gotten injured the previous summer, and the fur never grew back. I picked up the piece of bone that she had been chewing on, cracked it myself, and tasted the sweet marrow. This would do just fine. It was still fresh, and there was plenty of meat on it.

I grabbed the carcass and dragged it along the snow, past the landmarks, and delivered it to the den. White-Ears didn't even notice the smell of the stranger on the meat. She ate most of it. I took only what I needed from the bones and the ligaments, and I ate the skin too, fur and all.

Chapter 10

It was sunny and cold, and White-Ears was asleep, but I was wide awake. The stranger's smell lingered in my nose, and I saw her when I closed my eyes. She had a thin muzzle and a shiny black nose and an intoxicating smell that made her very difficult to forget. I wanted to find her again. Perhaps I could apologize for taking her kill. Perhaps I could introduce her to White-Ears.

White-Ears was doing fine. I made sure to check. Her nose was still dry and she was still too warm, but she hadn't gotten any worse, and she was keeping food down so she must have been fine. I snuggled closer to White-Ears and listened to her breathing and heartbeat. It was rapid but steady. She was still fast asleep when the tip of the sunlight had touched her butt and tail.

It was too bright to sleep. I carefully stood up and shook myself. I bent down to stretch, feeling the soreness in my legs from the past days and the chill of the snow against my paws. When I breathed, a cloud formed in front of my nose, but this time it drifted away in the air, floating up until it disappeared into the uniform blue.

The sound of distant crows echoed in my ears as I made my way through the thick forest and past the leaning tree. I smelled the base of the tree, hoping to catch the scent of the notch-tailed girl but she was never here, so I left my scent and I kept going.

When I stayed on the path, each step had a clean crunch against the fresh snow. But as soon as I left the path, I sank until the snow was past my elbows. I tried running, but it was thick and pointless, so I just walked.

The girl's tail had a patch to the right side, and it stretched all the way to the back. It was a brown tail with black dots that tapered to a black tip, and it was very fluffy. I could be friends with her, and maybe then I would get to pull on her tail. And her golden eyes would flash, and she would snarl at me, and I could already see it through my half-closed eyes. The sun was too bright in the snow.

I got to the place where I first met her by following the deer trail past the creek. The snow was flattened and hard, and the trees provided patchy shade, and the ground smelled like her. It also smelled like myself and meat. I lowered my head and circled the place where I took the carcass, and beside the blood, I could make out Notch-Tail's earthy scent. She went west, and she ran very fast because her prints were very far apart. About two hundred wolf-lengths out, she stopped, and there was a cluster of prints behind a tree.

She stopped here to sit down. From this spot, Notch-Tail had a clear line of sight to where I was yesterday. She sat here and watched me leave, and then she turned north and walked slowly, turning to and from trees in a big wide circle. She walked without a goal in mind, and she often doubled back, but she made progress north and kept going until the forest thinned out and became a barren slope. The snow that covered this slope was wind-blown and smooth. Her trail disappeared here. I climbed it anyway. It was rocky and unstable, and sometimes it was deeper than I thought, but I was strong, and I had a big weighty tail to give me balance.

The slope flattened out before cresting. I needed to catch my breath and drink water so I laid down. It was still sunny. There were dry mountains all around me, and in front of me, the rocky slope came to a stop right before a frozen lake. It was a small lake, round and uninteresting, with trees to the east and west that covered the shoreline, except the eastern corner where it was barren.

I thought I saw a movement near the lakeshore, but it disappeared when I looked again. I stood up and made my way down. My claws clashed against the unstable ground, and I slipped and tumbled and rolled. The snow was all over my fur. I climbed up and shook my face clean and found myself at the base of the hill staring at someone's shadow. I blinked. Notch-Tail was standing near a patch of trees about two dozen wolf-lengths away. Her tail was held horizontally, and she looked frazzled. She was close enough for me to smell her.

"Hello," I said with an open-mouthed smile.

"What do you want?" Notch-Tail hissed. Her eyes narrowed, and she raised her tail high in the air, and the bald patch stood perfectly still.

"I—nothing," I said. "I just wanted to explain myself."

"What's there to explain? You took my food even though I was willing to share."

"I said I was sorry."

"No, you didn't," she said.

"Well, I'm sorry, then," I said. She folded her ears and snarled at me. I could see that I wasn't welcome here, and there was no point in dragging it on any longer, so I lowered my head

95

and turned around.

"Go on," she said. I heard her take a step closer, so I turned and saw that she was actually quite a few steps closer. "Say what you have to say, stranger," she said.

"I took your food because my sister is very sick and without the food, she might die. If you want, once she recovers, I'll bring you a kill to make up for it."

"You could have just told me," Notch-Tail said.

"I really needed that food."

"And I would have let you have it if you just told me. It's not like you surprised me. I could smell you from very far away."

I looked down and up, and I saw her blink. Her expression was neutral and sad, and once I saw her face there was a sudden flash of heat from inside of my chest. We made eye contact and we both quickly looked away. I could feel my fur puff up, and the next thing I knew, I had bared my teeth.

"But you didn't surprise me either," I said. "I knew where you were, and I won the kill fair and square, and I am not sorry about it."

"Obviously," she hissed. "Go on, get out of here, and don't come back."

I turned and climbed up the same hill I rolled down. It really wasn't very steep. I didn't turn back because I knew she was still there, watching me, so I made sure to look as big and strong as I could and made it up in one breath. I came down the rocky slope, past the clearing along the deer trail, past the creek, and beyond. I made my way back to White-Ears, who was still sleeping, and I woke her up and told her to drink water, and she did.

Chapter 11

The wound on White-Ears's leg healed into an ugly, hairless scar that ran from the base of her tail down to her thigh. The skin was stretched taut between her grey and yellow fur, a valley of one-half of a paw width, a chasm, and a testament to the mistakes of the past. If it wasn't for her injury, our family would be at the ocean by now. Instead, the snow had started to melt, and Ma and Pa were nowhere to be found.

But at least she was better now. First, White-Ears limped around the tree trunk. And then she walked around it. And when she could run for a few steps at a time, we left at sunrise and headed northwest.

"We have a debt to repay," I told White-Ears. She was slow, and I kept pace with her. And although it was the middle of the day, she struggled in the snow, so I had to clear a path for her by making wide steps and brushing the snow aside with my front paws.

"Who?" she asked.

"A stranger. She gave us food so you could be fed," I said. I never told her about Notch-Tail. It was a lie, of course, but it was also mostly true. She did give us food, even though it was unwilling, and I did promise to make up for it. This was my last chance to see her before we left for the coast. I deliberated the whole night whether to make the trek and decided that it was safe for me to bring White-Ears. At worst, she would give me the cold shoulder again, and at best, she could join us. She was a competent hunter and would be a big help.

"That's very nice of her," White-Ears said. She sat down to take a break, and I noticed that she sat tilted, leaning on her hind legs in a way to shield her wound from the snow.

"Yes, it was," I said. "She was very nice. She wasn't like the strangers that attacked us."

"She must have been from the same family, right? We are not too far away from where we separated from our parents, and remember that night we heard the strangers' songs? How do you know she wasn't part of that family?"

"I don't know," I said. "All I know is that she was very nice and gave us food."

"Alright. How should we thank her?"

"I was thinking we can catch a hare and deliver it to her. She's not very far away from here."

"And then we'll go find our parents."

"Yes, of course," I said. I brushed aside more snow, and we walked slowly. We were past the creek, and I had my nose buried in the snow, trying for any hint of Notch-Tail. "Could we sing for them now?" White-Ears asked. Her voice was far away. I saw that she had sat down some ways behind where I was.

I shook my head. "I'd rather not draw any attention to us. You wouldn't be able to run away from anything."

"No, I suppose not."

"Keep an eye out for hares," I said, and she didn't say anything, so I kept walking. But as luck would have it, the forest was as barren as ever, and there was nothing. We walked past where

I took the meat from Notch-Tail, but it had been many days, and the place no longer smelled like anything except snow. Notch-Tail's scent was faint on a tree, and I held my nose there and inhaled three times.

White-Ears caught up to me. "Smell that." I gestured, and she did. "That's the stranger." White-Ears nodded understandingly.

"What about the hare?"

"I'm still looking," I laughed. "Finding food isn't easy, you know."

When we got to the rocky slope, there was still no hare. I told White-Ears that the stranger lived on the other side, and she asked me whether we should even go if we hadn't caught anything. I said it was fine. She shrugged, and we started climbing. I went behind her just in case she fell.

"I want her to come with us to the coast."

"What? No way we're taking a stranger with us."

"She's a great hunter."

"I don't know her at all, and you just met her."

"I'm sure if we just get to know her, it would be fine," I said.

"We'll see," White-Ears whispered. "Let's just meet this stranger first."

We climbed over the rocky slope, and the lake greeted us at the bottom of this landscape. It was still frozen like everything else, and it was clear and white and light blue. There was snow all over the treetops, and everything was silent, except our pawsteps. I helped White-Ears down the slope. She wobbled and gasped every so many steps, but she didn't fall, and soon we were at the bottom facing a row of trees. The lake sat calmly in the distance.

"Hello?" I barked. My voice echoed.

White-Ears tugged on my neck, and I turned to her. "You're too loud," she said. "You'll attract unwanted attention."

"We're trying to attract attention."

"What if this stranger brings her whole family?"

I hadn't thought about what she said until now, and the thought gave me a cold shiver. But I pushed it aside. "No, I didn't smell anyone around her. She doesn't have a family."

"That's even worse."

"How so?"

"What kind of wolf doesn't have a family? There must be something wrong with her then. Nobody in their right mind would be out here alone in the winter without a family to help them get food."

"She's a perfectly fine hunter," I said. "Hello!" I barked again, and this time I was loud enough to send a raven into the air. The black bird swooped from the trees and then soared above and behind the ridge. White-Ears shook her head and batted an eye at me, and then joined me: "Hello," she said quietly.

In the distance, there was a small movement near the ground. I felt my ears perk up and then I was fully engaged. The sound was no more than a hundred wolf-lengths away. Then there was another motion, and another, until I saw the gleam of Notch-Tail's nose against the snow. She came slowly and purposefully with her nose against the snow and her tail held high. Soon, she was standing in front of us. I wagged my tail.

"Hello!" I said again. "I wanted to introduce you to my sister." I gestured to White-Ears, who backed up a step and folded her ears back, so I grabbed her by the neck fluff and tried pulling her beside me, but she wouldn't budge, so I just left her and walked a few steps forward.

"Didn't I tell you to go away?" Notch-Tail said.

"Do you want to come with us?" I asked. "We're going to find our parents at the coast. I think it would be great if you came along. You don't have family here anyway."

"I'd rather not," she said. "I live here, and I don't want to go anywhere. Not with you or anyone else. Nice to meet you," she turned to White-Ears and smiled. "Now, please, I would like the two of you to leave."

"Why not?" I asked flatly. White-Ears shrank away uncomfortably, but I ignored her.

"It's really none of your business," Notch-Tail said, and she showed her teeth for a second, which were sharp but more yellow than White-Ears's. I hadn't realized that she was older, but now that I knew, it made perfect sense.

"My mother said there is always food near the ocean. If you come with us, you'll never be hungry. I still owe you a meal."

"You took it fair and square."

I felt my face flush with blood, and I turned my head to hide, but there was nowhere to hide, so I looked up again. Notch-Tail had lowered her stance, but she still wore the cold hard determination that she first greeted us with. Her mind wasn't about to be changed. I didn't want her anyways.

"Fine."

"Please leave."

"Fine, fine, fine," I said. "We'll go." And with that, I turned around and pushed my nose against White-Ears until she turned around, and we made our way up the hill. At the top, I looked down, and I hoped that Notch-Tail was still there, but she had long gone, and the lake was once again quiet.

On my daily walks, I saw a high, rocky ridge in the distance that overlooked this entire valley and possibly many more valleys behind us. It would be a safe and high place to sing for Ma and Pa. I ran ahead, leaping over a bush and feeling the tips of the new leaves rub against my belly as I flew. Then, I sat and waited for White-Ears. She was still weak.

"Are you coming?" I called.

White-Ears huffed.

When we finally climbed on top of the ridge, the moon was high in the air and full. Its bright white disk glowed in the purple night sky. I hopped on a dry ledge and shuffled my paw, knocking over a rock and sending it down the cliff-side. It flew until it landed below, a long time later, with barely a puff. Below, the valley opened itself to us. Splotchy snow and dark green canopies and bald patches of rocks. The ridge and cave where we first stayed was nothing but a dark spot, far to the east.

White-Ears's gaze lingered on the same place. I pressed my face against hers, and I tilted my head to the sky, and I felt her do the same. I inhaled and held it in. Then, when I felt ready, I exhaled, and a stream of white clouds came from my mouth. And then the first note, sending a shiver to the tip of my tail. We sang with our heads high and bodies tensed. We sang our story from then until now. We sang about how much we missed them. We sang about the mountains and the ocean. I stopped when my throat was scratchy, but White-Ears continued until she trailed off in a whisper.

Birds chirped and bugs buzzed but the world was quiet.

"Nothing," I said. I sat down, and then after a moment of hesitation, I laid down with my nose hanging over the cliff.

"We'll try again tonight," White-Ears said.

We tried many times over the night and the next day, but there was nothing, not even strangers—not even Notch-Tail. I would have preferred the reply from strangers, even if it was the same family that attacked Ma and Pa. Even that would be better than this silence. Every time I stared at the valley, it became bigger, emptier, until the mountains in the east pulled away into the infinite distance, and everything was this empty, lifeless forest.

"We should spread out. They must be close by."

"I searched as far as I could go."

"Was this when I was—"

"When you were sick, and the snow was still heavy," I sighed, got up, and shook my fur.

"What now?"

I hadn't thought about what I would do next. I always knew I would find Ma and Pa on this rock—this stupid rock, this stupid rock with dust and pebbles and lichen that smelled of elk piss. I didn't know what to do. I didn't know where to go.

"The ocean," I said. "Mother said we would find them there."

"Did she?"

I wasn't sure. But now that I thought about it, I was sure. Ma told us to go to the coast! Of course! We should have done it a long time ago if not for White-Ears's illness. "She did," I said. "You were too busy getting bitten." I grinned at her.

White-Ears snapped her jaws at me and then turned her head and rubbed her forehead against me as if she was scent rolling on my fur. Then, when I was least expecting it, she headbutted me, and I fell over.

I growled at her.

"Suppose that you're right," she said, looking down at me. "The ocean is huge. Where should we go?"

"We'll go along the coast like we did with the lake. Remember the lake?"

"And if it's bigger than the lake?"

"Then we'll take many days," I said. "They'll be there, somewhere."

And so with my assurance and against the vast emptiness of this valley, White-Ears and I headed for the coast, for the ocean where there was plenty of fish, for the ocean where Ma was waiting for us with more stories. And I would tell her stories. I had too many stories to tell.

Chapter 12

We left in the dark after the forest had been bathed in a purple hue, past the creek and then down from the rocks and into the forest. From there, we travelled west along a trail that smelled of deer and strangers. Both were faint. There hadn't been anything that passed through here for many days, but we wanted to be careful nevertheless, so we travelled at night.

"Only for a little bit," I told White-Ears. "Only until the strangers' scent disappears." She agreed.

The creek had partially melted with the snowcaps of the trees, and its bubbling concealed our pawsteps and voices. I decided to travel along it since we could talk without fear of being ambushed. The creek's shore was covered by rounded pebbles, smooth and soft on my paws, and the further we went, the smaller they became.

We stopped at a bend, where the creek gurgled relentlessly. I leaned over to drink the water, curling my tongue backwards and lapping it up. It was sweet and very cold and much better than snow. I dunked my head into the creek and allowed the water to flood my ears. Bubbling and crashing water drowned out everything else around me. I then opened my eyes, then my nose, then my mouth, and the water washed over every part of me.

White-Ears said something I couldn't hear, so I pulled my head out of the water and shook myself. I turned to look at her, and she repeated herself. "Any fish down there?"

"No," I said. "Too cold."

"What were you doing?"

"It's relaxing. You should try it," I said.

White-Ears leaned away and shivered. "I'd rather not. I'm already cold."

The bald patch on her leg shimmered in the moonlight. Looking at it, I had a brilliant idea. I jumped at her, and I nuzzled it with my cold snout, which made her jump in the air and scream and bite my nose. I laughed, and I couldn't stop laughing until she smacked my snout with her paw.

We ran down the creek together. I kicked up water with each step and heard the drops splattering on the snow far and wide. I chased White-Ears until I caught her tail, and then I took off, and she chased me to a wide curve. The unspoken rule was that we had to follow the creek wherever it went. A sharp bend in the creekbed allowed her to jump to the other side of the creek, and she took the inner path and caught up to me. I ducked out of the way when she tried to tackle me, but she claimed to have touched me with the tip of her outstretched claws.

She wanted to count it as a win, but I didn't think it was fair.

We slept, ate, and walked. Most of it was downhill. As we went further, the forest became thicker in smell, with greener pines and livelier birds. The days gradually became longer, with a stronger sun that whisked away the snow. And without snow, the still-white hares became easy to catch. The thin mice were even easier. They moved as if they hadn't eaten all winter, but there was still plenty of meat under the fur.

I sang for Ma and Pa every night, and every morning, before I opened my eyes, I would inhale and have Ma's scent fill my nose—but it was only for a split moment. The world always came flooding back: the pines, the grasses, the wet leaves, and White-Ears.

We hunted hares together. White-Ears ran slower than me, so she chased, and I flanked. The hares always made sharp turns away from me, and if we timed it right, it ran right into White-Ears's open jaws. Sometimes she killed it right away. Other times she only incapacitated it and left it for me to kill. The crunch was the best part. I liked to put my molars on either side of the neck and bite down, hard enough to crack the neck—but only about half the time. It was satisfying nonetheless.

We ate well. There were long stretches when we caught something every day. Sometimes we left the hard-to-eat parts behind and continued walking. There was no point eating it all since we would catch something else the next day. It would be something with a big liver, or maybe a fish, although it was still too cold for fish.

White-Ears's grey and white fur shone in the sun. It wasn't grease. I made sure of it. I groomed her and got all the dirt and knots out of her fur, one clump at a time. She started shedding soon after. We were both patchy, and the fur kept coming out, so I eventually gave up. A thought came to me as I pulled a patch of brown-grey fur from her shoulder. "Summer is coming," I said. She nodded and grinned with her mouth open.

I found a herd of deer late in the evening at the place where trees became grassland. There were at least ten of them. White-Ears and I were well rested from lazing around all day, and we hadn't had deer or elk since early in the winter, so we decided to follow the herd. We stayed downwind, a few hundred wolf-lengths away, and we moved quietly.

The herd was slow. None of the animals were remotely aware of us, and we tried to keep it that way. They would move for a bit, and then graze, and then move again. From this distance, I saw that the deer were eating the new leaves in the undergrowth. I lowered my head, smelled the shrub in front of me, and took a bite. The leaves were bitter. I didn't like it. White-Ears shook her head and laughed at me, and I told her to shut up before she scared our dinner away.

At last, after hovering around the edge of the forest for the whole evening, the deer moved onto the yellow grass. This was our chance. Open fields made it easier to identify the weak ones. Ma and Pa always preferred to hunt in the meadow. Ma had once told me that the woods would slow me down and I would eventually crash into a tree—and then she laughed and nuzzled my face.

"You chase, and I flank," I said, and we took off. We weren't as quiet as we thought: the deer bolted away the moment my first pawstep landed. No matter. We were fast and had an advantage on the flat plains. White-Ears ran straight at the deer, and I came wide in a semi-circle until I was running alongside the herd of deer. I ran along the forest, and every time the deer tried to turn into the woods, I stopped them. Behind me, White-Ears was gaining steadily on the deer, a couple paces at a time, until she was no more than a wolf-length away from the laggard of the group.

It was a small fawn, probably a newborn but definitely smaller than the rest of the herd. It was only the size of White-Ears, and it had white spots all over its yellow body. I pushed and panted until I got ahead of the fawn. Then, I made a sharp turn. The animal jumped and turned in the other direction.

Separate the one you want, Ma had said, separate and surround, and even if there were a hundred deer, they would not try to attack you. I barked loud and sharp. White-Ears turned with the fawn and moved to the other side of the animal. We ran beside it. The rest of the herd was far away now, and they didn't matter to me. The only thing that mattered was slowing down the fawn. With each step, I could smell its sweat and see it tremble. With each step, I was closer to dinner.

When we were close enough to grab on, the animal turned sharply and ran right into me. I jumped on its back and clung on with my teeth. It thrashed. I bit down on the piece of muscle just above its right shoulder. Panicked breathing filled the air, and hooves thrashed against the ground. I felt my back claws drag along the roots of the grasses, and I planted my paws, pulling the fawn into the ground. It squealed and crashed with a thud, and I tumbled with it. I closed my eyes and twisted my body to keep steady.

The deer tried to get up, but I had it firmly in my grasp. I kept it pressed down with my front paws, readjusted my jaws, and bit down. My fangs went right through the soft neck muscles of the deer. White-Ears bit into the belly of the animal. I gave it a clean crunch, and the animal twitched before passing out. Hot, sweet blood gushed out in spurts, all over my face and shoulders and into my nose, where it made the entire world smell like blood and meat.

By the time we got the skin open and the innards spilled out, the animal had stopped moving. White-Ears pulled the liver out of the belly and took a huge bite. I pushed her aside and snatched it from her. Of course, I had to! She was going to eat the whole thing if I didn't take it from her—or whatever was left of it, anyway. Splitting the liver was our celebration for a successful hunt. It was something only a fresh kill could bring. No amount of scavenging ever turned up innards.

The sweet bloodiness of the liver sent shivers down my back, and my tail started to swing in a circle. I ate it in two bites, feeling the warm slimy chunks down my throat. This was better than I could have dreamed and certainly better than I remembered.

We got through the kidneys, heart, lungs, intestines, and even the grass-filled stomach before we took a break. White-Ears laid on her side, and her chest came up and down, and her ears flickered once in a while. I laid down on my belly on the other side of the kill. I was very full, and I didn't want to do anything, so I stared into the dim forest in the distance.

Near the edge of the forest, the rest of the herd of deer looked at us blankly and grazed. Then, they slowly made their way into the forest, disappearing into the darkness one at a time.

I tilted my head and sang a short song. White-Ears joined, and our joyous voices filled the night air. The last time I hunted large animals, there was a chill in the air and a persistent nervousness inside of me. There was none of that this time. And though I didn't have Ma's soft fur to lean against nor Pa's strength to break apart the carcass, I was happy. White-Ears and I made a good team. We would be welcomed back to the family as hunting experts, and maybe then I would finally have something to teach Pa.

⌂

We ate a second dinner when the moon was high in the clear sky, and the carcass had cooled down. This time we tore at the ribs for the fatty pieces of meat in between. I broke off a rib bone and carried it with me until I found a place to sleep, not far from the carcass. I chewed it until I fell asleep dreaming of liver.

The sound of a pawstep jolted me awake. Immediately, I was hit with the pungent smell of a stranger. The stranger stood in front of the carcass with his head deep inside the open belly. Faint starlight gleamed off of his fur. He was black from ear to tail. My neck puffed and my tail stood high and an angry snarl escaped my mouth as I stood up. The stranger jumped high into the air and backed up. He smelled like blood.

I barked, low and deep. White-Ears scrambled up, and she stood with her teeth bared on the other side of the black wolf.

"Easy," he said with his ears folded, backing away a step.

"Get out of here!" I said. I caught a glimpse of his yellow eyes. I snarled again.

The black wolf shrunk himself to the ground and backed away, one step at a time, until he turned around and bolted into the trees in the distance. My fur relaxed, and my tail slowly fell back down.

"Are you all right?" I asked White-Ears.

"Fine," she said. "He scared me, though."

"It's okay," I said. "No stranger is ever going to take anything from us."

I slept beside her for the rest of the night, but I barely slept.

The next morning, the grassland was covered by a dense, hazy layer of fog. The stranger's scent lingered, and it made me uncomfortable, and I tried sneezing it away, which only made it worse. Later, the sun peeked through. Soon after, White-Ears woke up. We had breakfast. The carcass had frozen tips, and all the blood had dried into a dark crimson, and it stained the animal's fur like a sunset sky. I bit through the frozen layer, and underneath it all, the meat was still sweet and fresh.

I noticed a rib was missing. The stranger had taken it before we chased him off. I grumbled, and White-Ears stopped eating for a moment. She looked at me with her bloody snout tilted, then she licked my face and went back to eating. It wasn't long before we were full again. Even a small fawn was too much food for the two of us. We still hadn't touched the limbs or the rump of the carcass, only the innards and ribs. There were also the eyes and tongue and brain. Ma took a liking for those parts, so even though they were never my favourite, they were valuable parts to eat.

When the fog dissipated and the blue sky came into view, I saw a shiny black figure at the edge of the grassland. He was sitting down and barely visible over the patches of tall grass and bushes. I snarled at him, and I stared straight into his yellow eyes, against all the manners I had been taught by Pa. "He needs to go," I hissed.

White-Ears looked at me lazily, lying down on the pile of grass she had flattened. "If he's going to torture himself by watching us eat, he can be my guest."

I stared him down until he turned around and disappeared into the woods, but the air told me he was still nearby, somewhere, waiting to take our food. No way I was going to let that happen. I stood my ground and barely moved from this spot all day, and by the end of the day, the grass underneath me was warm. I rubbed my nose on the ground, feeling the warmth, trying to get used to the lack of snow.

Then, when the sun was low in the sky, the black wolf popped up again near the trees. I was furious when I saw him. "I've had enough," I told White-Ears. "We have to get rid of him." I bared my teeth and hissed as I approached the stranger, and in the corner of my eye, I saw White-Ears do the same.

"What do you want?" I yelled. There were still many wolf-lengths between us.

The stranger stood up, and his ears twitched. He answered while avoiding my eyes. "Nothing," he said, "I was just waiting for you to leave."

"You're not getting our food, so you might as well go away right now," I said.

"I won't bother you. I just want the bones and leftover scraps."

White-Ears stopped growling and came up beside me. "We should just leave him be," she whispered.

"He could be dangerous."

"We can take him on." White-Ears shrugged and lowered her tail. "He's all fur and bones."

"Go!" I bellowed once again. The intensity of my voice surprised me and made the stranger's ears fold back.

"Please, I won't bother you," he said.

I opened my mouth to talk, but White-Ears was faster. "Where is your family?" she asked. I hadn't thought about this question, and it took me by surprise. My tail lowered, and so did the fur on my neck. The stranger took a few steps closer to us, and White-Ears stepped towards him. The scar on her thigh had new fur, and though it wasn't the same colour as before, it looked good on her.

"They left," he said. "Nobody but me here."

"You're alone?"

"For most of the winter now. I'm weak and hungry. I'm no threat to your family."

White-Ears got closer, and I followed behind her. The black wolf had a weary face, and underneath his partially blown winter coat, there was the imprint of his ribcage. She turned to me and spoke with her snout right next to my nose. "The deer is way too much for us. Plus, we have to keep moving to the ocean."

"It's ours." I shook my head.

"Look at him. He's starving."

"We could be starving by the next new moon," I said.

White-Ears bared her teeth at me. Notch-Tail's face suddenly invaded my thoughts, and in White-Ears's, I saw the same mix of tiredness and weariness. White-Ears was right. We weren't the strangers that attacked our family. We had to be better than that. I nuzzled her and then turned and called to the black wolf. "You can come and eat!"

The black wolf lowered his head and folded his ears back, and approached us with his tail between his thighs. White-Ears and I parted to the side. Timidly, he walked towards the carcass and took a bite. He dug his snout into the ribs of the carcass, which had melted in the warm sunlight, and tore it out one chunk at a time. The stranger was voracious. He must have been starving.

After the black wolf had his fill—which was nearly half of the carcass—he retreated to a patch of grass away from us, where he laid down and fell asleep instantly. I kept an eye on him as I tugged on a broken rib bone with White-Ears. This went long into the night. Our bone-tugging game ended in a draw, two wins for me and two for her, and by the end of it all, we were both exhausted. That night was especially clear and cold, so, out of habit, I slept on White-Ears to keep her bald patch warm.

When it was morning again, my snout was on the ground, and I had drooled. I looked around for White-Ears with my left eye half-open. Something was stuck in my other eye, and I rubbed my face against my forearms until I felt better. A flash of grey and white in my peripheral told me exactly where White-Ears was. She was talking to the stranger near the trees. I shook myself awake and walked over. It was hard to know what to feel now. The anger of the black wolf's intrusion two nights ago had all but disappeared, and the wolf I saw in front of me wasn't a dangerous stranger but a hungry and tired wolf separated from his family.

White-Ears looked at me apprehensively as I approached. They sat close together and had been talking for quite some time, given the relaxed way they acted. I wagged my tail, and she relaxed.

"Morning," she said.

"Good morning," I yawned. I turned to look at the black wolf. "And to you too."

He looked at me and grinned.

I didn't have much to say to him. The black wolf's fur was shinier, and his grin told me he was genuinely happy. Oh well. I grinned back and allowed my body to relax. "Come and eat with us," I said, "I think we can finish the deer by today."

We ripped apart the carcass until there was nothing left except skin and fur and bare bones. White-Ears had taken on a liking for the black wolf, and they ran around together. Her white-tipped ears popped up over the high grass when they played, and so did his shiny black ones. They ran in circles and deep into the forest and then back around again.

I didn't join their game, but I didn't mind his scent anymore.

⌂

The wind howled and bent the trees, and the new leaves fluttered with cacophonic discordance. It was chilly. My summer coat had mostly come in except for the thick patches on my shoulders and thighs. At least those parts were warm.

White-Ears returned with the black wolf after some late-night frolicking. As usual, he stayed far away, and she came up to me. "It's cold," she said.

"Yeah. Maybe summer is over?" I laughed and nuzzled her.

"We should let him sleep with us tonight."

I shook my head and then my whole body from nose to tail. "I don't know," I said. "I don't trust him."

"He's quite nice, really. You should get to know him."

"You're sure about this?"

"Yes," White-Ears said. She buried her nose in my neck, and it tickled, and I jumped away.

"Okay," I said. "He can sleep with us."

I was too tired to argue, and it was getting colder over time. We piled together behind the dry bones of the deer, with White-Ears in the middle—just the way she liked to sleep. I put my snout over her bald patch but realized it wasn't bald anymore, so I leaned against her instead. It was a restful, warm sleep.

⌂

In the open grassland, we sang for Ma and Pa. As usual, there were no replies, but I wasn't worried because we would find them at the ocean. The black wolf joined us as well. He had a pleasant, low voice, and he sang his own story. He missed his family.

"What happened with your family?" I asked him. White-Ears looked at us with an open-mouthed smile on her face.

He came up to me and rubbed his nose bridge against my chin. "We were very hungry. My family fought, drawing blood over a field mouse. It was unbearable with all the teeth and snarls, so I left the same day and started heading south."

"You left them?"

"I didn't want to, but at the same time, I was terrified. And hungry. And tired." The black wolf folded his ears and shrank to the ground.

White-Ears bent over and nuzzled him. "It's okay," she said. "You're safe now."

To her touch, his smile returned vibrantly. "What about the two of you?"

"We were separated from our family—parents—in the winter," I said.

"We were attacked, and we are still trying to find them," White-Ears said. "But they told us to meet them at the ocean, so that's where we're going."

"I'm sorry to hear that," the black wolf said as White-Ears nibbled on his neck. "Where is the ocean?" he asked.

"West."

"How far?"

"I don't know," I said. "Far."

The black wolf licked White-Ears's face and smiled at me. "Thank you both for the food," he said, "I won't bother you anymore. Good luck finding your family."

White-Ears looked at me. I met her gaze, and I knew what she was thinking. I didn't mind. In fact, I was beginning to like the black wolf. I gave her a nod, and her face lit up. "You can come with us to the coast," White-Ears said as she jumped up and down with her tail spinning. "It'll be fun!"

"Plus, we could use some help bringing down elk," I said.

The black wolf happily agreed. He tackled us to the grass and we played for a bit, then we started heading into the golden purple sunset, towards the rolling hills and lakes in the west.

Chapter 13

With the warm weather came the longer days and the bug-filled air. We stopped at a small lake at the base of a hill. A chorus of buzzing and croaking stretched from one end of the lake to the other, and all around the shores stood tall grasses with brown tips. White-Ears bit one, and a white puff of grass sprayed everywhere. Both the black wolf and I laughed, but I wanted a taste of this grass for myself, so I got it all over my snout as well. It didn't taste like anything, and I didn't like it very much.

I leapt headfirst into the water from a dirt-capped ledge. It was cool and refreshing. Faint shapes of fish scattered about in the water all around me, but they were too deep and out of my reach. I tried anyway. I kicked my legs as hard as I could and sank into the depths, but the fish were much faster than me. I came up empty-jawed and shook myself dry, and I found a place to sit and watch the fish.

In the distance, loud rustling and the sharp scent of blood alerted me to the black wolf and White-Ears. He had killed a beaver, and they were eating it, and I wasn't about to miss out on fresh food. We ate together, and afterwards, White-Ears splashed around with the black wolf and me.

"If you're sick of eating rodents," he said, "legend has it there is a herd of caribou that migrates north and south along the coast."

"Legend?" I asked.

"Well, one of my brothers' wild stories," he said, shrugging.

"I've never had caribou," White-Ears said.

"They're like deer but better. Sweeter in the innards and meatier in the bones. It's my favourite food."

"Mine is liver," she grinned.

"You stole that from me," I said as I bit her nose. "Find your own favourite food."

She growled at me, so I pushed her into the water, and she did the same to me. The three of us played together in the water. I was glad the black wolf came with us. He often touched noses with White-Ears. He liked nibbling on my neck fur. He flanked deer better than me and had a knack for catching beavers. "When we find our parents, let's ask if he can be part of the family," I said to White-Ears, and of course, she was more than happy to agree.

We travelled west and south, through the grassland and into the flat shrubs. The big lakes dried up and they became small watering holes with stagnant water, and even those shrank as the sun beamed during the day.

We had plenty of food even as we entered the desert, but as the rolling hills became sharp and brown ridges, we started having difficulty finding food. Everything was prickly and dry. There were mounds of brown dirt with huge ants which smelled sweet. Between those, vast stretches of low dry grass covered the earth. Hidden among the grass were little green balls that were painful to touch.

We passed through the desert in a few days, and, in time, the full canopies of the trees obscured the hot sun once again, and the creeks returned, louder and fresher than before. We started descending through the cool, moist valleys with huge trees. Every day was downhill. Sometimes when the path was straight, we raced downhill. I was always faster, but not much more than the black wolf.

On a hot and windless day—most of the days were windless under the thick tree trunks—I stopped at a clear pool of water for a drink. White-Ears had gone ahead with the black wolf, but their scent trail was still strong, and I knew I wouldn't lose them, so I stayed for a bit to rest.

At the edge of the pond on the shaded side of an uprooted tree, there was a fish the size of White-Ears's snout. It had a striped back, tiny eyes, and a huge head. I stood on the edge and watched its mouth open and close silently, lazily grazing at the bottom. This was the one. My body tensed, and my tail flickered, and with a kick, I leapt into the water. Water bubbled all around me. My open jaws wrapped around the fish. I bit down. The fish tore away with ferocious energy, but my jaws were stronger.

I dropped the fish onto the ground on the moss between two haphazard logs. It flopped in place, and I grinned. It wasn't bad for the first fish of the summer.

Chapter 14

The massive tree trunks parted ways to reveal a deep blue sky, dotted with puffs of clouds, and as we came over the crest of the hill, the air became filled with the scent and the sounds of waves. Below me, beyond the vast swath of green trees, there was a sea of blue and white that glimmered under the sunlight. Sky and ocean met on the horizon, separated by tiny mountains. It was more beautiful than I ever imagined.

The ocean had the faint scent of saltiness, like the hooves of elk in the winter, but it also the smell of freshness—like fish. I inhaled again, and the same wisps of freshness filled my nose.

White-Ears's face lit up when she saw the ocean. She licked the black wolf, and he licked her back. I tilted my head back and sang a song of joy and relief, and my travel companions joined me, and our voices filled the skies.

We ran for the shore. Trees and shrubs and giant green leaves rushed past me as I bolted down the trail. The grey, rocky shore gradually grew larger until I burst through the last of the trees. I jumped over the rocks and crashed into a bed of sand and gravel. White-Ears and the black wolf emerged from either side of me. He stopped and leapt from rock to rock until he stepped onto the soft ground. White-Ears tumbled and rolled straight into the water. A puff of salty freshness enveloped us as a wave crashed into a nearby rock.

I raced towards her. The black wolf ran beside me, and we piled onto White-Ears at the same time. Water soaked my fur as I tumbled. It was cool, cold, and for a moment, it washed away all the suffocating summer heat. I stood up and shook myself, splattering water back into the ocean.

I chased the black wolf along the shore until he turned around and pushed me into the ocean. Half standing and soaking wet again, I snapped my jaws at him and he grinned. I heard a sound, and we both turned back up the shore. It was scraping of claws against rock and sand and mud. White-Ears had her head down in the sand, and she was digging. I glanced at the black wolf, and we ran towards her at the same time.

There was an unmistakable fishy smell in the sand. I stuck my head near the hole that she had dug, and she batted my snout away with her muddy paws. "What is it?" I asked.

"Something to eat!" White-Ears said with her tail swaying. She wiggled her nose into the narrow hole and pulled out a round, hard-shelled creature the size of her paw. It snapped closed as she pulled out. She laid it on the sand, smelling and licking it.

"Doesn't look edible to me," said the black wolf.

I laughed and said, "It looks like a rock," to which White-Ears glanced at me and picked it up between her teeth. She chomped down. The "rock" cracked in half effortlessly, and inside there was a yellow mass, wiggling between the shattered fragments of the shell and emitting a high-pitched squeal.

White-Ears dropped the cracked shell on the sand and tore the wiggling mass out of the shell. She tilted her head back and swallowed, and it slid down her throat. Her ears flickered. A wide smile grew from the tip of her snout to the sides of her face.

"I don't believe you," I said.

"Fine, starve. I'll eat them all."

White-Ears jumped to another patch of wet, smooth sand and started digging. I walked up to her. I tried sniffing the hole, but she growled at me. I growled back. She ate another shell before my curiosity and hunger got the best of me. I asked her how to find them, and she told me to look for holes and bubbles in the sand. It was a lot of fun to dig into sand. The soft, smooth grains wedged between my toes and made them tingle, and I liked it, so I wiggled them. My claws cut through the sand as if it was water. It took me less than five swipes to get to the round shell at the bottom.

I picked it up. There was sand all over my face, and I tried shaking it off, but it stuck there. A wave came and crested at my paws, so I dropped the shell on the wet sand and watched it roll back. I picked it up again and bit down. It went cleanly through and split the creature in half. White-Ears was right. The meat was delicious, like a soft and wiggly fish without the hard parts. Salty, smooth, chewy. I could get used to eating these things.

By the time we were done and overly stuffed, there were holes all over the sandy shores between the rocks. The water had dried off our backs, and the black wolf was puffy and shiny. He took a nap on White-Ears's back. His chest rose up and down, and in time their breaths synchronized and their bodies rose and fell together. In, and out, and in, and out, to the gentle crashing of the ocean.

I wasn't very tired, so I decided to walk down the shore instead of napping. I went north against the sun, hopping between rocks and stopping to smell the crevices between them. The ocean teemed with life, tiny little creatures that wiggled and twisted in the water, tiny shells, and blue plants that drifted back and forth. To the west, there was nothing but dark blue water, light blue sky, and in between them a row of island hills that stretched from one horizon to the other.

I walked until I could smell nothing but the salty ocean air. White-Ears was far behind me, and in front of me was an infinite unknown. It was quiet. Nothing but the gentle drumming of the waves and the occasional bird. I closed my eyes and sang. Two voices joined me, but not more than two.

I stood under a bright and yellow moon, a clear sky, and shimmering stars. The sky was filled with a long, thin band of silvery-white dots. Waves crashed and hummed, and the buzz of the summer insects surrounded me. I breathed out a long sigh, closed my eyes, and stepped into the waves.

The salty water lapped my paws and dewclaw and soaked its way to just below my elbow. It was cold, refreshing, and the air stung with a sharp freshness. I pulled back and licked my paw, which tasted faintly of fish.

Far ahead rested the dark silhouette of an island mountain. It sat directly under the moon, and below it, moonlight rippled on the surface of the water until it converged as a white line, a narrowing path, from the beach to the island.

I tilted my head and sang for Ma and Pa. They responded with their songs from the island, not so far away, so I stepped into the waves and allowed the water to come up to my chest, then my neck, and finally, the cool water wrapped itself all around me. I kept going, into the dim depths of the sea, breathing in the water and feeling its tendrils all over my fur.

After a few days of eating clams, we started searching along the shore. There was the occasional morning drizzle, but it was mostly sunny. The cool ocean breeze and the never-ending waves cooled me down, and the thick trees provided plenty of shade for mid-afternoon naps. The ocean wasn't good for drinking. It was salty and gross, and it made me more thirsty, and I ended up having a headache, a dull pain behind my left ear that would not go away with scratching. The black wolf found a creek that ran from the hillside down to the ocean, and we drank from it. It was sweet and refreshing.

We went south first. Our songs were unanswered, but that was fine because the coast was infinitely long, and Ma and Pa were probably out of earshot. I led White-Ears and the black wolf, who walked side-by-side and played with each other. When we were hungry, we stopped for clams. When we were thirsty, we went inland for water. We took many naps. The entire coast had a pristine smell that was unpolluted by strangers or bears. We sang for Ma and Pa many times during the day. Eventually, we settled on the song: "I am here, and I miss you." We sang in unison, White-Ears and I, "Come find us, family. We are here."

The black wolf sang with us. And although he sang his own song, it was still nice to hear. His voice was mesmerizing, low, and deliciously melodic. I nuzzled him and told him I liked his song, to which he said, "I practice a lot, alone."

To which I laughed and nuzzled him some more. White-Ears squeezed herself between us, so I bit her nose. She hissed at me, and we kept going.

It took three days before the rocky coast opened up to a vast, endless marsh. It was lush and green, with white flowers scattered across the wetland floor and yellow and black birds dotting the sky. The air buzzed with insects. I had to shake myself constantly to keep the bugs off of my ears and nose. It didn't smell like a marsh. It didn't have all the decomposing pockets of stagnant water, nor the half-submerged trees, nor the ravens. Instead, it smelled sweet like berries and fresh like the clams. I bent over and tasted the water. Salty, but not as much as the ocean.

White-Ears whizzed past me, splattering marsh water all over my butt. She stopped in front of a shrub that was freshly green. She nibbled at it.

"What is it?" I said. My voice caused a flutter of birds.

"Berries, but they're not very good," White-Ears said.

"They're not ripe yet," the black wolf said. He appeared out of nowhere, and I jumped, but I didn't want to seem skittish, so I pretended I didn't.

I looked at him. "What does it mean to be ripe?"

"The days need to get shorter and colder before the berries become sweet. I love these berries. They are plump and juicy."

"You've been here before?" I asked.

"Not quite," he said, "but for my second summer, my family came near the coast, and these blackberries were everywhere. My brother's mouth was purple for days."

White-Ears wagged her tail. "Can we come back here in the fall?"

"Sure," I said. "I want a purple mouth too."

At sundown, we faced a roaring river. It was wide and loud and crashed against the shore with a thunderous force. It was so wide that it was hard to see the other side—which was more marsh and more trees that shimmered in the heat. I stuck my paw into the water from the rock I stood on and felt the water tug against my toes. I pulled back. There was no way we could cross this river safely.

I looked at my sister and friend, my new family, and our eyes met for a brief second.

"What now?" asked White-Ears.

"We go inland," I said, "the river must narrow at some point."

We sang across the channel, but there was nobody else there, so we kept going.

The river splashed and glowed under the moonlight, but something else splashed under it. I saw and smelled them, and as usual, I desperately wanted them. There was still enough light to go fishing.

The black wolf saw me staring into the river from a mound of dirt, so he came over and stood beside me. "Hey," he said.

"Hey." I flicked my ears.

"What are you looking at?"

"Fish," I said. "Down there, see? The black shapes that seem to sway with the current. They have spots on the side, while the rocks are round and dull."

"I've never eaten fish."

I grinned and licked him. "You're about to have a favourite food."

I focused on a fish with a stripe down its side, big tail fins, and a curved mouth. It was barely visible, and sometimes I lost track of it. It liked to move around, though, and this was going to be its downfall: moving things were easier to see, so they were easier to catch. About half a wolf-length of fast water separated me and my prey. If I wasn't careful, I would be swept away into the ocean, and worse, I would lose my fish—and worse still, I would embarrass myself in front of the black wolf.

The fish darted forward. I jumped, mouth first with my eyes open. I made no splash against the torrential water. I pulled my body forward with my paws until I was fully submerged in the murky water. The fish was right in front of me, swimming, blissfully unaware until I wrapped my jaws around its slender body, but by then, it was too late for it. Fish blood squirted into the water and into my open mouth. I wiggled and kicked hard, using all of my legs and my tail, and I popped out of the water with the fish in my mouth. Deep breath. Inhale. Exhale. I climbed the shore and kicked my legs until I felt my claws take to the dirt.

The black wolf was standing attentively, tail swaying.

I threw the fish in front of him. "Go ahead," I said through my breaths. "Try it."

He smelled it and then bit the still-squirming fish and took its head off. It flopped on the spiny grass once, twice, and then stopped motionless. He tore a hole in the fish's body near the spine and ate a chunk of pink meat.

"Do you like it?" I didn't need to ask since the black wolf's tail and ears told me everything I needed to know, but I still wanted to hear it from him.

"Yes—" he chewed and said, "— this is amazing!"

I stepped closer to grab my fish back. His nose glistened and his ears half-folded, and his entire mouth was covered with fish blood and scales. The black wolf's entire body glowed with happiness, so I let him have the whole thing.

Chapter 15

We ventured a day and a half inland, followed the river, and watched as the forest thickened until everything was hot, misty, and green. The river wasn't getting narrower. It was loud, and the shores were rocky instead of grassy, but it was just as wide as before. White-Ears tried fishing with the black wolf, but neither of them had any success. I caught a small one with a hooked mouth and a big grey one the length of a wolf's tail. I ate the big one and left them the small fish, but that was what they deserved for being bad at fishing.

"I liked the ocean better," White-Ears said.

In the evenings, after the air cooled down, I taught the black wolf the game of find-the-bone. White-Ears had invented the game back at the den, but I was the reigning champion. We played with a beaver tail: a huge, stinky thing that flopped in my mouth as I ran. I hopped across a narrow creek and hid it behind a rock, and then I turned around and piled small rocks on it until it was barely visible. The rules dictated that the thing must be visible, but we never said how visible.

I came back and found White-Ears and the black wolf nuzzling each other, whispering in each other's ears. I came up to them and took a deep bow with my paws stretched in front of me. I wagged my tail back and forth and smiled at them. The black wolf tilted his head puzzlingly.

"I hid the thing!" I said. "Now you have to find it."

White-Ears smiled and stood up. "Come," she said to him, "I will show you how to win this game."

"That's not fair," I said. "There's two of you and only one of me."

He looked at her. White-Ears shook the dust off of her belly and wagged her tail and said, "Well, maybe next round I can hide it, and you two can find it."

"Fine," I said.

White-Ears went first. She lowered her head and swept the ground for scents. I had taken care to rub the lake mud all over the beaver tail, so I was sure she wasn't going to find anything this way. However, the black wolf had a different method: he smelled the air, and then the ground, and then the air again, and so on. I tried his method, but I couldn't tell the difference.

I stayed at least twenty wolf-lengths behind the duo. If I was too close, they would be able to use my body language as cues. I used the same body language trick on White-Ears to win two rounds before she caught on, so naturally, she was going to try to use it on me.

The black wolf's ears twitched. He whispered something to White-Ears and then tugged her fur in the direction that he was looking at.

"Oh!" she laughed.

Damn it. His up-and-down method definitely had merit. The two of them pointed directly at the creek, and they ran to it side by side. Then, they leapt over the creek in perfect synchronization. By the time I stood at the other side of the creek, the black wolf already clutched the beaver tail in his mouth.

"Round two?" I barked across the babbling water.

"Nah," said White-Ears. "I'm the winner."

"You didn't even find it. He found it."

"Still counts. We're partners, so whatever he found, I found."

"That makes it even less fair. I want a rematch," I said. I stuck my front teeth out for good measure. White-Ears shook her head and walked over to the black wolf. She started tugging at the beaver tail in his mouth. It split in half, and they both landed on their butts, and they stayed down and laughed.

"No round two, then." I shrugged. It was hard to play the game when there was nothing to hide and nobody to play with.

The air became dry, and the grass became yellow, but the river was still torrential. And then there was the summer heat. That nauseating, ever-present heat radiating from every corner of the sky made it impossible to run or even walk fast. I spent more time in the water than on land. Ma and Pa wouldn't have come this far, and they wouldn't have gone across the river when there was so much food and space on this side. Ma was cautious. She didn't do things this way. I decided that it was time to go back to the ocean.

We followed the shore and travelled north, weaving in and out of the rainforest, switching between playing along the beach and walking high up the cliff walls. Sea or forest, there was always something to eat. The black wolf was an excellent hunter of small animals. When I was napping, he brought back a fluffy creature with black rings around its tail. It wasn't very tasty, but it was a nice change from clams and fish.

It was many days, through rain and wind, chilling mornings,

and scorching mid-afternoon sunlight. Unfortunately, we never had any luck with our songs. There were no traces of Ma and Pa anywhere along the coast. No responses to our songs. No pawprints. Nothing.

We went north along the coast until it became rocky, sharp, and eventually impassible to all but the most agile wolves. It meandered into a river, and we followed it inland until we were no longer able to smell the ocean. It took many days. Some of the days, we sang for Ma and Pa, but most of the other ones we sang to each other. Our songs were joyous and fun, and we sang often. The coast disappeared over time, and then a line of stubby mountains came into view, and in time, the summer heat became a cool breeze as the days shortened. The vibrant, deep blue sky was replaced with a thin film of white, and along with the white clouds came the occasional rain. When we were up in the mountains, we had thunder, but when we came back to the ocean, the rain was fine and misty.

The black wolf was right. The blackberries were much better after they had ripened.

A puff of white cloud erupted from my nose and disappeared. I shook myself habitually and sat down. White-Ears sniffed the air with her head held high like Ma used to do. The chill accentuated the smell of the ocean, and everything had a sharpness to it.

"We'll stay at the ocean for the winter," White-Ears said. The black wolf nodded.

"It's so soon," I said, "hard to believe summer is over."

"I had a good time." White-Ears grinned.

133

"Me too," I sighed. I smelled the air again. I thought for a moment that I smelled Ma's fur. It was just for a moment, a wave of heat, nothing more. I leaned in and rubbed my nose against White-Ears's neck. Her fur was cool, and I could hear her rhythmic, steady heartbeat. Thump, thump, thump.

"We'll find them," she said as if she saw my thoughts.

"It's been so long. I barely remember what they look like. I mean, Mother had a dark patch on her back, and Father had a scar on his leg? Is that right?" I trailed off.

White-Ears sat down and her tail swished once against the bed of pine needles and dried yellow grass. She looked at me, her golden eyes glimmering. She looked at the black wolf, who stood to the side and pawed the ground.

"They had a good summer, too," she said. "It was a plentiful summer along the coast, not too hot, with plenty of food and no strangers. This is the best place to be."

I nodded. "Mother always said she loved the ocean."

White-Ears stood up, walked over to the black wolf, and bit him on the cheek. He turned around and half snarled at her, and she pushed him on the ground, and they yelped and rolled. The duo kicked up a cloud of dust. It drove away the smell of the ocean. I wanted to stay by the ocean, so I stood up and walked towards the shore.

I was going to try to catch something. White-Ears preferred playing with the black wolf, and I preferred leaving them alone. The two of them had a certain synergy to their movements. They heard each other's thoughts and wrestled with unnatural speed and gracefulness. It must have been love. It must have been, and I was happy for White-Ears.

Tiny waves lapped the sand. Lazy white foam brushed up against my paws, and back into the water, and back up. I bent down and licked the foam, which was mildly salty and not much else. A row of shallow hills dotted the distance, separated by a vast ocean. The sun, hidden behind the afternoon haze, crept towards the peak of the tallest hill. I laid down and faced the sunset, feeling the water come up to my snout and the tickle of the foam brushing against my whiskers.

This was okay. There was food here: fresh clams and fish and berries, squirrels, beavers, weasels, and other small animals the black wolf was good at catching. It was warm and temperate. The ocean was nice too. This was okay, and we could spend the next spring and summer looking for Ma and Pa.

"How do you know you love him?" I asked White-Ears.

She pawed at a hole in the ground. It smelled like hares, but the scent was old. "I just knew, I guess," she said.

"Since the beginning?"

"No," she said. "I wasn't sure then. I wasn't sure for a long time, but then one day I was."

I ran to the adjacent hole and stuck my snout in it, but I didn't find anything in there. When I pulled my nose out, White-Ears was standing above me. "Do you love anyone like that?"

"I don't know," I said.

White-Ears nuzzled me on my snout, and then she ran off into the distance, down the path, and into the forest. In the distance, I could hear the black wolf greeting her. They laughed and ran together.

Loons screeched their shrill song as the faint crash of the ocean came and went, and the ocean was bathed in a dark purple glow. I laid down on a soft bed of grass with my snout on the ground. Something tickled my nostrils. I exhaled, and it was gone, and then it was back. It was a leaf of grass that dangled in front of my nose and fluttered to the rhythm of my breath. I huffed, and it flew away, but it came back again. The grass swayed in front of my face, and I fell asleep to its rhythm.

My ear flickered before I heard it, and even then, I wasn't sure if I dreamt of it. "Come to me!" the song said. "Come come come come…" and then it was gone. I tilted my head and listened, and there was nothing but waves. My nose twitched, then I got up. Come to me, it said. Who said it? Who was it?

It must have been Ma. I recognized her smooth and low singing voice. Come to me? I had to tell White-Ears. I raised my head and sang. First, I sang a reply. I heard her, and I was coming. Then I called White-Ears and the black wolf. They appeared from the gaps between the trees. I rushed to greet White-Ears by nuzzling her neck. I also licked the black wolf on the nose and mouth, and he licked me back. White-Ears danced around me, and I had to keep spinning just to talk to her.

"I heard Mother," I said. "I heard her song, and she was calling us to find her."

White-Ears jumped at the sound of this, and she came in to embrace me with her wet nose and soft fur. Then she pulled away and tilted her head sideways. "What did she say?"

"She said, 'come to me.' It sounded like it was coming from over there." I gestured with my nose to the east, beyond the rolling rainforest.

"We came through there a few days ago," White-Ears said.

"And I didn't smell anyone, especially not our mother."

We sang together and waited for a response. Then, I ran up the slopes and into the rainforest. White-Ears and the black wolf followed. I didn't stop until I was atop the highest hill I could find, and there, through the trees, I sang again. Still nothing. White-Ears was panting, and she told me through hurried breaths that she was tired. I was also tired. I wanted to sleep. I wasn't sure I heard Ma, not anymore, yet something called me inland.

"I want to go back," I said.

"To the mountains?"

"Back into the mountains. We won't find them here."

"If they're close by, they must have heard us. We can look for them tomorrow, but I'm tired now, and I want to sleep," she said. She paused and then added, "You don't know if you actually heard her."

"No," I said. "I don't know." I shook my body and sat down. The excitement of the song had worn down, and all I remembered now was a stupid dream and a lot of needless running. The night was dark and chilly, and I felt the tug of sleep against my eyelids. "Maybe I was mistaken. Let's sleep for the night."

That night, I laid on the wet forest floor and stared up at the branches and the stars that glimmered above me. White-Ears and the black wolf were sleeping soundly. I counted the stars as they shined across the dark sky, disappearing behind clouds and reappearing again in the same spot. The stars were constant. They would hide behind thick rain clouds for many days, but they always came back to the same place in the night sky.

And soon, winter clouds would bring many days of snow, but the stars would still be there. It would be my second winter. I had spent nearly four seasons on the move and an entire summer looking for Ma and Pa. White-Ears found her love. We dug for clams and fished in the big river. I didn't want to believe that they were gone. I didn't want to stay here. I wanted to do another sweep for Ma and Pa before their scents disappeared in the snow forever. I wanted to go back to the den and figure out what happened, and find Scruff-Paw and ask him why he left without saying anything to us. I wanted to find Notch-Tail again.

The next morning, I woke up early and took a long walk by myself. It was something I hadn't done in a very long time, and it was nice. I followed a creek up the rainforest basin until I could see the ocean from afar. Then I sat, leaned against a tree, and closed my eyes to listen to the sounds of the world. The buzzing of the summer bugs had all but disappeared, and only leaves rustled and gulls called. I knew I didn't hear Ma, but nevertheless, I made up my mind.

When I arrived back at the shore, the sun had just set. I found the duo near the circular lagoon where the long clams were. White-Ears was splashing in the water with the black wolf. They were easy to find. Their scent was the only thing that stood out near the shore. Everything else was drowned out by the ocean.

I sang to get their attention, and they replied. White-Ears

came running with her ears perked and tail swaying. She came closer and nuzzled me. I greeted her back, and I sat down and sighed. "I'm leaving," I said. "I'm going inland. We left behind too many things, and I can't just stay here."

"Winter is almost here," she said through a puff of late-evening breath. "When will you be back?"

"I don't know. I don't have many days before the snow covers their scent, and I'll need their scent to backtrack the southern route."

"We're not going," White-Ears said. She looked at the black wolf, who came a step closer.

"I know."

White-Ears came up to me and buried her snout in my fur, and I felt the wetness of her nose. I nuzzled her back. I wrapped my neck around her, just like I did when we were children, and she whined quietly. She stepped back. "The winter is very harsh inland," she said. "We almost died last year, or at least, I almost did. I don't want to have to go through that again."

"I know. You will need the food and the warmth of the coast to start a family."

I looked at the black wolf. He blinked back at me, his eyes glowing golden green. White-Ears stood next to him and leaned on his narrow shoulders. She opened her mouth again, and for a moment, nothing came out, then there was a whisper.

"I know they're out there," she said. "I know they're trying to find us too, but I also know they would want us to have a safe winter."

"I'll be safe, I promise."

White-Ears looked at me with a warm, sympathetic gaze. She opened her mouth and smiled thinly. "When will you be back?"

"Before the first snow, if I'm lucky. Next spring if I'm not. I'll sing for you."

"Promise?"

"Of course," I said. I leaned in and kissed White-Ears on her nose. Then I turned around, took a deep breath, and ran, straight into the dark forest. I ran and ran up the hill and along the creek and through the prickly underbrush until I could smell nothing but trees. When the night was deep and the moon was high, I sang from the depths of the rainforest. A quiet whisper of a song answered, and I kept going.

Chapter 16

It was a chilly morning. Droplets of dew collected all over my nose bridge and snout. I shook myself, but the dew kept coming back, and soon, it was damp everywhere. The thick trees obscured the sun, and a wispy fog hugged the ground. All around me, it was quiet, except for the chirping of songbirds and the occasional tapping by a woodpecker. The red and white bird glared at me as I passed beneath it.

The night I left White-Ears and the black wolf, I slept in the open, on a soft bed of fresh yellow leaves, and I dreamt of Ma and Pa playing in the snow. It was sunny and cold and comfortable. I tried to join them, but I could not get close enough, and with every step I took, they faded further into the mountain. Ma's scent lingered in my nose as they disappeared, a soft, earthy smell, like a freshly dug hole or elk hooves. I later realized it wasn't Ma's scent. It was the smell of the autumn leaves. It was the smell of the den. I closed my eyes and rested my snout on a rock, and I didn't breathe at all. No scent entered my nose, and no scent entered my mind either. I couldn't remember what Ma smelled like.

I constantly walked uphill, and I was often hot and tired during the day, even under the shade of the forest. I preferred to travel in the morning and at night when the colours were

141

more vibrant, and the scents of the forest were stronger—all without the oppressive heat of the midday sun.

If I was lucky, I found a lake or a pond during the day. Fish and hares kept me full.

⌒

The trees were slimmer as the hills flattened out, and everything was yellow. Heat rippled from the yellow ground. Behind the farthest mound of dirt was a coyote's silhouette, a brown and yellow creature with huge ears. It stood attentively, its head turned away from me. It was looking at the hills in the distance, or the suffocating hot air, or something else. It didn't matter.

The last time I ate anything was two days ago. The dry plains didn't have any ponds or lakes, and the mice could see me from far away. Dried grass crunched under my paws, and jabbing thorns irritated my toes. I was careful where to step. The insects on the ground had an unpleasant sting to them—and they didn't even taste very good. I should have eaten something else, but there wasn't anything moving except the shimmering of the heat off the ground—and now this coyote.

There would be plenty of time to go east, but for now, a coyote would do just fine. The animal had a familiar smell which was like the wolves I knew, but also different. It smelled sour and earthy and warm. It was uncanny. I huffed from my nose, and the sound drew the attention of the coyote. It—he, a male—turned towards me. I stood still.

We made eye contact. The moment I saw his eyes, I leapt forward and started running. Parched earth whizzed past me, and hot autumn air brushed against my whiskers. The animal zigged between the mounds of dirt. It was incredibly fast and agile, running behind a tall patch of grass and disappearing under the hill, so I followed, bursting through the grass and feeling the ground give beneath me. I gasped and felt the world spin. A strange sound came out of my throat as I tumbled down the hill, crashing into a prickly bush with a thump.

"Augh!" I barked. I stood up. There were prickles all over my fur. Knotted, tangled summer fur filled with annoying and painful pieces. Now I had to get him. It was too late to give up. I was eating a coyote for dinner.

A rustle in the grass was all the sign I needed, so I ran towards the moving grass. The air lingered with the coyote's scent, along with a bit of my own blood. The prickly bush must have my skin cut somewhere. This was distracting. I needed to focus on the scent and the movement. The coyote turned left and silently parted the grass. It ran on dry dirt, taking huge strides as it hugged the plants and dunes, around and around. I tried to do the same, but I was too big, so I jumped over the dunes, but it was too tiring, so I ended up running through them. Bushes scratched my forearms and face, and I tried to shield my nose and eyes. This slowed me down, and soon, the coyote was getting away.

The hill gradually flattened. Flat land was better to run on, and I didn't need to turn as much because there were no dunes or gopher holes to dodge. The coyote was still far away, about a hundred wolf-lengths. I watched it duck under a bush, and suddenly it was running back up the hill. I exhaled sharply and turned and suffered through the exact same thing as before, except it was more difficult in reverse.

I was panting and dizzy at the top. The heat seemed to hug me, compressing my fur from nose to tail, a heavy, dry heat that made it difficult to breathe.

The coyote looked back at me. Its ears twitched. I closed my left eye, then my right, and then with a deep breath, I took off running again. I didn't get any closer this time. Once again, I was out of breath, and he looked at me with his brown eyes. Big brown eyes and a twitching black nose. He looked uncomfortably wolf-like in this rippling heat.

I sat down, and I couldn't stop panting. He wasn't tired at all. He just kept looking at me.

"Hey! Run away!" I said as it kept looking at me with the same blank expression. "I'm going to eat you. You just watch."

The coyote breathed and didn't speak. Maybe it wasn't able to speak, or maybe it didn't understand me. I growled instead, and its ears just twitched. I got up again and lunged forward, but the entire world started to spin, and I had to catch myself before I hit the ground. When I looked up, the coyote was gone. Its smell was gone too. Only the hot sun remained. I was still dizzy. My mouth was dry and felt like sandpaper. My teeth were sticky against my tongue as if flesh and teeth were melting together. I needed a water source, fast.

With one eye closed, I stumbled down the hill to the bottom one step at a time. There was more likely to be water on lower ground, Pa said. Marshes and ponds can be hidden.

"Right on," I whispered. My front paw caught a rock, and I tumbled, but I didn't feel much. Water. I need water.

"Hey, where are you?" I said, but Pa kept talking about marshes and ponds.

"Ponds," I mumbled. "Ponds and lakes and marshes and creeks and raging rivers and the ocean. Let me guess, you're going to meet me at the pond? Do I have to wait another three seasons this time?"

I wobbled my way down to the bottom of the hill. Around the right side, it was shaded, and there was thicker grass and bushes, so I went in there. It wasn't much cooler here. The air smelled dry and hot, but at least I wasn't in the sun. I took a few more steps and found a nice shaded crevice to lie down in. I should sleep for a bit. It would be easier to find water at night.

A crescent moon greeted me to the east. It was a tiny sliver that hung in the sky, silently chilling the air. There was dew on my nose, sweet, refreshing dew. But there was also an itchy spot. I reached my nose under my right paw and scratched with my dewclaw. It went away but came back every time I pulled away, so I kept scratching. I hated this feeling of raw itching on the tip of my nose. Every time I sniffed anything, it would itch incessantly, painfully, swollenly. I solved the problem, though. The tip of my nose was dripping with blood, and the itching finally stopped. Now it was time to find some water.

Trees appeared once again in the place of those horrible thorny bushes. I enjoyed trees. They provided shade, and they didn't hurt, with an added bonus that I could rub any itchy body parts against the rough bark. The wound on my nose healed and scabbed over, and the scab fell off, and now there was a smooth patch of whitish-pink where it used to be black.

It was cold on some nights. My winter fur wasn't warm yet, and the chill of the wind pierced through me.

I followed a wide path as it led me through the thick forest. White-tipped mountains grew taller in the distance, and the trees became narrower and taller. I mostly went east, towards the mountains, up, along the ridges and the hilltops. There were lakes here, each with their gorgeous white-blue water that tasted sweet, like the water from the den.

Each lake was a place to stop, to drink some water, and rest up before continuing. There were no fish here. Not since the rainforest, and to be honest, I didn't want fish. I didn't know where I was going anymore. East. I had to keep going east, up these trails and mountains. I would sing for Ma and Pa, but there was no point. Nothing here smelled like wolves, which only meant I should keep going. East. Towards the mountains. Maybe I could retrace our steps all the way back to the den.

Patchy grasses lined the cliff that towered steeply from south to north. A trail ran along the grasses. The dying sun illuminated the entire trail and cast a purple hue on the dirt and rocks in front of me. Ahead, the trail split with one path leading away from the cliff, so I turned east and went into the hillside, leaving the sunset behind for more progress on my journey. When I came around the bend, a ravine carved the earth in front of me. It was both sharp and wide. There were rocks and broken branches in the debris, along with mud. And, on top of it all, the newest light dusting of snow. I tried to find a way around the ravine, but it cut all the way from the peak of the mountain down as far as I could see.

North it was, then. I meandered back to the mountainside trail and kept going north. The path narrowed until I had to carefully dig my claws into the dirt with each step. It took me higher and higher until the moon was hovering behind me and the stars twinkled and the entire mountain range opened up below me. It was beautiful. I had never been so high up in my life.

146

At the peak, where the trail disappeared, there was a plateau with a thin layer of snow and colourful flowers. I sang. When I stopped, my voice kept reverberating in the mountain ranges.

I kept going north. A path led me down the mountain until I stood in a valley once again. This time, the valley had thin and tall trees, just like the trees from my childhood. It was pristine here, so I decided to rub my scent all over the trees.

Let it be known that I was here and that I have laid claim to this land.

Chapter 17

The snow fell in wet clumps. My winter fur kept me warm, and the snow kept my scent hidden, and this was how I got close to the small herd of elk that grazed on the still-green grasses in the clearing. There were six of them. The big one had a set of antlers on its head, while the smaller ones grazed peacefully. The black wolf's recommendation for caribou meat rang in my ears as I approached the herd.

When the nearest elk was twenty or so wolf-lengths away, I introduced myself. I snuck around a tree until I was perpendicular to the animal, and I charged at it. The herd took off in the other direction. The big male first, followed by the others, galloping through the forest, hopping over icy logs with no trouble.

I followed closely. The cold air filled my lungs, and it felt refreshing, exhilarating to be chasing elk once again. My front paws bounced off the snow as my hind paws landed on the same spot. Branches rushed past my face, and shrubs flew behind me.

I closed the distance at first, but soon, they were further away. I had to run around big rocks and thick bushes while the elk simply leapt over them. The elk were faster than I remembered. When the elk veered to the east and headed up a hill, I had to dodge many rocks, and it soon became steeper than I was prepared for. My breath was shallow, and I was lightheaded, dizzy, and the taste of blood lined my mouth. I gave up and laid down on the hill facing the crest with my butt hanging over a log. The elk settled down just out of sight, and the faint grinding of jaws resumed as they grazed.

For the next day, I followed the herd. I stayed far enough behind so I wouldn't be seen. There was nothing I could do about my scent. Nothing out here was worth rolling in. There was nothing but the scent of dirt, snow, and elk. The herd didn't seem to mind my scent if I stayed far away, or maybe they couldn't smell me.

The animals moved north along a narrow band of forest on a hillside ridge. The ground dropped sharply away on one side and sloped gently down the other, with gnarly trees and wide-leafed bushes that led all the way down into a valley. In the afternoon, I tried to get closer, but I couldn't start running. My legs and shoulders were sore: not a jabbing pain, but a slow and persistent ache. I really just wanted to lie down and sleep for a few days. But I should probably eat. I would eat first and then take a long break. I had been searching for two whole moons now, and I really just needed a break.

The world was silent except for the rustling of pine needles in the cold wind. The sky was clear to the east and grey and dreary to the north. Snow covered everything. The elk settled down for the night, and so did I. I slept between two bushes on a rare piece of flat ground on the hillside. The snow was soft and cushioned my legs.

I woke up before the sun had come up. It was still dark with tiny wisps of light to the east behind the white mountains. I was sure the elk were still asleep, so I followed the scent trail across the ridge and down the side with the steeper slope. At the bottom of this landscape the bull elk rubbed his big antlers against a tree. The entire tree shook violently, rustling, trembling, dancing in the morning light and casting long shadows down the ridge.

That's my food for the week. I grinned at that thought, panting, feeling the cold wind on my tongue. I could almost taste the animal's hot, sweet blood pulsing in my mouth.

"It's not worth it," Ma said. "Don't go for the big dominant ones. They can hurt you badly."

I shook my head, and then my whole body and snow splattered on the ground. I turned to look behind me. I wasn't expecting to see her, and there was nobody there, but I replied anyway. "You'll see, Ma. I'll get that damn elk, and I'll tear its throat out."

"You'll get hurt," Pa said. His voice was husky from a summer of hunting and singing.

"I don't think so," I said—well, whispered. The elk was still within earshot. "You haven't seen me for the whole summer. I'm bigger and stronger now. I might even be as strong as you, Pa."

Ma and Pa stayed silent, so I left them behind on the ridge. I leapt down the first drop, catching a moment of airtime and feeling the excitement of freefall. It was like falling from the boulders at the lake. My paws slammed into the ground, and I saw the elk turn its head upwards to look at me. I ran down the steep hill, flinging my tail to the side, turning around bushes and small trees, until I was face to face with the muscular animal.

I lunged towards it, but it didn't move.

"Run away!" I barked. I didn't know what to do if the prey

150

didn't run away. Maybe I could just go for it? The animal's neck was right there with its skin dangling, ready for my jaws. It lowered its head and huffed. A stream of hot clouds came out of its nose and rose to the sky above, which had just begun to brighten. I circled the bushes, and its beady eyes followed me. It turned to face me with its antlers and tamped its hooves against the ground. Snow flew everywhere, and then everything was quiet. Light shimmered at the horizon.

I shuffled a step left, and so did the elk.

It was a deadly dance between the elk and me. I moved, it turned to face me. Step for step, it always stood its ground. The rest of the herd was gone, somewhere else, and it was just myself and this animal that stood in front of me. It was at least twice my height, with legs the width of a tree, a stubby tail, and a huge head with antlers as thick as my paws. It huffed angrily, swaying its head back and forth, threatening me with its huge rack of antlers.

I snarled and charged at the animal, who swung its antlers at my face as I approached. With a swish of my tail, I turned and ducked under the elk. Its neck was right above me. I was so close I smelled its musky scent and heard its heartbeat. It was much bigger up close, towering over me like a tree.

I lunged for the neck. It moved aside with a guttural grunt, and the antlers came down again with the force of a snowstorm. I missed. Pulling back, I tried to run around, but before I could move, I felt a searing pain on my thigh and rib cage. The tip of the antler stabbed my right side, and pain shot through my body like a bolt of lightning, like a white-capped wave battering the shore. I backed away a few steps and snarled through gritted teeth.

"Go!" Ma said. "Don't stop until you're safe!"

Her voice echoed in my mind as the pain flashed in front of me. An angry elk swung its head back and forth. The world spun. It was lighter, then darker, then lighter again. The sun had crept above the horizon and everything was dim and orange. My ribs throbbed, but I thought I was okay. I could still move. I shifted my body around until I was facing the elk again.

"No, Ma. This time I'm not leaving."

I came at the elk again. My entire body was on fire. The animal bellowed, and its entire torso shook violently. It swung its head and kicked its hooves towards me, but I was faster. I ducked around the head and grabbed the animal's butt with my paws and teeth. The smell of blood punctured the air, and all of a sudden, there was blood everywhere. The bull contorted its body and kicked its legs. I held on as it thrashed, and its muscles twitched and trembled between my teeth, and I knew that it was weakening. Panic was taking over, which meant I had won.

I wanted to shout. I wanted to yell and scream and sing, to tell Ma to look at me, I did it. I did it! But the fight wasn't over yet. I had to cling on until it bled out. The elk was a huge, tenacious creature, and it did not give up.

Fine! I would make it give up.

With this thought in mind, I bit down hard on the hind leg, right where the thigh met the torso, and I gnawed. I gnawed and crushed, snapping muscle fibers between my teeth.

The whole animal buckled with so much force, I felt the jolt from my teeth to my tail. This was a mistake. I should have let it fling me off. It was badly injured, and I knew I just had to wait it out. I clung on, and moments later, a searing, screaming burst of pain shot through my body as the animal's hoof slammed into my ribcage.

The whole world felt like looking at the sun. Hot, dizzying, with a loud ringing in my ear, and I couldn't focus on anything except the all-consuming burst of pain coming from my chest. It wasn't even pain anymore. There was just something there, ever-present, something, and everything.

The sky spun. I had to close my eyes but only for a moment. I could still take it down if only I tried harder. But no, my jaw loosened. I couldn't hold on anymore, not with my claws and not with my fangs. It just all loosened at once. All the strength flowed out of me and was replaced by this sensation. This…pain? Was it pain? It was bright. Hot. Disgustingly hot. So hot that it melted the ice below me and replaced it with thick, syrupy blood, and it smelled of blood everywhere. Hot. Disgustingly hot.

The elk galloped away. Its hoofsteps crashed against the ground, and the sound burrowed into my ears, but I couldn't turn away or open my eyes.

⌂

I wanted to puke but nothing came out. The sun was high in the sky. It was cloudless and windless but I couldn't open my eyes. The pain was my entire world and I felt nothing but the jagged, open hole in my chest. The blood dried, and no more came out, and all was quiet. But the blood wasn't mine. It smelled like elk. There was elk blood all around me, soaked into the snow and staining the air. I wasn't bleeding. I was okay. I just need the pain to go away.

Earth shifted beneath me, the sky tumbled, and everything was turning again. I pressed my nose into the snow to cool down, and as I moved, a burst of pain shot through my neck and chest. I took a deep breath and opened my eyes, and the light seared into my eyes. Thump thump thump thump, my head was pulsating faster now, so I closed my eyes again. The ground stopped moving, and the pain was better. Better, but only a little bit.

I took small breaths. Whimpering made the pain worse. Breathing too. I just needed to wait it out. Wait until tomorrow. That was what I must do. I will feel better tomorrow.

"Get yourself somewhere safe," Ma said. She stood in front of me, and her grey, aged face glowed with life. I stood up, but I didn't really. I couldn't move at all, but she was there, and I nuzzled her face, but I didn't really. Ma smelled like lavender, those purple flower bulbs in the alpine fields in the summer. It was summer here.

"Why are you here?" I asked.

"You need me," she said, "I'll be here when you need me."

"Will you come back again?"

"I will."

I nuzzled her again, rubbing her scent all over me. Ma was a wonderful mix of lavender and elk blood. I was back on the ground again, and there were tendrils of pain poking into the summer meadow, and Ma was fading away, a bit at a time, fainter and greyer.

I opened my eyes. It was evening now, and the sun glowed behind clouds in the west, and dark clouds raced past the orange glow. The flash of pain made Ma come back, and she stood in front of me again. She smelled of fish and grassland this time. Pa stood behind her. He had a full white mane that billowed in the wind, and he smelled of elk blood.

"Hi," I said. I went up to him and licked his mouth.

"Get off the ridge and find shelter. A storm is coming," he said.

"Will you stay with me?"

"I'm here," he said. "But you have to go. Go now. Get up and head down the ridge."

I took a deeper breath and took a step down the elk trail, but I didn't really. Pain. There was so much pain, I didn't know where I was anymore. I was on a flat landing with a broken ribcage facing a snowstorm, but I also stood on the meadow with Ma and Pa, and they were right in front of me. They were smiling.

"I couldn't find you," I whispered.

"You tried your best," Ma said.

"It didn't matter."

"Yes, it did. You took care of your sister. You did good."

I tilted my head to look at her. Her eyes glimmered with their deep, golden orange. The twin white peaks that surrounded us—the peaks that looked like White-Ears—reflected off of Ma's eyes. The field bloomed with white, blue, red, yellow flowers, like splashes of water all around me. Ma's fur was shiny, but there were now patches of white around her eyes, and her whiskers carried the same grey agedness. We made eye contact for a split second, and then I looked away. At the ground, at the flowers, and then at the snow and the setting sun.

"I did good," I breathed. My voice was barely audible, and my rib cage shook in pain. The pain was there, but it had always been there, and I was okay. "I have to go now," I said. The meadow didn't come back. Ma and Pa didn't come back. But I knew they were there. I was going to be okay. I have to get somewhere safe.

One step at a time.

One step was all I could manage before the pain overwhelmed me. The moon peered through the rapidly moving clouds, casting shadows on the hillside that disappeared as quickly as they came. One step. One more. One more.

I made my way down the slope until I was in the forest. It was a thin forest full of overturned trees and bare bark, charred stumps partially covered by snow. Burning pain radiated from my chest with each step. The hoof landed on my right side, and even the slightest motion was unbearable. Thankfully, my claws were sharp, my tail gave me good balance, and my winter coat kept the cold away.

Wind picked up when the sun crept below the horizon. The moon rose and disappeared behind the clouds. Flakes of snow smacked me in the face, and it collected all around my nose bridge, ears, and eyes, but I couldn't shake it off. Shaking would have killed me on the spot, right then and there. I laid with my eyes closed and felt the snow melt on my nose. Pa was right all along: a snowstorm was coming.

My legs trembled. Each step I took was more difficult than the last, and I found it hard to keep my eyes open. I had walked far enough, and I needed to sleep. The icy wind blew north to south. I found a huge fallen tree that leaned east to west, and I pulled myself around it to get to the south side, near the base where it still had branches and needles. I was warm here. The tree blocked the snow and the wind.

At the base of the tree, my front paws weakened, and I collapsed on the ground with an intense burst of pain. There was snow in front of me, a fresh bed of snow with flakes steadily drifting, smelling of lavender and elk blood and long razor clams with their skinny shells and crunchy bodies. And blackberries. Frozen hares. There was no pain here.

I just needed to sleep.

⌒

I woke up shivering, and I didn't have the strength to even lift my snout. The burning pain was mostly gone except for a dull but ever-present ache on my ribs and deep within my chest. My entire chest burned, but it wasn't sharp anymore. Keeping my eyes closed, I shuffled my snout in the snow. There was snow on top of me too, but not too much. There was snow everywhere. I wasn't cold, but I shivered anyway, and the shivering wouldn't stop, and my entire body burned.

There was sunlight again. It was only the beginning of winter. I must keep going, or at the very least, I could find some food. Standing up, I shook myself lightly, wincing at the pain shooting up from my chest. The pain burrowed into my brain, behind my eyes and under my ears, where it stayed, lingering, oozing into every other part until it consumed my consciousness.

Sour berries. It was a clump near the tip of the overturned tree. They were white, and they made my face scrunch up, but at least it was something. There were mice around me, hares too, I smelled them in the air and along the ground, but I couldn't even run. Sour berries and a nap. Tomorrow I could catch something.

"Go home," Ma said. "Your sister is waiting for you. Go to the coast where it's warm."

"Will you come with me?"

"I can't, but I'll be there with you," she said.

Walking. Two steps at a time now, with a few shallow breaths in between. I was making ground, going west, into the deep valley that rested silently below. But I really needed a nap. I could keep going at night, it would be easier and less hot and fewer sounds to drill into my skull, the way a woodpecker drilled a tree. I was okay with it now. I couldn't find Ma and Pa. They were not here, and they were not at the coast. Maybe they died that night when we lost them. Maybe they were stranded in the mountains. Whatever the case, I was okay with it. It was my fault, and I accepted it.

"Go home, my love."

"I will, Ma."

"Tell your sister I love her."

"I'm sorry, Ma."

"You did good. You did good."

My whole body was hot. It was too hot to sleep, too much ringing in my ears, and too much head pain. I was sick, just like the time I puked up elk innards as a child, all over Scruff-Paw and White-Ears, and they slept far away from me for a few nights after.

It was still dark, with glittering stars between the trees and shiny white snow lining the forest floor. I walked west. West, towards White-Ears and home. It was too hot, and with the gusts of wind, it was too hot and too cold at the same time.

I found a hole to sleep in. It was a pit under the root of an upturned tree. It was probably the wind that blew it over, and the entire set of roots were pulled from the ground, leaving a hole just a bit bigger than me. It was a makeshift den: warm and earthy and quiet. I leaned over and smelled the entrance first. Nothing had been in it for some time, so I squeezed through the opening with great, burning pain all over my chest, and I let sleep overtake me once again.

I was too weak to move. It was cloudy again with whistling winds that picked up the snow and swirled it. I didn't have enough strength to lift my head, and everything I did made it hurt. There was no way I was going west today. Maybe tomorrow. Tomorrow I would travel to the edge of the valley, but I would sleep today in this comfortable hole. The hole was pungent and earthy and warm, and it smelled like the elk blood caked on my face.

When I woke up again, it was bright and sunny. I took a few gulps of snow. It cooled my body down.

And then it was cloudy. Then snowy. Then it was sunny again. I didn't leave for days. There was light during the day, and the shadows that were cast into the den danced across my eyelids, and I dreamt that I was sleeping under the broad leaves of the great oak tree. I stood at the top of the boulder above the lake and played the game with White-Ears, and I won. Then I opened my eyes in the grasslands and…

It was night again, and in the darkness of the den, I came to understand that I was dying.

I forced myself out of the den for a brief moment, when the moon was but a thin crescent, and the air was light and crisp. I paid no attention to the pain. It was meaningless at this point, and I was used to it, and I had something more important to attend to. It was now or never. I was dying. I had a fever like White-Ears, and I was dying like the deer that gave up after I tore into its belly. It was dying, and it knew. I knew too. I wasn't ready. I needed to see White-Ears again. I needed to see the girl with the notched tail again. But I couldn't because they were too far away and I was dying. I closed my eyes and kept them closed, counting my breaths until I lost count in the hundreds.

I was ready. I would tilt my head back and sing my life to the stars, and then I would sleep, and that was that.

"Hear my voice," I sang. Steam billowed from my mouth, and the whole forest was filled with song. "I am here and I am alive. I came from the mountains, and I went to the coast. My ma is a strong, grey wolf, and my pa is a big white wolf, and we were a happy family." I told the story of my fishing at the lake, and of the journey to the sea, and White-Ears and the black wolf and everything that happened since.

I let my voice dissipate, and I closed my eyes and listened to the forest, and listened to my song bounce between trees until there was nothing left. And finally, it was all quiet. The mountain was quiet, and so were the trees and the sky. Nobody was listening, but that was okay. Keeping my eyes closed, I slowly pulled myself back into the den. The pain didn't bother me anymore. I curled with my nose against my tail, and the calm darkness of sleep overtook me.

Chapter 18

A day passed, and then a night, and then another. When I woke up, I wasn't dead yet. The pain was still there, and it was just as red-hot as it was before. It didn't get better, but it didn't get worse. I tried moving from the hole, but each step sent the world spinning. There was water on the ground. The snow had melted around and above me just enough for there to be a small puddle of muddy water.

She first came after I sang my song. I had fallen asleep, and when I woke up, the air was filled with the smell of meat. It wasn't good meat, and there was very little. A mushy, half-frozen, rancid piece of rabbit. She laid it quietly in front of me without waking me up. I recognized her smell. It was strange and familiar at the same time. I knew this wolf from somewhere, but I wasn't sure where, and it didn't matter. I pushed my body forward and reached with my teeth until I felt a tuft of rabbit fur on my tongue, and then I pulled it into the hole slowly, wincing at the pain radiating from my chest.

It was delicious. I hadn't eaten for many days.

I slept through most of the next day. I faced the opening of the hole, hoping to see the stranger if she came again so I could thank her. When she came in the evening, I was asleep once more. She brought a fresh liver from some animal, fresh enough to fill the air with coppery sweetness. It woke me up, and I pulled myself up just enough to see a silhouette looking back at me. She stood tall with her tail swaying slowly, towards the direction of the setting sun. Her tail had a bald spot. Her eyes glowed orange as if the setting sun had pierced right through her.

I opened my mouth to say something, but the pain in my chest wouldn't let me. I opened my mouth anyway. We made eye contact, and she turned her head and ran to the south along the trees. She was quiet and agile. When she was gone, and her smell disappeared, I leaned forward and picked up the liver. It was still warm, soft, and chewy. I shivered, which made the pain worse. I ate the whole thing in two bites.

I slept during the day. I slept because I wanted to be awake when the girl with the notched tail, golden eyes, and sweet smell came to visit me again. When I woke up, the sun was setting, and I stuck my head out the entrance to get at the fresh layer of snow. The pain wasn't so bad anymore. I could move. I couldn't walk, but I could move, one step at a time, without blacking out.

I laid down at the entrance and waited for her. The sun crept behind the purple and grey clouds between the trees and then behind the horizon. The sky darkened slowly, and there was only the sound of rustling pine needles and the chirping of birds. Purple turned to blue, and then blue to grey until there was only a hint of light coming from the west. Maybe Notch-Tail wasn't coming.

The call of an owl echoed in the forest, followed by the quiet flap of wings. I looked up just in time to see a black shadow glide across the sky. I opened my jaws and tried to sing, but I heard only a weak squeal. It was painful, too, but not unbearable. I needed to see her again tonight, so I kept trying.

On the third try, I managed a wavering song. "Come to me," I sang. "I need you."

There was an echo and then silence. I rested my head on the sloped entrance to the hole, careful to shift the weight away from my chest. The ground was cold. I closed my eyes. I gritted my teeth and buried my nose into the dirt, enduring the pain from the movement, and I stayed there and listened to my own song echoing at the back of my mind. She had to come back. I needed her.

⌒

I wasn't fully asleep when I heard the crunching of pawsteps.

My eyes snapped open, and there she was, the girl with the notched tail, a few dozen wolf-lengths in front of me. She had her tail held high, and she looked at me. Her eyes glowed faintly. Notch-Tail looked at me again, tilted her head, and then sat down. She smelled of wildflowers and carrion, and it was a sweet smell, like a muddy river. I opened my mouth, and a croak came out with a puff of hot air.

"Hi," she said. She was far away, and she spoke quietly, and I wasn't sure whether she actually said anything.

"Hey," I said. I whispered it. I imagined the whole thing, but she stood up and came closer before sitting down again. Notch-Tail nudged something on the ground, so I pulled myself up, wincing until I was at the level of the dirt and snow. She had left another piece of meat for me, this time further away from the entrance.

I stood up and grunted, and I limped on shaking legs towards

Notch-Tail. It took twenty-four steps, it hurt less, and I was getting better. "Thank you," I said as I got closer. She nodded, and I laid down in front of the meat, less than a wolf-length away from Notch-Tail. It was the same animal as yesterday, except this time it was a chunk of rib. It tasted very good.

"Thank you," I said once again after finishing my meal.

"How are you?"

I looked up. I hadn't seen her at night before. She had a thin, energetic face and a shiny black nose and a pair of sharp brown ears. Her mouth was open, and her tongue hung out just a bit. Brown, patterned fur twisted around her thin torso, glimmering in the moonlight.

"Why would you help me?"

"Because you were injured," she said. Her mouth was open, and she smiled. Her smile was warm and contagious and it made me want to smile.

"I took your kill last winter." I closed my eyes and waited. I relived the moment when I took the carcass from her mouth, and when I went to her lake, and when White-Ears and I left in a huff of anger. I expected her to say something. I expected her to stand up and leave, but when I opened my eyes again, Notch-Tail was still there.

"I know," she said. "I didn't think I would see you again."

She laid down in front of me. We kept our distance. I closed my eyes again and took in her smell. "Will you sleep here tonight with me?" I asked.

"Of course," she said.

I slept in the open. Notch-Tail slept in front of me, facing me. She kept her distance, and I didn't mind it. I woke up many times at night, and it made me feel good to see her in front of me. She was sound asleep. Her chest rose and fell, and her ears flickered occasionally. Later in the night, when the sky started to clear and the temperature dropped, I got up and moved next to her. She radiated heat, her heart thumped with a regular beat, and her fur was soft. I had the best sleep of my life.

In the morning, Notch-Tail was gone. The sun filtered through the rolling bands of clouds. They were like logs of white and grey that stretched from one edge of the sky to the other. The air was cold and wet and smelled of pine needles. It snowed last night. There were snowflakes all over my nose bridge, and I licked them off.

Notch-Tail left not too long ago. There was an indentation in the snow where she slept, which smelled like her. A trail of pawprints pointed north, winding between the trees until I could no longer see them. Her prints were ruffled around the edges. She stepped softly, and she was careful not to wake me. I turned my gaze north, past the trees, towards the rounded hill that stood not too far away. There was a ridge there too, and mountains behind it. The mountains were brilliantly white.

I stood up. Burning pain streamed through my chest, but there wasn't a hole there anymore. I could feel my ribcage. I knew my heart wasn't going to fall out. But even then, I couldn't shake myself, so I stood there and looked at the white peaks in the distance and waited for the snow on my back to melt in the sunlight. Between the hill and the peaks, there was a ridge that slanted up into the mountain. I last saw Ma and Pa there, on the lush green meadow full of wildflowers. They told me to come down here, so I did. I opened my eyes again.

The rolling clouds had moved on, and the sky was a dark, rich blue.

The base of the tree—my shelter and den—was the center of a small clearing. I took a few steps in each direction, testing the fresh snow with my toes and letting my body rest before continuing. I made a full circle around the shelter, and I left my tracks and scent. There were trees with unique smells, and I rubbed my head and neck against them. And then I laid down again, and I waited for Notch-Tail.

She came back before sundown. Her paws were muddy and dark against her light brown fur, and she smelled like bog water. I stood up and wagged my tail, and she came up to me and licked my mouth. I licked her back.

"You look better," she said.

"I feel better," I said. "Less pain." She grinned at me.

Notch-Tail came up to me and pressed her neck and back against my face and told me to inhale. I took in the new scents she was carrying, and then I showed her mine. There was no meat on her fur, no animals, or even freeze-dried fruits. It was just bog and old water.

"It's okay," I said. "I'm not very hungry."

"I tried," she said with a flick of her tail and then sat down and started licking between her toes.

I sat down. "Where is your family?" I said.

She didn't raise her head. "Somewhere out east, gone, dead. I don't know."

"You've been alone all this time?"

"Two summers," she said. Notch-Tail was older than me, but she didn't look old.

"One."

"Were you still with your family last winter?" she said.

I shook my head. "No, just my sister. We just separated, and I've been looking for my mother and father ever since."

I turned towards the ridge to the north, past the barren, snow-covered earth towards the brilliant white peaks, yellowed by the setting sun. Ma and Pa were out there somewhere, but I wasn't going to find them. Once the pain went away, I would take Notch-Tail and go west. I would find White-Ears, and we would be a big family again.

I slept beside her, and she made me feel good. Her smell was intoxicating, sweet like wildflowers and musky, like fresh innards. Her brown fur had light patches on the edge of her ears, down her face, and around her eyes, and it was soft, dense, and smooth. Her thick neck fur became my favourite headrest. I fell asleep to the quiet thumping of her heart and to the up and down motion of her chest, breathing in and out.

It started snowing again. It was colder, so I snuggled closer to Notch-Tail. The snow drifted from the uniform grey sky and landed on her nose, where each snowflake melted into a tiny puddle on top of Notch-Tail's shiny black nose. I took a deep breath and stood up, bracing for the searing pain that wasn't there anymore. I shuffled, quietly and carefully, until I stood over her snout. I lowered myself on top of her until the outer layer of my belly fur covered her mouth and nose. She stirred but did not wake.

Lying down, I turned to face the sky. I watched the snow drift from the sky until it stopped, and then I watched the clouds part until patches of dark blue opened up, and then I watched the light dim and the sky turn purple. I watched as the stars appeared in the sky. Notch-Tail was still sleeping. I wasn't tired.

☁

Earlier in the day, Notch-Tail spotted an old moose from atop the south side of the valley, and she sang to me. She stood at the southwest corner of the valley, waiting for the wind to change directions, and when I got there, the wind was coming from the north. I licked her face, and she asked me about my injury, so I jumped to show that I was fine. We started slow, but soon we were running at a steady pace.

I was ready to hunt again.

The snow was heavy, and we were silent and low. Notch-Tail went first, a couple wolf-lengths in front of me. We followed a trail without any tracks, surrounded by thick and barren bushes on either side, with dead trees jutting out and logs splayed across. Notch-Tail jumped quietly over a log, and I followed. I balanced myself on the log for a moment before tumbling down, catching my weight on my front legs and feeling the dull ache pound against my chest. She looked behind as I stood and panted. I gave her a nod, and we kept going.

Her pawsteps were wide. She dragged her paws through the snow to clear a path for me. Her tail twitched so I could follow through the dense thicket. We moved fast. We came across the moose on an island between two creek streams that ran through the valley. The bubbling water concealed our approach. It was an old female that stood tall and thin without antlers. It was loud and clumsy, and its ribs were showing. The moose reached up and tried to eat the thin branches, but it tripped and stumbled forward. We stood side-by-side and watched it lean against a tree to stand back up.

Notch-Tail looked at me and gestured with her head. Go forward. Go around. I understood. I pressed myself against the snowy ground and made my way across the creek to the east, around the back of the moose while keeping parallel to the wind. Flank from both sides, Ma said, flank them, and they will panic. When I got in position, I watched as Notch-Tail crossed the creek directly in front of the old moose. She was as quiet as an owl, with a face full of determination. I inched my way closer.

She bolted, crashing through the thick bushes and sending powdery snow in every direction. The moose jumped and ran in the opposite direction, and I revealed myself. I barked low and loud, and the moose made a sharp turn into a pile of snow. Then, with a thunderous thud, it tripped and tumbled into the creek against the sharp rocks that separated cold water from fresh snow.

I ran for it and so did Notch-Tail. She got there first, and the moose thrashed and tried to get up, but Notch-Tail jumped around it and tore at the neck. I bit the animal's thick hide around where its ribcage met its spine, and I held it down, and Notch-Tail made a clean kill. We stood in the frigid creek with our heads down, and we didn't look up until we finished all the innards. Notch-Tail loved the kidneys and liver, so I let her have it all.

It was late. The moon was high in the sky, our bellies were full, and our mouths were bloodied. I licked the blood off her face tenderly, letting my tongue linger on her cheek and letting my saliva soak into her fur. I nuzzled her face and neck and nibbled on her ears, and we pressed our bodies together until

169

our heartbeats synchronized. I pulled her closer to me and then climbed on top of her. Notch-Tail trembled, and she tried to pull away. I bit her scruff and pulled her head back. She whimpered and then screamed.

The air was full of her scent—that dizzying, earthy smell that made me crazy for her. I pulled on her neck and bit her ears, and she squealed in pleasure. We mated. When I was done, I was stuck inside of her, and I felt her heartbeat slowly calm down.

We fell asleep hugging each other, and I had a very restful sleep.

Chapter 19

As the days became longer, Notch-Tail's belly rounded. Food was plentiful, and we were full of energy. The moose lasted us many days, and its nutrients helped me get better, and we spent days wandering the forests and slopes. I showed Notch-Tail where the bull elk nearly killed me, and we smelled the ground under the trees where the elk slept, and we rolled around in the snow and grass until we both smelled like elk.

When the moose was nothing more than sun-bleached bones and tough skin, we left and headed west. We hunted for deer. The thick snow slowed them down, and they were weaker, but I was also weak. My body still hurt whenever I moved, but the pain wasn't so sharp anymore. I ignored it. Notch-Tail was also weaker. Her belly was large, and it dangled and dragged against the snow, and she couldn't have ignored it.

We walked down and through the valley, where we found food. The winter wasn't so harsh here, and the animals were easier to catch. At first, the hunting effort was mostly Notch-Tail, but as her belly grew bigger and I recovered, I took the lead in the hunts. We took down deer and a few hares. The winter was good to us.

When Notch-Tail couldn't sprint anymore, we walked across the vast forested valley until we came across a secluded patch.

It was obscured by trees on one side, and on the other side was a knob of earth sticking out of the ground. Between the two, a hole led into the ground at a shallow angle. It smelled faintly like badgers and urine. Notch-Tail stuck her head into the hole and explored the inside, but it was too small to fit a wolf. After a few moments, she pulled out of the hole.

"This is fine," she said, and we took turns digging. The hole could fit only one of us. I stuck my head into the hole and pulled the dirt out with my claws until I was tired, and then Notch-Tail did the same thing. We dug until the den was spacious inside. It was enough space for many children.

☖

There were strange smells in the forest. I was more agile than Notch-Tail, so it was my responsibility to find and clear out potential threats. I walked in circles around the den, and I investigated every tree and rock and crevice. Most of the strands of fur and urine were very old. A fox visited this area, and I wanted to get rid of it, so I followed its scent trail in the middle of the night until it disappeared into a snowy cliff. Coming back, I walked in a criss-cross pattern through the trees, and I left my scent everywhere. There were no strangers here, but I still had to be cautious.

Notch-Tail was still awake when I got back to the den. The moon was out, and it was thin, but there was enough light in the forest for me to see that she was tired and her belly was bulging. I greeted her by licking her snout.

"It's coming," she said, "I can feel them."

"Go inside and rest," I said. Our eyes met briefly, and hers glowed bright and green. She tilted her head back and sang a song, and I joined her, and then she slid into the den on her belly.

I laid down outside near the entrance. The forest was silent, warm, and the moonlight filtered through the trees, casting patchy shadows on the snow and dirt. Clouds drifted in and out of the sky until the moon disappeared behind the clouds, and then the moonlight disappeared behind the mountains.

I woke up to sunlight, and my neck fur was standing on its end. My shoulders were tense. A strange scent lingered in the air, and it stung my nose, and I wanted to growl at it. I followed the scent north as it weaved between trees and over rocks. There were tracks, but the snow's surface was very hard, and they were faint. At the base of the slope, there was a tree well with fresh snow, and there was a perfect track inside, so I bent down and smelled it. It was fresh. Whatever animal left these tracks was large; it sunk into the snow deeply.

My chest bubbled with pain as I climbed the slope. I used the snow as traction, and I took the long way up, stopping for the pain to fade away before continuing back and forth in long stretches until I rounded the crest of the hill.

At the top, there was a large, flat meadow. Snow covered every feature on the meadow except a faint set of tracks, going halfway into it before doubling back to the steep hillside where the animal sat and faced south. I sat in the same spot, and I looked down, squinting against the sunlight. The den was visible. The intruder sat here last night and watched us sleep, which meant I had to find this animal and kill it.

The sun was strong and warm. The snow had begun to melt

and harden again, so I hurried ahead before I lost the tracks. I scanned the ground with my nose against the icy surface until I found the scent trail again, and I followed it to the edge of the meadow and down another hillside full of dried bushes. There was a path here, and the animal followed it, leading me to a rapidly flowing creek.

And then I saw it. A lynx, two hundred wolf-lengths ahead and behind a tree. It had a big head, a short snout, and a stubby tail. It stood still and looked straight at me. I raised my tail and lowered my head, and a low snarl came out of my throat. There was a torrential creek between the lynx and me and many trees, but I could smell it, and I could see its piercing green eyes, looking at me expressionlessly.

"Go away!" I barked. It heard me, its ears twitched, but it stood unphased. Of course, it didn't understand me. I stepped closer. One step. Another. Frigid water washed over my paws, and it came up to my dewclaw and then my elbow. I kept the low snarl in my throat, and it was as if it echoed in the entire forest.

"This is my home now. Go away, or I will kill you."

The lynx came out from behind the trees, and its fur was puffed, and its head was held high. It was the size of a wolf. It wasn't afraid of me, and it hissed threateningly, but deep down, I knew I could take it on and win. Because I had to. Because I didn't have a choice. Because my children were coming soon, and it was too dangerous to let this lynx stay nearby.

My snarl became an open-mouthed growl. "Go away," I said. "Final warning."

I jumped towards it with my teeth bared, and I let myself land on the snow on my front paws with full force. The old wound in my chest sent a pulse of pain straight into my skull, and I winced. The lynx had arched its back, and it backed up a few steps and kept hissing at me. We were only a few wolf-lengths away from each other, and I could smell its sweat and hear its heartbeat.

Still growling, I paused. I shook my head and waved my tail and took a step closer. The lynx hissed louder. It wasn't leaving. I was within attacking distance, and it had no intention to flee. Its back was arched, and it took a swipe at me, but it was too far away. I jumped back and landed on my hindpaws with my tail planting solidly into the hard snow. Enough was enough. I needed this animal away from the den, and I made up my mind to kill it, so I lunged, and it swiped at me again, and I dodged back. The snow crunched under my paws as I ran around the backside of the lynx. It simply turned around and hissed at me some more, but it did not move from where it stood.

I ran head-first, teeth bared, feeling the wind against my neck fur. My heart pounded. My eyes locked on the animal's neck. It jumped back as I came down, and from the corner of my eye, I saw a massive paw fly towards my shoulder. Sharp, stinging pain erupted where it slashed me, but my jaws made contact with fur and skin at the same moment. I bit down as hard as I could.

Claws thrashed all around me, and there was pain, and the sound of fur ripping, and I had to let go. The lynx pulled away from my grip and darted away. There was blood in the air and on the ground. There was blood in my mouth, and it wasn't mine. I ran towards the fleeing animal, but it was fast. Its thick paws glanced off the icy snow, and its stubby tail waved, and it disappeared into the rocks and bushes on the other edge of the valley, blending in with the brown and white until it was gone. I stopped chasing. There was blood all over my shoulder and neck. I sat down and licked myself. It stung. A gash on my left shoulder was the width of my claw and as deep as teeth. I licked it, letting my saliva soak into the gash and cleaning the blood.

I waited at the edge of the forest. It was silent again. I waited a very long time until I was convinced the lynx wasn't coming back. Slowly, my fur flattened and my tail lowered. I marked my scent all over these trees, and then I laid down and licked my wound some more, feeling the warmth above, the smooth and slippery snow below, and the intermittent stinging pain everywhere in between.

The sun sat low, just over the horizon, and I still needed to find some food for Notch-Tail. Maybe I could explore the meadow, maybe find a hare to eat.

I started heading back slowly, listening to my paws crunch against the snow as I held my head low, nose against the ground, looking for anything at all. The forest smelled like lynx and blood. There were patches of bushes and stubby trees and dark green clusters of pine. They were big and towering and cast long shadows in the snow. The smell of lynx had lingered, so I shook myself head to tail, trying to get the smell out of my mind. It got stronger. I paused and scanned my surroundings.

Up ahead, close to where I had fought the lynx, there was an overturned tree with its roots pointing at the sun. Its trunk faced north, and at the very end it had gnarly branches with yellowed needles, balanced precariously on another pine. A deep indent in the earth connected the upturned roots with whatever was still in the ground. The smell of lynx was stronger here. I sat down and closed my eyes and turned my ears.

A tiny, high-pitched squeak came from behind and below the tree. I opened my eyes and walked towards it. I was careful to step where there were pawprints, where the ice was too hard to break so I didn't make any noise. Every step brought stronger smells, and I realized that it wasn't an adult lynx at all. The hole in the ground was small, well hidden, behind a tangled mass of roots and under the part of the trunk closest to the ground. It smelled like regurgitated food and urine all around. The lynx had its young here, and they were still in the hole. It was quiet. The lynx cubs had probably heard me approach.

I stuck my nose in the hole and sniffed it. There was more than one lynx cub in the hole. The sun had begun to set, and I was very hungry. Notch-Tail needed more food than usual, and here it was, deep and hidden under these roots. The lynx cubs would keep us fed.

Spreading open my toes and curling my claws, I reached in with an arm and pulled a clump of dirt out of the hole. And then another, and another. The earth was soft and cold, and it smelled. Soon, the hole was big enough for my head and shoulders, so I wiggled deeper and kept digging. I was close. I could smell them. I could hear them. Finally, when I had dug enough, I saw they were pressed against the back wall where they frantically scratched the dirt, and I heard it all. I was close. The dirt was softer now. They started squeaking, tiny whimpers and loud squeals. As I pulled the last clump of dirt out, there was a hiss. Barely audible. *Hssssss...*

I stuck my head and chest all the way in. The cubs were

small, each the size of my snout, with golden brown fur and eyes that glowed faintly. They had both retreated to the very end. One of them stood between my snout and its sibling, and it hissed with its ears folded back. It was ready to strike. The other one tried to disappear into the dirt and made itself as small as it could. The hissing cub took a swipe at me and nearly hit my nose, so I backed up until I felt the chill of the outside air again.

I spun my head and twitched my ears and looked around and saw nothing but wind and trees and snow melting, dripping from the branches and puddling on the icy surfaces. But it wasn't sunny anymore. Dark clouds rolled in from the west and the wind whistled past the trees. The weather was worsening, and tired pines trembled all around me.

The mother lynx wasn't coming back.

I stuck my head back into the wide-open lynx den, and I pulled out another clump of dirt. The braver cub hissed at me once again as her brother whimpered. I pressed down on her torso with my right paw and took her head and throat in my jaws, and I pulled her out and sunk my teeth in her neck. She fought to the last moment, scratching my nose and mouth. Then, when she stopped moving, I went back in for the other one. He only whimpered and shook, so I killed him inside the den. His neck cracked and squirted blood, and he stopped moving.

I took both lynx cubs in my mouth and started to head up the rocky slope, through the meadow, and back to Notch-Tail. Their limp torsos dangled on either side of my mouth, and thick blood dripped between my teeth and down my chin.

Chapter 20

When our children were born, it was spring, but it felt like the depths of winter. The sky was dark, with rolling bands of black clouds and wet snow, and the winds billowed and howled. I sat at the entrance to the den, shielding Notch-Tail from the biting wind with my left side—the side that didn't hurt. By late evening, my fur was a solid mass of icicles, but the wind had stopped, and the snow gently drifted from the grey skies.

I set out in the intermittent moonlight after Notch-Tail and the kids had fallen asleep. There was a path from the den's opening that led across the valley to the base of a shallow hill. The path was used by deer before the most recent snowstorm. Even in the wet air, I could still smell the deer, but the scent wasn't strong enough to follow. With every step I took, a faint and dull ache pushed against my ribcage. I stuck to the middle of the path so that my left side bore most of my weight. It wasn't so bad anymore. With time, the pain became dulled until it was just another memory, and then the memory itself would fade. Life went on. I barely remembered how I got injured, and it didn't matter. I needed to find food for Notch-Tail and myself.

I inhaled. The air was wet, mossy, with a hint of deer and

wet wolves and the faint scent of blood. Yesterday, Notch-Tail licked our children clean, all three of them, until there was no blood left anywhere. But the scent always lingers. I shook myself and listened as pieces of wet snow splattered against the trees.

A bird called. It echoed once. I looked up in time to see an owl take off from the tip of a dead tree. The tree trembled, but the owl was utterly silent. It headed east, across the bare undergrowth and deeper into the valley. I turned and ran after it, and as I took the first few steps, a branch wedged under my paws, and I crashed into the undergrowth, chest first. I got up and felt the pulsating ache in my ribcage. The thumping matched my steps until it merged with my heartbeat and became a continuous wave of pain. I had to take a break. The owl soared past the treetops until it disappeared behind a dense mass of trees into the clouds before becoming one with the dark sky.

There was nothing to eat around here. However, I was well-rested, and I could keep going. I would go as far as the ridge before the sunrise and bring something back by midday. It was the right weather to find frozen hares. So I took a long walk through wet snow and dark green patches of trees and watched as the shadows lengthened until the moon disappeared to the southwest.

At the foot of the ridge, I raised my head and smelled the air. There were wildflowers at the top, rocks covered with lichen, and everything was hidden under a blanket of wet snow. The sky had brightened to the east as I limped up the ridge, winding back and forth, careful to make sure my claws caught the densely packed undersnow with each step. I swung my tail against the hillside. It was slippery. I knew if I slipped, I

180

wasn't going to make it back up again.

But I made it up, and I was okay. I sang for Notch-Tail from the top of the ridge. She replied. Everything was fine, so I kept going. I would be back by sundown.

When the sun was high in the southeast, I caught a hint of musky sweetness in the air, wafting from the other side of the ridge. There was rotting meat somewhere. Notch-Tail was hungry, and I needed to find it. Along the ridge, the thin snow had just begun to melt from the sun's heat, revealing a strip of earth. My claws gripped solid ground and made it easier for me to follow a path down the other side of the ridge into a narrow valley surrounded by steep hills.

A narrow creek bubbled and weaved down the valley, shielded by the hills on each side. I walked beside it. My paws plopped against the wet earth, a mixture of snow and mud, and if I stood still for too long, I could feel the mud pull against my claws and wrist. The trees were small, gnarled, and tilted. That sweet scent of rotting meat was stronger now. It was pungent, sour, and sweet, with hints of freshness.

Just ahead, the carcass stuck out of the gap between two large rocks, bridging across a sharp bend in the creek. It must have been washed out from above the frozen ridge before ending up in the valley. I walked around it. It was grey with patchy brown fur, partially rotten, and partially eaten. Its chest and belly were open, and there were only ribs left. I didn't know what type of animal it was, but the meat smelled good, so I found a piece of rib and pulled the meat off of it. The taste of meat sent a shiver down my back and through my tail. I had my fill, just a little bit, and just enough to get back to the den.

I pulled on the carcass and tried to tug it away from the boulders. It cracked, detaching from the rock with force, and soft, mushy skin and flesh splattered onto the creek. I watched as the pieces floated away in the current. There was a leg stuck in the rock crevice, but it was nothing but tendon and bone, so I left it.

I dragged the torso by the first rib, between the shoulder blade and where the head was supposed to be. It tried very hard to sink into the mud, and so did my paws, so I had to jump every few steps. I whipped my head to move the carcass. Sharp pulses of pain accompanied every step, and it slowly intensified, and by the time I got out of the valley and onto the narrow ridge trail, it was everywhere. The carcass threatened to roll down the steep slopes. It pulled against my neck and shoulders, and my claws were bloodied from digging into the rocky terrain.

A tendril of pain against my chest made me wince, and I let go of the carcass, and it rolled until it came to a stop, a few wolf-lengths ahead along the path. Skin and fur came off. I left it there. The sun had started to set, and the world was bathed in an orange glow. I sang once again for Notch-Tail to let her know I was coming back with food. She replied with a short song with excitement in her voice.

It was easier now. The carcass slid smoothly on the wet, snowy ground on the valley floor. It was better than going uphill, but even then, by the time I could smell the den, the sky was dark again.

Notch-Tail's head emerged from the den when I approached. Her eyes were wary, but she had a wide-open smile on her face. Her fur was matted, and there were patches of dried blood under her chin. A droplet of sticky liquid dripped from her neck. It was saliva, but it probably wasn't hers.

She crawled out of the den, her tail swaying back and forth in a wide circle. I dropped the carcass and ran up to her. I licked her mouth. It tasted like old blood and morning breath. She nuzzled my neck and sighed. "I was beginning to get worried," Notch-Tail said.

I buried my nose in her neck and shoulder and wagged my tail. "I got food for you," I said. She pulled away from me and jumped towards the grey chunk of rib meat that sat tilted in the snow. "Eat. It's all for you."

I sat a few wolf-lengths away and watched Notch-Tail dig into the carcass. The sound of crunching filled the air, and the ripping of soft, waterlogged flesh, and Notch-Tail's squeals of pleasure. Then she looked at me, and I nodded and smiled, and she ate some more. It wasn't the best-tasting meat, but it was something.

As she ate, I laid down on the wet snow and licked my claws. There was sand and rock grit under them and a blob of dried blood on my middle toe, which hurt when I touched it. I licked there anyway, wedging my tongue under and getting all the dirt out. The crunching slowly stopped, and Notch-Tail came up to me and licked my nose. I looked up at her.

"I'm going back now."

I gave her a swish of my tail and watched as she stuck her head into the den, disappearing into the well-concealed entrance. Standing up, I shook the water from my fur and inspected the rack of bones on the ground. There was still something to eat, so I dragged it near the entrance of the den, and I laid down and chewed the bones, getting my tongue into the crevices and sucking out the pieces of tendon that Notch-

Tail had missed. When the moon was high in the sky once again, and the entire forest was illuminated, I left the carcass where it was, and I shuffled to the mouth of the den. There, I sat down and wiggled until I covered most of the opening. Snow could come at any moment, and I had to keep them warm.

Chapter 21

I had three sons. Each was a tiny ball of black fluff and fur that smelled like Notch-Tail. She left to stretch her legs, so I kept my children warm and safe. It was dark. I faced into the den with my tail sticking out of the exit, and I grabbed each child by the neck and pulled them together in front of me.

Each of them had their eyes closed and ears folded, and the smallest one trembled when I put him down, so I licked him first. He was muddy from tumbling around in the dirt. My tongue covered most of his back and face, and I stopped to drag my whiskers across his nose, and he giggled. Clumps of dirt came off with each lick and I scraped it off my tongue with my teeth. When my smallest child was clean, he stopped trembling. I stuck my nose in his soft fur and inhaled, but all I could smell was Notch-Tail and the den.

There was a light-grey patch of fur on the back of his ears, and he reminded me of White-Ears. I closed my eyes for a moment and tried to imagine White-Ears when she was small, but the memories were fuzzy, my eyesight was poor, and all dens smelled alike. In the summer, I would introduce my child to White-Ears. He would be better than she was at fishing, and we would hunt together, and I would show him how to catch beavers.

My other two sons were more active. They started playing while I cleaned the smallest one. Both were bigger. The biggest one had a light-coloured nose, and the smaller one was grey all over. They tumbled against each other. They had tiny teeth and tiny paws and folded ears and no eyes, yet they fought ferociously. I put my nose and snout between my two sons and wiggled them apart, and I grabbed the light-gray one with the bright nose and started to lick him. The other one tugged on my whiskers. I said, "Stop that," but I didn't think my children understood me, and it didn't matter since they were so small. They could tug all they wanted.

Notch-Tail came back not long after. She pawed at my tail, and I hissed at her, but she squeezed her head into the den anyway. The air outside was cold, but it was warm and moist inside the den, and when Notch-Tail entered, she brought a burst of cold air. The children shivered. I pushed them aside and moved further into the den so that I was fully pressed against the dirt at the end. We were both able to fit. Notch-Tail laid down, and we formed a circle around the children. The small one wobbled up to me and rested his chin on my left paw. I turned my paw around, palm facing up, and tickled him with a claw.

"He likes his father," Notch-Tail said.

I smiled and wagged my tail which kicked up a cloud of dust. Notch-Tail nuzzled the child with the grey fur and whispered, "Well, I like all of you equally."

I rested my head against the soft dirt and closed my eyes, and I heard Notch-Tail do the same. "Should we sing them a song?" I said, and she grunted in agreement, so I opened my mouth and breathed a quiet song about the ocean, and she hummed along.

I woke up before the sun was up. Steady heartbeats filled the den, and the children were fast asleep. I nudged Notch-Tail on the butt and woke her up so I could leave the den. She grumbled about it being too early, but I ran my teeth along her winter fur and nibbled her until she got up. She backed out of the den, shook herself, smelled the air, and went back into the den without saying anything.

I needed to stretch, walk around, and find something to eat. I never liked the dawn. It was too bright, too early, and too cold. But now that Notch-Tail was taking care of the children, I had to hunt alone. Hares were less active in the early morning. Deer were asleep. Even the pheasants, which usually ran too fast and darted too quickly, had an unusual sluggishness in them at sunrise.

The air smelled the same in every direction, so I decided to go south. It was a gentle slope at first, and as it became steeper, I started to have pain on my right side. I weaved down the hillside, using the trees as support and feeling the wet snow beneath my paws, which acted as a cushion. I came down to the creekbed just as the sun started peeking from the mountains. It was warmer in the sun, and suddenly I was very tired, and it became hard to keep my eyes open.

There wasn't much to eat here. The forest was silent. Dead and silent, with no rodents or birds, except the occasional squirrels scampering up the smooth tree trunks. I made a big circle around and then decided to come back up the slope. I didn't want to leave Notch-Tail and the children for too long. Ma had always said that you can't wait around for food to show up. You have to find it yourself.

I came back around midday. Notch-Tail stood in front of the den, and I looked at her and didn't say anything. She looked rough and tired and hungry, and her tail was drooping. I knew she had hoped for food and I let her down, but it was more than that. Her fur was ruffled, and her head was lowered, and her legs spread just a tiny bit further apart than usual. Notch-Tail was scared of something. I walked up to her and nuzzled her, rubbing my scent all over her face and neck.

"What's wrong?"

"He's trembling and warm, and he's barely moving," she said.

I immediately knew which child Notch-Tail was talking about. I pulled away from her embrace and walked towards the den, and the echo of my pawsteps on the hard, compacted snow pierced my ears. Notch-Tail followed. I let her enter the den first, and then I went after her, with my back facing the hole, trying to ward off the cold air.

Notch-Tail nudged my smallest son gently with her glistening nose. He stayed in place. He was curled up in a ball, and I could see his fur tremble, harder, softer, like the bubbling of a creek. I felt his face with my snout. It was warm, and he smelled different from the previous night. I nudged him, and he laid perfectly still, eyes closed and ears folded.

"He'll be fine," I said. He reminded me of White-Ears, and she grew up to be a fine wolf. "He'll be just fine," I said. I went nose-to-nose with Notch-Tail, and I licked her face. She cracked a smile and nodded.

"Stay with us for a bit?" she said.

"I should go find food."

"Stay with me."

"He'll be fine," I whispered. "We need food."

"Okay," she said, and I left the den and headed north when

188

the sun was hanging low above the mountains, and by the time I crossed the meadow, it was already dark. Food was my priority. Notch-Tail needed to eat so she could take care of the children. I needed to eat too. Fresh meat was what I needed.

I sat on a rock and listened. I scanned the meadow, rocky and sloped with an imposing, barren mountain towering to the right. The path that led down to the forest branched left. There wasn't anything to eat in the forest so I went right, up the rocks, until I could see everything. Everything in the meadow and valley glowed orange from the dying sunlight. Nothing moved. I jumped off the rock, splattering snow all around me. I walked from where I sat, through the middle of the meadow, and up the sloped, rocky path until I couldn't go any higher. From there, I came down and around the edge of the meadow. It was dark when I came back to the rock. There was nothing on this plateau.

I came back and circled the den, looking for intruders and animals. There was nothing for me to find and nothing to kill, so finally, I stuck my head into the den. Notch-Tail had fallen asleep. She rested her snout on her tail, her nose twitched, and her ears were erect and alert. In the center, I could see my children, each motionless, sleeping. The sound of breathing filled the den, and four heartbeats in perfect synchronization.

I found softer snow on the northwest side of the den, and I circled the spot before lying down and going to sleep.

I dreamt of nothing in particular, but something hung heavy over me, like a blanket of wet snow, soaking into my mind and vision and making everything blurry. I woke up in the middle of the night to urinate, and once again as the sun was coming up. The sky was dark blue, then bright and brilliantly blue with only the shadow of stars that lingered in the west. I closed my eyes for a moment, and then when I opened them, the first rays of the sun had come.

I poked my head into the den, where it was warm and moist. Notch-Tail slept peacefully with the children. I pulled my head out and circled the den, but the smells were no different from the day before. The day felt like a westbound day. Westbound, through the infinite valley, until I could find food. There had got to be something to eat. The animals were more active in early spring. I had a good feeling about today. I followed the main trail to the west. My steps were loud and wet. The ground under my paws squelched, and I felt the water seep between my toes, in my claws, and into my belly fur. As I came across a creek, the trickling of water filled my ears. It was not here a few days ago, so it must have been from the melting snow. I crossed it and continued walking. I walked all morning until the sun was warm on my back and the squelching had been reduced to pitter-pattering.

There was a scent trail for a hare between two jagged rocks. I stuck my nose in there and found a tuft of white fur, so I picked it up and chewed on it. The hare was shedding not long ago, and it probably heard my approach and fled before I could get close. The scent was strong. I followed it. It winded around trees, getting stronger and weaker and stronger again, but never strong enough, never close enough for me to give chase. I ran anyway.

Around the trees I ran, brushing against the rough bark and knocking off pieces and filling the forest with the scent of fresh pine, throwing up mud and splattering it, leaving deep pawprints and filling the space under my claws with more mud. The wind blew into my whiskers and past my face. I pulled my lips back and allowed my tongue to dangle, feeling the cold air in my throat. I ran until the bottom of my throat burned, and my lungs were tingling, and there was mud all over my fur from toe to tail. I hadn't run this hard since my injury, and it felt good.

The hare's scent lingered. I shook my head, then my body, and told myself to focus. I had to focus because the sun was high in the sky, which meant Notch-Tail hadn't eaten for two days. I tried every day, but the hunt was unpredictable. The nature of the hunt was unpredictable: sometimes we got moose on the first try, and other times we had to eat old bones and mushy, freeze-burned rhubarb for many days.

If there was a hare here, I was going to catch it.

A noise. I paused in the thicket of bare branches, and I stood high and then low, smelling the air. I closed my eyes and listened. My ears swirled in opposite directions. There was a crackle. I heard it, and I was sure of it, but I couldn't pinpoint where it had come from. I lifted my left paw and planted it in the waterlogged ground in front of me, and it made a squelching splatter that echoed between the trees.

The hare took off running. It was a blur of grey and white, a dozen wolf-lengths away. It was hiding under a log, and now it ran fast. I saw a trail of prints. The hare made shallow prints, two in the front and one in the back, and the one in the back was shallower and had two dimples. I chased it. Wind brushed my face fur back, and the thunderous sound of running flooded my ears, so I folded them back. The muddy earth slowed me down, but it slowed my prey even more, so I pushed ahead.

It turned. It didn't turn very well, and now the gap was only a wolf-length away. I pushed forward with each step. The ache was gone, and I was feeling energetic, alive. Half a wolf-length now. The mud had tired out the hare, and it was slow. I was close, and I was toying with it. I faked a lunge, and it turned in the other direction into a tree where it glanced off and kept running. Towards me now. I reached out and clawed at it, and then I lunged and bit down. The first bite missed the neck and only broke its hind leg, but the second bite went straight through.

I sat up with the dead hare under my left paw and panted, feeling my lungs fill with air and then pushing it all out and repeating it, over and over, until the ringing sound went away. I bent down and tore at the underside of the hare's neck, pulling on the exposed strands of flesh until it snapped apart. It was fresh and sweet. It was good.

I sang for Notch-Tail, to let her know that I was coming home with food. My voice trailed off, and so did the echo. There was only the sound of meltwater. Drip. Drip. Drip. I waited for a few moments. I licked the blood from the edge of my paws and tried to get my tongue around my face. When I was mostly clean, I picked up the hare and started walking towards home. The sun was behind me. Wind blew in my face. My back was warm, but my face was cold.

When the sun was lower and the air colder, I dropped the hare, tilted my head back, and sang again. "Are you there? Tell me you are okay," I said. Then, in the same breath, I said, "Are you there? Are you there?" and I repeated it until the tune was stale.

I got nothing back. Orange turned purple and purple turned navy blue and all of a sudden it was damp and cold and I could feel the dampness seep into my fur, like water through snow. I picked up the hare and started walking again, but I ran instead. I ran with the hare dangling in my mouth, heart racing, water splattering all around me, my breath fogging up ahead of me, waiting for her reply. I needed to hear from her. Something bad had happened, I didn't want to hear it, but I needed to hear from my Notch-Tail.

I cleared the thick patch of pines and crossed the meltwater creek when I heard her voice. It was soft, quiet, and it trembled in the air. "Come, come come come," Notch-Tail said. "I need you. I need you. I need you."

I ran for the den. When I got there, it was quiet and dark, and there was nothing and no sounds and no smells. I dropped the hare by the entrance and stuck my head in. Notch-Tail was there, and so were my children. Her eyes were wide and glowed green, and she looked at me intensely. The den smelled different. It sent shivers down my spine, and I tried shaking myself, forgetting how small the space was. I wiggled closer and Notch-Tail bared her teeth and growled a broken growl with her ears folded back. They didn't come back up.

Beside her, my youngest son lay in the dirt, curled into a tiny ball of fur. He didn't move at all, so I reached with my nose to touch him. I nudged his head, taking in his scent and letting all the smells flood my nose. His scent was wrong. I felt my heart speed up, and I smelled him again. "Wake up," I whispered. "Let me see you."

He didn't budge. I heard a whine coming from Notch-Tail, and I leaned to lick him, and he didn't move. "Wake up." But there was nothing. No little heartbeat and no tiny, quick breaths. My youngest son was gone. There was no mistaking it. It was the scent of death that made my fur stand on end. "Please wake up," I said.

193

I leaned forward to grab my son by his neck scruff, but before I could get to him, Notch-Tail darted forward. She covered my son with her snout and snarled at me. Her voice was broken and it crackled. She snarled at me still, and she laid her snout over our dead son, and the den trembled with her snarls.

We made eye contact, only briefly, and then the growling stopped, and she looked at me with those glowing green eyes. Her eyes lingered on my face, and she blinked, and she closed her eyes, and her eyes stayed closed, and she covered our son with the soft underside of her face and kept him from everything that could hurt him, and it broke me.

I pulled my head out of the den, and I laid down outside and curled up, and I buried my head in my tail. I needed to sleep. But I couldn't. His body kept flashing in front of me. Notch-Tail's sorrow. The smell of the den. The dreadful cold seeping into my fur. Those green eyes that told me everything. I couldn't stop seeing it all. I couldn't sleep, so I tilted my head up and sang, and I sang so the world could hear, and I sang so Notch-Tail wouldn't have to bear the burden of it all.

And the forest was silent except for the dripping of meltwater.

And then it was morning once more. Notch-Tail had stood in front of me, and she blocked the sunlight, and when I opened my eyes, she bent down and nuzzled my face, and she rubbed herself all over me. "Wake up," she said. I looked at her, and I didn't say anything. Notch-Tail turned and grabbed the hare that had sat frozen on the wet ground and retreated into the den. I stood up and walked over to the entrance of the den, feeling the wetness on the tip of my tail and all over my belly and paws.

The den was dry. I stuck my head inside. Notch-Tail gnawed

on the hare in one corner and the two children fed on her nipples. In the other corner was my son. I shuffled on my belly until I got to him and picked him up carefully, by his neck fur, and I pulled him out of the den. It was warm in the den, and he would rot, like all dead things, so I pulled him out and walked to the nearest tree, a knotted and leaning pine, resting him against the snowpack on the leeward side.

I sat down, and I pressed my nose against his cold fur and nudged him. Of course, he wasn't coming back. I knew this, but I groomed him anyway. I licked every inch of his fur clean until my son was grey and black and shiny in the sunlight.

I laid down beside him and closed my eyes.

Later, Notch-Tail came back out. She had saved me some hare meat. There wasn't much except bones and connecting tissue, and it was still fresh, but the blood had dried, and it was cold and chewy. I took the meat and walked to the space between three pines, and I faced the pine with the mottled bark and ate my kill. I ate every piece of skin and flesh and left only the femurs, skull, and ribcage. It was too bright to sleep, too warm, and the sky was too blue, so I decided to take a walk.

I grabbed my son by his neck fur with my front teeth and pulled him away from the snow. He didn't want to come. His body was cold and hard, and it didn't dangle in my mouth. I took him anyway. Muddy wetness was part of the ground, and it infused everywhere, but I kept him clean. I went east, up the gentle hills until I was at the foot of the ridge, and I leapt up to the closest piece of level ground, and I kept going up until the entire forest revealed itself to me.

The ridge sloped northeast, high up in the sky until it intersected with jagged grey mountains. I kept going until it was too rocky to climb. Until the sharp rocks tumbled down with each step. Until the rocks jammed into my paws and pulled me down with them. This was the top of everything. I placed my son on a flat surface and pointed him west.

"Look," I whispered to him, "all this is yours. Out west, there is a great big ocean, and this summer, I will take you there and show you how to pull clams out of the sand." But I couldn't do anything like that. He died before he could see the world, and it wasn't fair. I couldn't take him to the ocean. I couldn't teach him how to hunt and fish, and it wasn't fair.

I stood up and nuzzled my son, and I buried my nose in his fur and remembered his scent, and I tilted my head back and sang until my throat was scratchy and raw. And I turned around, and I left, down the narrow path, feeling the dry rocks turn into soft wet earth and then slushy snow, and I didn't want to turn back until I was back at the den, and I didn't turn back at all.

Notch-Tail's heartbeat drummed in my ears, so I snuggled closer to her. My children slept between us against Notch-Tail's belly, and I felt their tiny breaths brush against my chest and ribs. I shuffled my head again. Finally, Notch-Tail woke up, and I touched my nose against hers. She whined weakly, and we went back to sleep.

Chapter 22

Notch-Tail told me that the child with the patchy brown fur and blue eyes was born first. He was a few moments older than the other child, who was pure grey from head to tail. They were both bigger now. My older son was the bigger and stronger one, and he often pranced around the den and kicked up a dust-storm, which got everywhere, all over my fur and all over Notch-Tail and his brother. Sometimes he stumbled and fell, and my younger son would come up to his brother and bite him on the nose. They fought in the dirt, and they got back up and ran some more.

I raised my hind paw and scratched the side of my face all the way up to the top of my head. The fur came off in clumps. I was shedding, and it was too hot during the day, and I couldn't wait to lose the heavy outer coat. I turned my head and watched a clump drift to the ground, where the warm spring wind carried it off the ground and around a tree before disappearing into the leafy bushes. In the afternoon sun, everything was light green. Even the pines had shed their grey needles, and in their place grew soft and green ones. I stood up and brushed my face against a branch, and it tickled.

"I want it!"

I looked down. My younger son had snuck up on me. He

jumped up and down, looking at the branch directly above me but far out of his reach.

"You want this?" I gestured. He nodded, so I bared my front teeth and pulled at the branch, severing it where the green needles were still soft. I bent down and handed it to him. My younger son took the branch in his mouth and ran off behind the bushes.

I smiled with my tongue out. The pine tasted surprisingly pleasant. It was sweet and tangy and bitterish. It was fresh. I thought about pulling another branch for myself, but I decided against it. Later, I changed my mind, so I jumped for the highest branch I could reach and pulled the entire thing down. Pollen covered my face and nose, and I sneezed. I shook myself until the pollen was gone, and then I laid down to chew on the branch. It was a very enjoyable flavour despite the bitterness. The greener the branch tips, the better it tasted, and I found myself pulling each needle, chewing it for a moment before spitting it out.

Across the clearing, my two children were tugging on the branch I gave them, and Notch-Tail walked back and forth between the den and the patch of aspen trees. She made a very big oval, looping around a few aspens before returning and repeating it again. I got up and joined her.

"I just need to stretch my legs," she said.

"Go run around. I can handle them just fine," I said, "I might even show them how to catch something."

"You're gonna teach them to be bad hunters."

"Still better than you." I reached in to bite her on the neck, but she laughed and jumped away. She ran west and disappeared through the trees, but the pitter-patter of her pawsteps remained for a while longer.

I turned around, and my sons were standing attentively. They had both been looking at Notch-Tail run. The older son pushed the younger son to the ground, and they started wrestling each other, yipping and tugging until the younger son was pinned to the ground on his back. Then they righted themselves and repeated the exercise, this time with the opposite results.

I wiggled my snout between the two children and felt the older son tug at my whiskers, so I stuck my tongue out and licked him, and both of them stood up to touch my snout. "Children," I said. "Enough playing for now. Come with me, and I will show you how to hunt."

"Wow! I'm so excited!" said the older son. He jumped on his brother and knocked him over, and I noticed that both of them had white patches under their chins. They were still small and fuzzy, but their ears were straight, and their eyes were bright.

I bumped the older son with my nose and told the two to follow closely. I took them up the deer path until we hit the clearing. The old leaning tree had collapsed in the spring snowstorm. I jumped on the slippery log, holding myself steady and then pulling up my children. I pulled the younger son first by his neck scruff and then the older son, who insisted on grabbing onto my paw. "On three," I said as I counted to three, and we all jumped from the log at the same time. Both of my children were brave. My ribcage was fine. It really wasn't very high up.

At the center of the clearing, I sat down, and they copied me. The ground was still wet, and there were patches of snow, but the children didn't mind the wetness. The younger son stood up and ran around his brother before sitting down again. He could not sit still, not unlike when I was a child and I knocked

White-Ears down whenever I had the chance. I smiled at them and told them to quiet down.

"Father, could I go kill something now?" the older son said.

"You need patience," I said. "Hunting and fishing are all about patience, and unless you can sit still, you won't get anything."

"Okay," he said. He sat still and looked at his brother, who fidgeted with his paws.

"Now listen," I said. "We're hunting for rodents today. You stand still or move silently and wait for the prey to show up. They always do because they can never stay underground for too long. It's moist and suffocating down there, and they always come up."

"Okay, Father," the younger son said. He looked at me, and I took a glance past his eyes, which had just begun to turn a pale golden yellow, partly from the sunlight and partly from his getting older. Just a few nights ago, I thought I saw a glimmer of blue, but it might have been Notch-Tail's teeth reflecting in the moonlight.

"Close your eyes," I said.

"Done."

"Okay."

I dropped my voice to a whisper, "Listen for their movements. When the ground is too wet or too cold, and you can't smell them, you can still hear them."

"I don't hear anything."

"Me either," I said. "That is fine. Sometimes there is nothing, and we have to move on." I stood up and started walking, and then a thought flashed through my mind: even though there was no prey, I should show them the motions anyway. I stopped and turned around. "Would you two like to learn how to kill a rodent?" And of course, they liked to.

I sat them down again and showed them how to leap into the air and land on a spot on the ground. I told them to practice. They took it to a puddle and made it a game. Whoever made the biggest splash was the winner. Surprisingly, the younger son was a much better water-splasher, and I congratulated him by jumping into a puddle, splashing water on both of them.

In the distance, Notch-Tail's song wafted through the trees like a wisp of fog, and our ears perked up. "Your mother is calling," I said. "Let's go home."

We fed the children the best meat we could find. The innards of elk, the lungs and liver, the stomach, and the strips of fat between the ribs. All of it was their favourite. As the weather warmed up, they grew. The older son had a thin face like Notch-Tail, dark patches around his eyes, and a white chin. The younger son was greyer and had a twinkle to his eyes. They both had luxuriously soft fur, with no knots and no dirt, except the occasional bloodstain, of course.

It was still too early for them to hunt. The younger son went around and caught a mouse, and as far as I knew, that was the only thing either of them had caught. They were still young, and they didn't need to hunt. But maybe, when Notch-Tail and I were out during the day, the children went fishing just like I did when I was a child. I imagined the older son pushing his brother in the water. They were having fun, I was sure.

Notch-Tail took the lead on this hunt. She found a scent trail earlier, and we followed it. I kept my nose near her tail patch so I didn't have to think. She took the lead, and I followed, and when there was something to chase, I rushed and she flanked.

We worked in perfect harmony whenever there was prey, but of course, there wasn't always prey. When we realized there was nothing to eat in the forest today, Notch-Tail slowed down, and so did I.

"I lost the scent trail," she said.

"Let me check." I walked ahead and scanned the ground, and there were no deer scents anymore.

"Let's head back," Notch-Tail said. "We'll regroup with the kids. We've left them for too long anyway."

"We should head out," I said.

"To the coast?"

"It takes an entire season. Two, perhaps, if the children are slow."

"It's not too early?"

"I'm sure they will be fine." I shrugged. The children were miniature versions of us, each with perky ears and sharp teeth, and I didn't think anything would harm them. "Not under our watch, anyway," I added.

My two sons were fast asleep when we got back. They were big and barely fit in the den, but it didn't stop them from trying. The older son had his fluffy butt hanging out, so I nudged it, and he jolted awake. Inside the den, I heard his brother whine, and both of them growled, and then the older son disappeared into the den. Moments later, two heads stuck out the entrance.

The older son yawned. "Hello, Father."

"We're going on an adventure as a family," I said. In the corner of my eye, I saw Notch-Tail nodding and wagging her tail, so I continued. "We're taking you to the ocean, and you can meet my sister."

"Your aunt and her mate are going to be part of our family," Notch-Tail said.

"And the coast will be full of food, and it never snows there, and you'll never go hungry," I said.

The two children shot wide beaming smiles at us and yapped in excitement. "Adventure! Adventure!" And they bolted out of the den and ran in circles until they were tired. "We're going on an adventure!" said the younger son as his tail flung specks of mud everywhere. I smiled and nodded and told them we would leave in the morning. The older son said he wouldn't be able to sleep, so I wrestled him to the ground until I had my jaws around his neck and told him that sleeping was good for him. Notch-Tail laughed, and we then sang as a family.

"Huddle around," I said after the chorus, and the kids pressed themselves against me, and Notch-Tail laid down and did the same. "It will be a dangerous adventure," I said. "You two must promise to always do what we say. If I tell you to run, you run. If I tell you to hide, you have to hide, and you can't make a single noise until we come back. Do you promise?"

"We promise," mumbled the two sons together, and moments later, they fell asleep. I looked down and saw their chests rise and fall, up and down in perfect unison.

"So," Notch-Tail whispered, "what now?"

"Now we sleep?" I turned to kiss her on the nose, and she laughed quietly.

⌢

In the early morning, I woke up to stretch my legs. I slept in an awkward position, and both my legs were tingling, so I stood up and shook them separately. It was a very bright morning with a blue sky and no clouds. The sun had just peeked over the mountains to the east, casting a pleasant warm light on

Notch-Tail and the kids curled up in a bundle and fast asleep. I thought about waking them up, but then I decided it was best to let them sleep some more. A walk would be nice this morning, I thought, so I stretched my legs again and started down the trodden path southbound.

This trail looped east at the creek junction before veering north again, then back west, and then south. A small circle. I was familiar with this, so I walked with one eye closed, half asleep, downhill, and then up again until I was back at the den. Dew had collected on my fur. I licked it off my paws and belly and left the rest of the fur to dry in the sunlight, and I laid there on the grass and enjoyed the morning.

The children awakened and came over to greet me. They smelled like Notch-Tail, and it was really a wonderful smell. My younger son grabbed my nose and pulled too hard for my liking, so, reflexively, I growled, and he backed off. "Can we go now?" he said. "Adventure! Adventure!"

"Adventure, sure," I yawned. I closed my eyes, and the sun filtered through my eyelids. A shadow flashed across, and I opened my eyes to see Notch-Tail standing in my sun. "Good morning," she said. I greeted her by licking her nose. She and the kids went to gnaw on the bones of the deer we had killed a few days ago, and I laid there and sunbathed some more.

We left before midday. The children were well fed, and the sky was clear, the path was dry, and the forest was silent and open. I took the lead, and Notch-Tail covered the back. This way, we kept our two sons safe in the center where nothing could get to them, and they wouldn't be lost. I promised Notch-Tail that we would not separate until we found White-Ears at the coast.

On the first day, we cut a clean line west until the valley

melted away to a thicker and lusher forest, along a shallow river, and we kept going until it was very dark. The second day the kids were hungry, so we went hunting, and we took them with us, and Notch-Tail and I took down a white-tailed deer. Then, on the fifth day, when the food ran out again, we kept going, and the same day we passed the furthest scent-marking I had made during the winter.

We took the same path to the coast as I once did with White-Ears. It was the second spring since we made that journey, through countless rainfalls and snowstorms. I was surprised our scent was still noticeable along the path. I lifted my leg and reinforced the scent, and I told Notch-Tail to do the same thing, so she did. Our scents would last another year.

It was late afternoon when we passed the place where the forest became grassland. The sun was hot during the midday, but now it hid behind towering white clouds, and as we came down the grassy hill, the sky began to darken, and soon the sun had disappeared completely. After that, the sky was dark and grey and heavy raindrops flew in all directions. I turned around to see the children huddled in a ball, shivering under Notch-Tail, who shook herself frequently.

"Let's go find some shelter. Follow me!" I said, and I ran for the bottom of the hill, listening carefully to the footsteps of Notch-Tail and my sons. They followed closely. The rain had picked up the pace, and suddenly, the sky was aglow with strings of light, crackling and twisting, disappearing back into the clouds with an ear-piercing boom.

The younger son screamed, and I turned around and took

him under my chin. "It's okay. It's okay. I got you." It was raining hard now, huge droplets smashing into my fur and soaking it. Burning wetness lingered in my nose. I pushed my sons under my belly and then turned to scan the grassland. Rain was falling in sheets now, crashing into the grass like waves against sand, and it came over and over again, faster each time. And the sky lit up once more and I couldn't focus on the grassland anymore. I closed my eyes and crouched down on my children and braced for the thunder, which came and shook the earth.

"We have to go!" Notch-Tail said. It sounded like she was very far away, but I could still feel her right beside me, her voice drowned out by the rain. She tugged on my neck and ran towards the nearby grove of aspen trees. I got up, nudged my children to go after their mother, and then ran behind them. There was rain and hailstones, which were heavy and painful. Lightning and thunder came regularly. Boom. Boom. Boom. It echoed and splashed, and suddenly there was too much rain in my eyes, so I ran with my eyes closed. Moments later, I slammed into a warm and wet shoulder, knocking her over and rolling on the ground.

Then the rain was less. We had made it to the grove, which was denser than it looked and kept away most of the hailstones. I shook myself dry. "We're okay," I breathed. "Is everyone safe?"

The children nodded and shook the water off of themselves. "Come closer," I said. Notch-Tail and the two sons came to my side, and we huddled together, wet and cold, and waited for the rain to stop. The younger son twitched whenever the thunder came, and the older son made fun of him for it. Notch-Tail told them to hide underneath her, and they did.

The storm kept going late into the night until the wind

lightened up and the rain became snow. Snow turned into rain again as the air warmed, and then the morning light pierced the clouds. The rain stopped, then the wind stopped. Finally, the skies were blue again, and I fell asleep to a warm blanket of sunshine.

Chapter 23

In the full blossom of late spring, when the air shimmered in the sun, and the sky buzzed with flying insects, we reached a pond covered by water lilies. My older son jumped onto a lily pad and promptly sank into the water, and both his brother and his mother laughed as he clawed his way out. He shook himself dry, and some of the water got in my mouth. It was light and fresh and good tasting. I smelled the pond before lapping up more of the same water.

Beyond the pond were patches of brown cattails on the edge of a marsh that blended in with the forest. I wanted to scout it out, so while my family stayed behind to rest near the water, I followed the dry patches of marshland, hopping between water until I reached forest ground. Spongy earth made my steps bouncy. I loved the feeling of flying, so I jumped extra hard with each step for maximum airtime. After I had my fun, I found a tree stump and marked it with my scent, and then I sang to the family to converge on my location.

Three quiet shapes emerged in the distance. The children were about half the size of Notch-Tail, and they ran around her, around and around. I sang another short burst, and Notch-Tail called back in response. "We're coming, we're coming," she said.

"Too slow," I said. I started jumping on the soft ground again, and when the children got closer, they joined me.

"Fun, right?" I laughed.

"Real fun," Notch-Tail said. "You think this is a good place to stop for a few days? It's quite open, and I prefer a bit more shelter."

"We probably need food more than shelter."

"You're right," she said. "Let's see if we can find an overturned log or something. Children," Notch-Tail turned and pulled the kids towards her, "come with me, and we're going to find somewhere safe. Your father will scare away all the bad animals."

I started with the marsh, and I made my way around it, smelling the grass and marking my scent where I could. I went around the pond, up the hill and back down, and then from one end of the forest to the next. There were many smells here: at least two families of beavers and the occasional deer and a pile of moose poop from the previous winter. Not a lot to eat, but also nothing that could harm my children.

Once I was done, I sang for Notch-Tail, and she replied, and I followed the song until I found where they had decided to shelter. It was a small clearing surrounded by dense bushes, and in the center, there was a massive overturned tree. Notch-Tail had dug under the tree enough for the two sons to sleep and be hidden from the rest of the forest. I beamed her a smile. "Nice," I said. "This is good."

"Did you find anything?"

"There are a few beavers in the marsh. No large prey. I think it's best if we split up," I told her. Notch-Tail agreed and trotted into the forest.

I told the children to stay put and then made my way towards the marsh. The sun was high in the sky, and I hoped to find a beaver during the day when the watery foreign landscape was easier to navigate. The beavers had the upper hand at night. Following my own scent, I walked back to the marsh. I smelled the bushes until I found beaver tracks. I followed it, and it took me through a convoluted path, into the water, and back out, looping around until I was at the very edge of the marsh. And it kept going. With dry ground underneath me and a strong scent trail in front, I took large strides and followed quickly. The landscape blurred behind me until it was unrecognizable, but I wasn't paying attention. The scent was strong, and I was close.

Suddenly, water splashed underneath my paws and onto my belly, and I felt myself sinking. I stopped and looked up. I was surrounded by trees, but they were small and sickly, and the air smelled like rotting plants, and there was water everywhere. I lifted my paw and the tepid, greenish water dripped from my toes. I shook it off and leapt to the nearest piece of dry ground, which was the exposed root of a thick poplar that only had leaves on one side. The swamp smelled like a large animal, but I couldn't make out any details. Everything smelled like swamp, and the longer I stood here, the less sure I was.

I followed it anyway, splashing every step. There was a patch of dry ground further ahead, and I waded through the water until I stood at the tip. It was very muddy and wasn't dry at all, but at least I could finally smell things here. Pungent, sour sweetness hinted the air and then lingered. I hadn't noticed it until now, but it became impossible to ignore. I thought it was food. It must have been some kind of decaying meat, a wispy, delicious smell, and it was straight ahead. Not too far.

I walked with my head held high in the air, tail twitching.

CHAPTER 23

The mud squealed under my paws and the stickiness infused into the gaps between my toes. The smell was stronger now. It was definitely meat, very good meat, and not too decayed either. This would make for a very nice meal for my children.

Then, whoosh! My neck fur puffed up and I felt a jolt of alertness flood my body. Of course! It was a bear! I was over two hundred wolf-lengths from the carcass when I saw the bear. It was large. Large and muddy and brown, lumbering about in the knee-deep water, splashing and grunting, crunching and gnawing on the overturned elk carcass. Occasional cracks echoed in the air, popping, joints snapping, and tendon breaking deliciously. I hid behind a tree and watched the bear eat, and the longer the beast fed, the hungrier I became.

I stood and watched and waited for the bear to leave. It fed greedily, slapping and tugging, spraying bits of blood and fat in all directions. It smelled like a bear. I hadn't encountered one before, yet I was sure of it. So sure that my neck fur started rising whenever the wind wafted towards me. Run, my body said. Leave it. Be gone! But of course, I couldn't. My children were hungry, so I stayed and waited.

After a while, the bear stopped eating, climbed out of the wet swamp, and laid down under a tree. It shuffled and then got up again, walking northward until it retreated out of sight but not out of smell. It was still nearby, I could still hear the shuffling, the splashing, and I still smelled the bear as vibrantly as ever.

This was my chance. It couldn't see me, and I didn't need much meat. A few chunks of rib and it would feed the children enough for us to get out of this marshland. In and out. I would be quick.

I turned and sprinted, tail swinging, splashing water on my

belly. The two hundred wolf-lengths became hundred, then fifty, until I was half-submerged in swamp water and out of breath, and the carcass was right in front of me. The innards had been eaten clean, and all that was left were rib bones and legs and the fatty parts that lined the back. I darted my head around to check for the bear, and then, as quickly as I could, I dug my snout into the meat gnawed. Pulling, tugging, feeling the characteristic snap of skin and tendon breaking. Then I pulled back with all the force I could muster.

Zsssh! It ripped clean, and a snout-sized chunk of meat dangled in my mouth, and just as I was about to swallow it, the bear roared. The roar, deep and terrifying, shook the entire forest.

I turned around to see the bear charging at me full speed.

The bear's paws thundered across the swamp. It had a large, ugly scar across its entire face, and its eyes glowed an unknowing, predatory hue. A long and high-pitched whimper escaped my throat. Suddenly, I felt small again.

Meat in my mouth, I tucked and turned and ran. My tail didn't want to swing, but I didn't need it. I ran in a straight line, floating on the mucky wetness, bounding off of each dry island. I ran until I couldn't hear the bear anymore, and when I turned around, it was far away again. The animal had turned around long ago. There were prints in the mud and a shadow of a bear in the distance.

"Breathe," I said to myself. My heart wanted to leave my body, and my lungs were on fire. I gasped for breath before I realized a piece of meat had dangled in my throat. I spat it out and it plopped to the ground. I was okay. The bear had no interest in chasing me, and I managed to get a small chunk of meat for the children.

I took the long way back, around the southeast side of the swamp, behind the forest, and then all the way around to where we left the children. I turned around to check for the bear along the way, and I went around trees, doubling back and around the same trees in the opposite direction. I even rubbed the meat in the opposite corner of the forest, just in case I was followed.

Before entering the clearing, I stopped and barked a "hello," and I immediately heard shuffling. My two sons came to greet me, and when they saw the meat in my mouth, they went crazy and jumped all over me. I dropped the chunk of meat on the ground and watched my children feast. Their tails swung wildly.

"This is really good," said the older son.

I nodded. "It's all for you and your brother. Eat it all."

I walked around and listened to the forest. There was no bear anywhere, but I could still feel the danger. "Listen to me," I said. The children didn't look up. "This place isn't safe, and we have to leave. Where did your mother go?"

Chapter 24

I huddled with my sons behind the log, and we watched the sun slowly creep behind the trees. The sky became redder and the air colder until the sun had set and there was only a faint blue glow of light coming from the west. The children told me that Notch-Tail came back in the afternoon before heading out again. I didn't want to sing for her because I didn't want to draw any attention to the children. There could be more bears. Even the one bear was too many.

"We'll wait for your mother," I said. "And then we leave together as a family. Sleep now, and I'll stay up and keep watch."

"Were you scared, Father?"

I smiled and nudged his grey fur. "Of course," I said. "But fear is what keeps us out of trouble. It was a very big bear."

"Could you have killed it?"

It was an interesting question. I wasn't sure. Maybe I could have distracted it and then attacked from the back. A few bites, and it would bleed out. Or maybe Notch-Tail could have attacked it from the back, she was an excellent hunter after all, and the bear couldn't have been stronger than a fully grown moose. In the end, "I don't think so" was what I said. "Not by myself anyway. Once you two are fully grown, we can go kill a bear together for messing with our family adventure."

"Yay! We'll kill a bear together!" The younger son buried his nose in my fur and snuggled closer.

"But only if we work together as a family," I said.

My older son licked me on the snout and wagged his body back and forth. "I get to deliver the killing bite."

"I'll distract the bear while you do it!" my younger son chimed in.

"No, no," I said. "Your mother and I will distract the bear. We have to keep both of you alive."

"Okay, Father," he said. His ears lowered a little bit.

"You two must keep each other safe, do you understand?" I nuzzled both sons until they were both in front of me and I saw their vibrant faces. This was good. My children would be fine. They snuggled against my fur. I leaned back against the log and looked up at the sky and watched the last wisp of light disappear into the hills of the west.

I had almost fallen asleep when I heard a shuffle, then silence, followed by the faint crack of a tree branch. I leaned forward and looked ahead. The sound was too faint for a bear, too soft for a deer. "Hello?" I whispered. Notch-Tail answered with a low-pitched whine. I stood up, careful to not wake the sleeping children, and then trotted over to greet her.

"Come with me," she said. "There's caribou nearby, and I need you to help me."

"Close by?"

"Very close. Half a day's walk and they're not going any-where. So if we hurry, we can make it back by sunrise."

My tail started wagging on its own, and I couldn't help but grin at her. "I guess we have to go, it's a good opportunity, and they are hungry," I said, looking back at the children sleeping.

"But we must be back by the sunrise. We have to leave here as soon as we can. It's not safe here."

"Of course," Notch-Tail said. She came up and licked me on the mouth, and I took in big gulps of air filled with her scent and the caribou droppings she rolled in. Then I bent down and kissed the children good night, and Notch-Tail did the same thing, and they didn't even stir.

We left in the cover of the night. I rolled in the mud before we left, and Notch-Tail smelled like caribou, so there was no way anything could trace our steps back to the den. I made sure to step with my toes, one paw at a time, pressing lightly on the dry dirt to not make any sounds at all. I had no reason to be silent, but something gnawed at me on the inside and I couldn't stand the slightest noise. I walked one small step at a time. I followed Notch-Tail as she swung her tail side by side. The bald patch was right there, and if I wanted to, I could have nudged it with my cold nose, which would have made her scream, but I didn't want to since it would have been too loud. I smiled at the thought of Notch-Tail screaming in the darkness

She walked fast. We were almost jogging, and her fur bounced up and down as she walked. Cold wind brushed past her back and blew caribou-scented air in my face. It was a new smell, I realized, I hadn't ever smelled caribou before, and it was earthy, musky, and slightly sweet. Then, Notch-Tail turned west, and we passed my scent markings from the day before. It seemed like an unending forest, and it was darker than I was used to without moonlight. I stuck closely to her at first, and when the path widened, I sped up and walked alongside her.

It was the middle of the night—closer to dawn—when the

forest thinned and became a field. A mountain stood towering to the south in complete darkness. To the north, a treeless slope flattened out into a plateau. Notch-Tail paused and turned around. "We go up," she said. "The herd is sleeping up there."

I wagged my tail absentmindedly. "Okay," I said. "Any newborns or crippled ones?"

"Not that I know of. I couldn't get closer without alerting the entire herd, and I didn't think I could kill one without your help."

I smiled and yawned and watched Notch-Tail yawn as well. We fanned out and I took the eastern side of the slope while Notch-Tail came from the southwest. The hill was shallow and dry, with bits of rock and lichen between the grass, and knobby shrubs, barely knee height. It was still early in the season, and the shrubs weren't very prickly, so I used them as cover. I hopped between each shrub until I was over the crest of the hill. In the distance, parallel to me, I could see Notch-Tail doing the same thing. She was an excellent hunter, after all. I lifted my head and looked up.

Notch-Tail's eyes glowed in the darkness. She gave me a nod and looked ahead so I followed her gaze. In the distance was a mass of black shapes on the ground. It was windless. If not for Notch-Tail, I would have walked past them, and I never would have known they were caribou. I looked back at her and then at the caribou again. They were still too far away. I had to get closer.

I curved east, around a patch of trees and then back forward, hiding behind bushes until I was no more than a hundred wolf-lengths away. I had lost Notch-Tail, so I ducked behind a skinny aspen tree and tried to look for her. A flurry of motion started on the opposite corner, and I saw a black shape zip across the field. I took off running as well. We closed in on the caribou, and at seventy wolf-lengths away, one of the adult animals jumped up and bugled his call. He swung his antlers side by side before taking off in the opposite direction, and the entire herd converged on him.

Fifty now. Wind brushed against my whiskers. I opened my eyes wide to see better, and everywhere smelled like caribou.

Twenty.

Ten.

Notch-Tail was running beside me, and her breathing was deep and powerful. She veered to the left and I followed, and with the sudden movement, the herd had scattered forward and right. She had locked onto a female caribou, no antlers, slight limp towards the front left. I kicked my legs and picked up speed.

Five.

Pulling air into my lungs, sprinting.

Three.

One.

I leapt onto the animal's back and clamped down with my jaws, snapping muscle and drawing blood. The caribou tilted against me and flew into Notch-Tail, and I watched as she weaved to the front, flying in the air and grabbing the caribou by the neck. We tumbled together in the grass and skidded to a stop.

I tugged hard on my end, and the caribou punched the air with all four of its legs, but it wasn't enough to shake us off. Notch-Tail delivered the lethal bite to the neck, and in a flash, blood squirted in all directions, and the animal stopped moving.

"We did good," I panted. "Good, clean kill."

Notch-Tail tore at the neck of the animal and swallowed a chunk of tendon and fat. "I'm very hungry. We'll eat and then bring the kids here." "Before sunrise." "Sure." We ripped into the animal's belly, ate the innards, and left the rest for later. After having had my fill of meat, I tilted my head and sang a short tune, and Notch-Tail joined me. Our song echoed and fell silent.

"No response," I said. "See, our children are clever."

Notch-Tailed smiled. "I never once doubted that."

We walked east, in the dark, for a long time. My belly was full, and I felt a spring in my step, and I bounced on the dirt to the beat of the swaying of my tail. A bare sliver of light peeked through the trees to the east. Then it was suddenly very bright. The sun had started coming up, one ray at a time, quietly piercing the dense moisture in the air and scattering the fog and making my nose tingly and warm.

She smelled like caribou blood. The mix of caribou blood and Notch-Tail was one of my favourite scents in the world, next to Ma's. In this gentle morning breeze, I got a face full of it, and I loved it. She also bounced as she walked, in an almost singsong manner, joyously up and down. "The children will love this fresh liver," she said, swinging her tail.

"Is it really fresh if it's coming from your belly?"

"Fresh enough," she said. I caught up to her again and bumped her butt with my face, and she laughed.

We passed the scent marker when the sun was barely over the horizon. The forest was still dark, and the fog obscured most of the smells. It was dense, like wet grass, and hung over us incessantly. I knew we were almost there so the smells didn't really matter. "Let's take the direct route," I said. "The children are hungry, and we should get out of here quickly."

"Of course."

I walked ahead now. I felt a certain urgency with each step, and as I came to the triple-jointed poplar tree, I started to run. I didn't like being away for so long. I just needed to see the children and touch them, and then we could get them out of this forest and take them to the food. I leapt over a pile of branches and heard Notch-Tail call to me. "Slow down. I just ate."

"Come, come, come," I said.

I stopped at the ring of bushes surrounding the den. The fog was irritating, dense, so irritatingly dense. I couldn't see or smell anything. I barked, "Hello." It was low and quiet. No reply from the children, so I barked a bit louder. "Hello!" Nothing. Notch-Tail had caught up to me, so I turned and touched her face. "Something is wrong. I can feel it," I said. I felt uneasy, tense, and my heart was slamming against my eardrums.

"I feel it too," she said. "Go. Quietly. I'll go around."

I pressed my belly against the soft earth and wet grass and walked towards the den. I called again, very quietly, with the quietest bark I could muster. The sound that came from my throat reminded me a lot of Ma's warning bark. It unnerved me. Dense branches parted in front of me as I pushed, nose first, past the shelter and into the small clearing. We approached from the southwest, and at first, all I saw was the overturned tree trunk. I inched closer, step by step until the mist parted and my nose was pressed against the log.

Bear. The air smelled like the bear. The log had scratches

on there, fresh and deep. The bear was here.

I barked loudly. "Danger! Where are you?"

"Come around!"

I ran around the log to where Notch-Tail was and saw that the ground had disappeared. There was no more ground. The log hovered over a massive, freshly dug hole. Claw marks sank deeply into the ground, leaving gashes where dirt and branches used to be. "Where did they go?" I said.

Notch-Tail tilted her head back and sang a song. She was loud, and her voice trembled, and she called for our sons over and over again until her voice cracked and she had to breathe.

"Where are they?" I asked again. "Where did they wander off to? We have to get going. The bear was here." Then, as I spoke those words, a wave of cold stillness washed over me. My children were gone. The bear was here. And then the thought filtered through the fog: *my children are in danger.*

"Where? Where? Stay there, and we'll find you!" I sang into the misty air.

Notch-Tail ran around the log, hopped on top, and then down into the hole and back up. I closed my eyes and smelled the ground. The bear was here recently. Probably just before the morning. Our children were here too, but they left. They went that way—I looked up and saw a path of flattened grass. Good boys. They heard the bear and ran away.

"Follow me," I said. I took off in the direction of the scent trail without looking back, and Notch-Tail did the same. Her pawsteps were heavy, uneven, and her breath was hurried, and my heart was pounding. My sons were clever: they turned right, then left again, and I could sense that the bear had fallen behind. Keep going. Don't stop. Don't even think of stopping. You can outrun this animal, or at least you can lose it. I know it. I believe in you. Keep going. Don't stop.

Notch-Tail stopped sharply and sang once again. She asked them to reply if it was safe and that we'd come to find them. They were probably scared half to death by now, all alone and lost and…A song came back. Faintly. It was the younger son's voice, and he was weak, and he called for us. "I'm here. Help me," he said. Keep going. Don't stop. We're coming.

I ran again, towards the source of the song, forgetting the smells, trees, and mist. Shapes flew past me. Notch-Tail caught up to me, and we went to the edge of the scent markings and then some more until we passed the dried creek bed and then, in the space under the sprawling roots of an old pine tree, came a tiny voice. My younger son didn't say anything that I recognized. He just squeaked.

"I'm here," I said. "I'm here, and you're safe now." I pushed my nose under the root pile and started digging. Dirt flew behind me and the hole enlarged until I could stick my head in there, and I did, and in the back, there was a grey ball, curled up and trembling. "It's okay. It's okay," I cooed. "You're safe."

"Really?" he said. His voice wasn't right. I pulled myself out a little to give my son some space. He turned around and I saw that there was a long gash from the base of his neck down his backside. His fur was tattered and bloody, and the entire air was filled with blood.

"Oh no, no. Come out and let me see you." I pulled out of the hiding place, and Notch-Tail jumped in. She stayed in the hole with him for a few moments. She was licking him when they came out, and I could see him wincing every time her tongue went over the open gash. "It's okay," she kept saying, over and over again, softer each time. They laid down, and he rested his head against Notch-Tail's belly.

"Where is your brother?"

There was a silent rasping. "He kept me safe."

"Where?" I pressed. We were going to leave as a family, and I had to find the older son as soon as I could. The sun was already a good deal above the trees, and soon it would be storming, and soon it would be dark.

"Gone," said the child who had closed his eyes and whimpered. "He's gone. The bear took him. It killed him and cracked his bones and took him."

Thunder crashed through my body, and my legs trembled, and then I collapsed on my hind legs and tail. No. I didn't believe it. He was a clever boy and he would have gotten away. "No…"

"He saved me," my son said.

Notch-Tail looked up. Her golden eyes flashed with despair. "Find my child," she whispered. I bent down and rubbed my face against hers and nuzzled my younger son. I stood up and ran. I didn't know the direction, it was just where my instincts took me, but I needed to go somewhere, anywhere. I went somewhere and anywhere. My child had to be found, and I needed to find him. I followed the scent until it took me to the wetland. The bear was gone. The scent was gone, so I went through the water. Cold, stinky, brown water splashed over my knees and onto my belly and shoulders.

I had to see it for myself. I wouldn't be able to leave without seeing his body. And then I would kill the bear. I would take its neck in my throat and tear it open until the entire swamp was coloured like blood. I would tear it to pieces and leave it to rot in the swamp. My son was a good, clever boy.

I stopped and stood with my eyes closed for a moment. Water sat still, just above my dewclaw. All around me, the fog had dissipated, sunlight streamed through the gaps in the trees, and everything was silent. A faint hint of blood lingered in the air to the north. Not too old. I followed the trail with my nose just above the water, getting fainter and stronger and fainter as I looped around trees and shrubs until it was right in front of me. A jagged piece of land that smelled like bear. A trail of blood. I hopped up and shook myself off and followed the trail to the opposite edge, and I saw it, a mangled pile of blood and bones, deeply red, with ribs sticking out and tattered fur in patches all over the ground. I smelled the fur, and it had his scent on it, and that was all I needed to know.

I sat and waited for the bear, but it never came back. I wanted to stay. I wanted to dig my fangs into where it hurts and twist it until the bear died from the pain. But I couldn't. The sun was high in the west, and I knew that I wouldn't be able to kill the bear. My last child was still injured and we had to get out of here. I sang for Notch-Tail, and she called for me to come back, so I did.

"We have to go," I said to my child. "Can you walk?"

He rested against Notch-Tail. His head moved up and down with her breath, but he did not otherwise move or speak. I bent down and nuzzled his shoulder, pressing into the blue-grey fur and inhaling. I noticed that he had grown much bigger. Bigger, stronger, and braver. He was going to be fine.

"He's in shock," Notch-Tail said. "The injury is very bad, and he's been drifting in and out of sleep the whole day. I gave him some food, but he wasn't awake enough to eat."

"We should leave before nightfall."

"I know. The bear could come back any time. Can you carry him?" she said. I looked at Notch-Tail's tired face and saw that she had gone to a very dark place. She looked back blankly. "Yes, I'll carry him," I said.

Notch-Tail got up carefully and made sure she didn't disturb our child. I nudged him with my nose and rubbed my whiskers over him, and whispered to him, "I'm going to take you. This might pinch a little."

"Okay, Father," he breathed.

I grabbed him by the patch of loose skin and fur at the top of his neck, where ears became neck, and I pulled on it slowly, feeling it stretch in my jaws until all of his weight was dangling from the scruff, slowly and carefully hoisting him into the air until I was eye level with Notch-Tail. My son whimpered loudly. He trembled. He was in pain, but there was nothing I could do.

I gestured to Notch-Tail, and she took the lead. We walked slowly through the forest and into the wider path and followed it as the forest became the field, up the slope until I could smell caribou in the air.

It was dark now. Stars glimmered overhead, and the moon had just begun to rise to the east. I took my son to a dense grove of aspen trees, and Notch-Tail prepared a bed of leaves and soft branches. I laid him down on this bedding. Notch-Tail laid beside him, licking him until his whimpering went away, then she closed her eyes and fell asleep.

Moonlight filtered through the leaves, making tiny round shadows on the ground in front of me. Notch-Tail and my child were asleep, so I rested my head on the ground and closed my eyes for a moment. And then, feeling the wind, I shuffled until my child was warm and cozy between the two of us.

I wasn't going to sleep tonight. Instead, I would stay awake and count the leaves and wait for something to happen because my son was horribly ill, and someone had to keep watch. I would stay up and keep watch and make sure nothing bad ever happened again, even if it meant not sleeping, for as many days as necessary.

Chapter 25

I had stories to tell, but I didn't have the time to tell them. I had places to show, but I didn't have time to show them. I could have told the stories earlier, but I didn't, and now it was too late. A thin, yellow film formed over his wound, and then, in less than a day, it began to smell. By the next morning my child had a fever and he shivered profusely. He didn't wake up for three days, and in that time, the smell worsened. He wouldn't eat anything. He wouldn't drink. I brought water in my mouth and splashed it over his snout, but it only rolled off his fur, soaking the earth below before the sun took it away.

We stayed with him every day. Notch-Tail tended to him while I brought chunks of caribou from the carcass. Notch-Tail took short walks, but she always came back before sunset. We always slept together as a family. It snowed at night, and then the snow melted in the morning, but we kept him warm and dry. It was the fifth morning, the sun had come up and risen high, and Notch-Tail had left to stretch her legs. I felt a stir near my chest, and I turned my head to see my child looking at me.

"Father?" my child whispered. The grey fur around his neck trembled as he spoke, and he spoke effortfully.

"I'm here," I said. "I'm here. What do you need?"

"What will it feel like?"

"It's not time yet."

"I can feel it," he said. His orange eyes glimmered, and he looked away, wincing at the pain.

I leaned in and licked him on his soft whiskers. "It's okay," I said. "I'm here, and I won't let anything bad happen to you."

"Will I see you again?"

"Of course. You'll have all the meat in the world, and you'll never be cold or hungry, and we'll be there. Of course, we'll be there."

"Really, Father?"

I curled my body so that I could touch his nose with mine, and I rested my head on the ground. "I don't know," I said. "I really don't."

"Where is Mother? I want to smell her again," he said, so I tilted my head and sang. I told Notch-Tail that our child needed her, and she replied with her song.

"I'm coming," she sang. "I'm coming I'm coming I'm coming." And my son tried to sing to his mother but he couldn't.

"I don't want to die."

I pulled him close to me and covered his snout with my neck fur. "It's okay now. You're safe," I said. I hummed the tune of the ocean and felt him relax. I closed my eyes. The sun was warm on my back. The forest was quiet. The world was quiet. Notch-Tail came back running, splashing, galloping across the field. She stopped, shook herself, and laid down beside our child, and she pressed her nose against him. I didn't want to open my eyes, but I heard the whole thing.

"I'm here," she said. My child moved a little. I lifted my neck and let Notch-Tail squeeze in.

"He wanted to smell you," I said. I made eye contact with

her, and though it was only a glance, I told her everything, and she understood. She told him to inhale, and he did. "Mother," he whispered.

My child never spoke again.

He died peacefully, and it took only a moment for his body to become perfectly still, no breathing, no heartbeat. We kept him warm for as long as we could, but by the time the moon started to rise, the cold ground had crept into him, and when the moon was high in the sky, my son was as cold as the air.

I took him in my jaws and stood up. Notch-Tail followed me silently, claws tapping against slate, as we walked up the narrow mountain trail. We walked until the trail became too steep to follow. I set him down on a flat rock facing the open sky at the place where the drumming of the mountain stream slowed down to a trickle.

We slept beside him that night. And the next. And the next. We slept beside him until his body began to bloat, and his fur began to tatter. Until his eyes turned grey and rain-bleached. When the last of the caribou ran out, I kissed my child goodbye, and we left.

Chapter 26

We sat on a ledge, looking west towards the setting sun and the vast mountain range. The dying glow of the sun illuminated the valley and cast long, grey shadows against a thousand treetops. The air was moist and earthy, and it shimmered and hummed in an orange hue.

She leaned over and rested her snout on my neck and shoulders. Her cold nose dug into my skin. She took a breath. I turned and nibbled on her face, and soon, I found myself taking in her sweet and comforting scent. It had hints of creek-water and wet rocks, and it was orange and warm, like the sky. I closed my eyes and nuzzled her. Her face was soft.

We stayed like that for a moment, and then she said, "We'll be okay."

"I know," I said. I wiggled my nose deeper into her winter fur, and she pulled away. She looked away from me, away from the setting sun and the rolling bands of magenta beyond the mountains, and above that, the orange tufts of clouds—it was puffy, like fur. She sighed and then turned back around.

"I love you," I said. I leaned in and touched her nose with mine. She smiled and licked my mouth. We both laid down at the same time, side by side, on this warm flat rock, overlooking the world. She faced the sun, and I faced her. Her fur glowed orange, and her golden eyes glimmered, and, as the sun crept beneath the mountain and under the sea, her eyes slowly pulled shut, and finally, all I could hear was the slow, slow rhythm of her breath, in, and out. I leaned against Notch-Tail, and I fell asleep to her breathing.

It was deep into the night when Notch-Tail suddenly stood up and made me tumble backward. She told me she wanted to go hunting. "Hunting for what?" I asked, but she just grinned and told me to follow her.

"Gophers," she said finally. "Come on, it'll be fun."

She walked slowly. I could tell that she was exhausted. Not physically, and not mentally either. She was exhausted deep within her body, in the place where the heart beat too fast. I was exhausted there too. In the mornings, I wanted to sleep forever, feeling the sunlight on my back and Notch-Tail's hypnotic breathing under my snout, leaving the world behind me for the warmth of the safe place.

"Wait," I said. I pulled her tail, and she yelped before twisting around to bite me on the nose. We made eye contact, and I stuck my tongue out.

"What am I waiting for?"

"Sing with me," I said.

I tilted my head back and sang, and before long, Notch-Tail joined me. Our voices intertwined and rose up in plumes, and it billowed in the moonlight until finally, it became part of the dark blue sky. I sang about nothing in particular. It has been a long time since I sang about anything. There wasn't anyone to hear these songs anyway, there was nobody here except Notch-Tail, and she sang about how hungry she was. We finished on a high note about elk livers, and when we were done, I looked at Notch-Tail and licked her face.

"Where are we going to find gophers?" I said.

"Up this mountain. There is a path that takes us to the alpine meadow at the very top. Have you ever hunted for them?"

"Once or twice," I said. Notch-Tail trotted along the narrow mountain path. On the right side, to the east, there was a steep slope dotted with patches of rainwater, and with each step, cold water splashed on my legs, seeping into the gaps between my toes and wetting the tip of my tail. She moved gracefully with her tail swaying side to side, the thin, bald patch on her tail dancing with its black tip.

At the plateau, Notch-Tail stopped and smelled the air. Then she smelled the ground. At last, she turned to look at me. "The first one to get to three is the winner."

"What do I get when I win?" I said.

"If."

"We'll see about that."

"You get bragging rights," she said, smirking. Her mouth was open, and her tongue stuck out, and I could have bitten it, but I decided not to.

So I sat near the edge of the plateau, and I waited, silently, waiting for any sound or scent of the gophers. Notch-Tail took off running, and she bent down and sniffed every hole in the ground, clawing at the ground. I smiled. I knew she would lose.

Chapter 27

Notch-Tail had never fished before. I promised to take her a long time ago, and now that the air had cooled down and the skies cleared up, it was time. We stopped at a lake after a thunderstorm. The waters were as clear as the air and shimmered a light green, and we ran around the entire perimeter. On the far side of the lake, a thin sheet of blue ice piled against the mountain. On the closer side, there were rocks, some of which were the size of a wolf. I motioned for Notch-Tail to join me on a large rock that overlooked the lake. She hopped up, her claws clacking.

It was a bright autumn day, the air was still cool, and the rock I stood on was wet and slippery. I stood aside and dug my claws into the crevices, leaving room for Notch-Tail to balance herself. It was a windless day. The storm had passed in the early afternoon, and the accompanying cold winds blew until the sky was clear. When the winds stopped, the songbirds returned with the squirrels. Notch-Tail tried her luck with a pheasant, but it darted into a thick and prickly bush.

I told her fishing was half skill and half luck. The skill half, I said, involved identifying the fish, and jumping silently, and biting tightly. The luck was everything else. It was an art of waiting. To catch fish, you had to be perfectly calm in the head and at peace with a clarity of mind rivalling the water. We weren't ready. I wasn't calm, and I wasn't at peace, but I didn't know if we would ever be ready—so, in a sense, we were as ready as we would ever be.

"What are we looking for?" Notch-Tail said. Her head was locked onto the ripples on the water below. Her tail swayed, whooshing against my thigh.

"We're waiting," I said. "We're waiting for the wind gusts to stop."

"So we can see the fish?"

I nodded.

As expected, the wind ceased, and moments later, the ripples disappeared beneath the surface. The afternoon sun glared—big, bright spots of light obscured the lake straight ahead—but the rest of the water was clear. Near the shore, the lake bottom was mossy with scattered weeds, and I knew the fish hovered among the weeds.

"Look there," I said. Notch-Tail looked at me instead, so I guided her eyes with my snout towards a round dip in the lakebed where long shapes moved in the water. "In the dark patch, do you see them?"

"I see them. Are they fish?"

"Big ones, at least the length of your tail," I smiled and wagged.

"I'm going to go catch them," she said. She leapt off the rock and landed on the wet shore, splashing rainwater everywhere.

"Wait, let me show you how it's done."

"I want to try it."

"You're going to scare them away, and we'll be eating nothing tonight."

"Nonsense," Notch-Tail said. She arched her back and

234

readied to leap into the water.

"Fine," I said, half smiling and half sighing. "We can do it together."

She nodded, and we both jumped into the water at the same time. The lake water was bright and cold, and it soaked my fur. I kicked my legs back and exhaled, sinking into the depths where the fish were, and Notch-Tail did the same thing. There were three fish just below us, and none of the three seemed to notice us. This was part of the luck: having light bounce off the lake surface in a way that mimicked movement made the fish less alert.

I kicked once more, and suddenly, Notch-Tail bubbled and rose to the surface. I ignored her and opened my jaws, and with one last kick, I came right above the fish. They darted away at the same time, but one of them swam directly into my teeth. Perfect luck.

I dropped the fish in front of Notch-Tail, and it flopped on the rock. It was large, not quite the size of a wolf's tail, but it had more girth: a huge head and a meaty body. It had a slippery layer with the pungent smell of old clams. Notch-Tail had just shaken herself dry, and she looked like she was panting.

"Needed air," she said. I looked at her with my tongue hanging out.

"Try it!" I said. "Every part is edible."

She leaned over and bit squarely in the middle. The fish squealed, and blood squirted out, and the air instantly took on the scent of fish. It had a delicious, sweet, meaty flavour. It was filling and rich. Our mouths were both red when we finished eating, but I was wrong about the edibleness: the skeletal bones were too sharp to eat, so we had to eat around it. Notch-Tail nuzzled me with all the fish guts and blood still hanging off her whiskers. I licked off whatever I could, and then I walked over to the lake to rinse my face.

"Come play in the water?" I said.

"Too wet," she said. There was a moment of quiet, and I burst out laughing. And she laughed as well, and we stood beside the lake and sang about nothing and everything.

I stood up and pawed the remaining fish skeleton into the shimmering water, and I watched it flutter as it sank, back and forth, until it was buried by the moss. The sun had begun to set, setting aglow the mountain peaks. I motioned for Notch-Tail to follow before jumping around a rock and following the trail up the slope. It was still wet, but so was I from the lake water.

"Where are we going?"

"Somewhere high up," I said. "Somewhere we can watch the stars."

Chapter 28

Autumn came and passed quickly, and the days shortened, and the snow came in heavy and wet dumps, but it was warmer, lighter, and food was more abundant, and the skies were brighter. Then the darkest days of winter passed, and the days lengthened and the snow melted. And then there was no snow at all. And then there were bursts of snow, and then rain, and finally at the place where the mouth of the raging river met the ocean, there was nothing but clear blue skies and turquoise waves.

Chapter 29

"What now?"

"I don't know," I said. I spread my toes in the sandy puddle. It cooled me down and took away some of the heat from the sun that bore directly over us. The spring sun had beaten the path dry. A lone cloud drifted overhead and cast its shadow over the yellowish-green valley to the south, but then it passed, and it was sunny again.

We started down a narrow trail along the crest of a ridge, with steep valleys down each side. I smelled the elk a ways back, and so did she, and we both knew there were newborns in this herd because late spring was a good time to find calves. We walked quietly for some time, and I followed Notch-Tail, but not too closely. I thought I could smell the elk better if I was far enough, but I also didn't want to be too far behind, just in case Notch-Tail started to chase.

"It doesn't matter," I said. "She's not here anymore. They could be anywhere."

"We can keep looking." Notch-Tail bent to smell the ground. We came down from the ridge, and it wasn't steep anymore, but down at the forest level, it was still wet. "Nothing," she said. "Just day-old tracks and poop."

"We keep looking," I said. I took another step and then

stopped. I thought I heard rustling in the trees below, but it was just the wind. We should have been getting close to the elk now, but I was beginning to think that we were going the wrong way altogether. We kept going.

When the sun lowered behind a narrow band of clouds, and the wind picked up, we found the fresh scent trail of the herd. It was far and faint. I ran beside Notch-Tail, and we leapt over a fallen tree in perfect synchronization. Fresh air filled my lungs, and wind brushed past my face, and I kept my tail just high enough to feel the breeze tug at the tip of my tail. I gulped the air, feeling every scent and every temperature change, stealing glances at Notch-Tail, who ran with a smile.

The elk were less than a hundred wolf-lengths away. Notch-Tail slowed down, and I stopped to catch my breath. Then we ran again. I took the right side, and Notch-Tail flanked left. The elk saw us and started to flee. They were fast. Calves were nowhere in sight, and the rest of the adult elk were too alert and too fast for us. I put up a good front, and I managed to scare one loose, but the animals quickly regrouped and kept running.

In the center of the herd, a female ran with a limp on its left hind leg. I thought we could catch it, but a large male ran beside her and made sure she did not fall behind. We closed in. Notch-Tail snipped at the protecting male and distracted him long enough for me to close the gap, but I wasn't able to grab on before he came back. He charged at me and took a swipe at me, antlers swinging. I ducked. Notch-Tail came to my help.

The herd kept running, and soon the gap was two hundred wolf-lengths. Two-hundred-fifty. My lungs burned, and to the south, I heard Notch-Tail stop running. I sat down and panted. It wasn't worth expending so much energy when there was so much food near the ocean. We didn't need elk. We could eat beavers, clams, and fish.

"Almost had them! We were so close." Notch-Tail said.

"We can follow them if you want," I told her. "We'll tire them out and wait for a better time."

"No, it's fine," Notch-Tail said. She walked up to me, and we touched our noses. "We did good. There's always next time."

She was right, of course. There was always next time. I was no stranger to failed hunts, and I knew to simply move on and hunt another day. There was no point dwelling on what happened yesterday when all that ever mattered was what to eat tomorrow. Everything else was bygones—remnants of the past in wispy strands of memory, getting hazier by the day until one day it would snap, and that was that.

Chapter 30

Notch-Tail ran ahead and left her pawprints on the soft sand, where it was lapped up by the waves. Her prints were washed away, and by the time I got to them, the sand was smooth again. I pressed my hind legs into the sand with force. Then, I stepped away and watched the next wave take it away. There was barely a dimple after the first wave, and no traces were left by the third. I waited until the sand was smooth again, and then I took off running. The ground shifted below me, and salty water splattered all over my fur, and I caught up to her and pushed her into the water. Notch-Tail jumped and shook herself dry.

"Very funny," she said. "Now there's sand all over me."

"You're welcome. Now you smell like the ocean, so you can blend in."

A small wave crashed into a rock just south of us and sent plumes of salty air in all directions. We kept going. The beach narrowed and curved with the coast until it was only a wolf-length wide, with a towering green cliff on the right and the ocean on the left. The sun shone brightly behind me, and soon, there was a burning feeling at the back of my ears. We walked beside each other, even though we barely fit on the narrow beach.

Notch-Tail stuck her nose in the holes on the cliff wall, but there wasn't anything to eat. We tried the seaweed on the beach, but it wasn't very good. The clams were good, but they weren't very fresh. The tide had retreated earlier in the day, and most of the leftover clams were dried out by the sun.

"You've never been to this cave?" I said. The strip of sand was too narrow, so I led the way, and Notch-Tail followed behind me.

"No. I saw it from the coast, though. It never looked accessible."

"It's only accessible at low tide," I said. "I went once. The clams were very good."

"I'm excited," she said. She smiled, and her tongue dangled from her open mouth.

The sandy shores began to undulate, up and down with each step. I knew we were close, so I started running. The path widened, and when we turned a corner, I saw a large and shallow cave at the end of the sandy path. It was buried in the cliff walls, which made it impossible to get to when the tide was high, but during the midday in autumn, the tide was low enough to reveal a long path into the cave.

I shook myself to get the sand off my fur before stepping over the rocky threshold onto the wet sandy floor. Inside, the vibrant colours of seaweed glimmered in the sunlight reflecting off the ocean. There were pools of trapped water dotted everywhere, with patches of seaweed and rocks with holes.

I turned to Notch-Tail. "Watch out for the lobster claws. They can really hurt."

She nodded, and we got to work. White-Ears always found the good stuff in the trapped pools of water, especially when there was sand at the bottom. I found a large pool, and I started digging on the north end, and soon my claws found a round clam. I dug until the hole was large enough for my snout and then I plunged my face into the warm water and pulled it out. It was a huge clam, but it was no match for my teeth, and it tasted very good.

Notch-Tail had equal success with the clam harvest. By now, she was used to the ocean. She loved the coast. We had spent the summer here looking for White-Ears and her partner, without much success or even a trace of them. White-Ears had disappeared, but I understood. I was gone for over a year, and food was scarce, and things always changed, and if they were chasing the black wolf's caribou herd, then they were happy, and if they were happy, I was happy.

"We're not going back inland," I said. "I don't like snow."

"No, of course not." Notch-Tail had a mouth full of clamshells, and she spat it out while talking.

"We can't stay here."

"Why not?"

"I don't want to," I said. "There are too many memories here."

"We don't have to stay here."

"How's your hunt?"

"The clams are very good, exactly like you said."

The setting sun lit up the cave in a pinkish glow as I cracked my last clam and ate the fleshy parts, and then I stood up, shook myself, and walked towards the threshold of the cave where it was rocky and wet. Water splashed, and then Notch-Tail stood beside me. The sun had just begun to glow orange and it threw long shadows of the mountains on the sea. The shadows danced on the surface of the ocean, and they grew, ever so slowly, with the setting sun.

"How about there?" I said. "It really isn't very far."

"Have you been?"

"No. It'll be an adventure. Those hills look very green in the distance, and it might be nice. Can you swim?"

"Better than you," she said, smiling. "We'll go. It does look very nice."

I motioned at the round hill directly ahead. There was an orange channel of calm seawater between us, and I estimated it to be no more than a thousand wolf-lengths. I was full, and there was no pain anywhere, and if we left now, we could make it before the last bit of sunlight disappeared to the west.

"Ready?" I said. She nodded.

I leapt into the water from the threshold of the cove, and I let the water caress my body until I was fully enveloped by the cold current. There was still sand underneath, but as I stuck my snout out of the water and started paddling, the sand disappeared, and then there was nothing but water. I turned around to see Notch-Tail swimming effortlessly, so I picked up the pace, kicking and pulling and swishing my tail for good measure. Water crested over my nose, and I exhaled, pushing out a puff of mist and tasting the saltiness of the sea. And with each push and pull, the island became closer until Notch-Tail caught up to me, and the island was right there, right in front of my nose. It towered like a green sand dune, and it was bigger than I thought, and it was further away too, so we swam some more until the sun was a thin slice of redness on the horizon.

My paws touched sand again as the light receded. I stuck my head out of the water, then my neck and shoulders, and I shook very hard to get the water out of my fur. Notch-Tail did the same. I was very tired. My tongue was dry, and I couldn't stop panting, so I walked only far enough to find dry ground, and I laid down and closed my eyes. I felt Notch-Tail snuggle beside me, but I didn't open my eyes.

"Adventure, right?" I whispered.

"Adventure tomorrow," she said. "Good night."

In the morning, we walked around the island until we found a grouse nest. The birds were flightless and dumb, making for very easy prey in the sparse island undergrowth. The trees towered over us, their canopies too high to see, and the entire island smelled like the sea. We ate, drank from the pools of rainwater at the peak of the island, and went back to the beach to nap. When the sun was low above the horizon, I woke her up and pointed towards the next island. It was closer than this one was, yet still, the mountains shimmered behind it just out of reach.

"Another adventure," I said, and we jumped into the water and swam. It was still daylight when we arrived, so we swam to yet another island, this time to the northwest with the sun directly in our face. Again, I was very tired and sat on the grassy, mossy shore and stared at the mainland. The clam cave was nothing more than a big black dot on the cliff walls, and above it were the trees, and then hills, and then snow-capped mountains. White-Ears was probably out there hunting caribou, and though she wouldn't be as tired as us, she was still missing out on the fun.

"What about caribou?" Notch-Tail said. I hadn't realized I was thinking out loud. Nuzzling her face and feeling her whiskers, I told her about the black wolf's tales of the caribou herd, and she looked at me hungrily, so I told her we could eat more clams, but we were both tired, and soon we went to sleep.

"Do you know the secret to catching fish?" I said while treading water. The seawater was unusually calm, and it was a nice reprieve from the hot sun. I swam well, but the main stretch of mountains was as far as the previous three islands combined, and we couldn't have made it in one breath. We needed a break. Notch-Tail bobbed up and down in the water, and her entire face was wet, dripping water. Under her wet fur, there was a thin contour to her face I hadn't noticed, and my eyes lingered on her face for a moment before I started to sink. I swallowed a mouthful of water and had to pull myself back up.

"Surely that's not the secret." Notch-Tail laughed.

"No, no. I'm just being silly," I said. "The secret to catching fish is to be like a fish."

"Uh-huh."

"Seriously. I move like a fish before jumping into the lake. Somehow this makes me invisible to the fish, and they'll never know I was there before I wrap my jaws around them."

"You're kidding," she said. "You wiggle your butt before jumping in, and somehow that's the secret?"

"Not kidding," I said. I started swimming forward again, and Notch-Tail followed closely behind. She alternated between laughing and breathing, and before I knew it, my paws touched sand again. The wind had picked up, and it chilled my body and dried my face. I walked up to Notch-Tail, who had just laid down on the sand to sunbathe, and I licked her salty face. "Get up," I said. "The day is still young, and we have entirely new land to explore. Should we go fishing? I can show you what I mean."

Notch-Tail opened her eyes and looked up at me, her snout

still on the ground. "We have all the time in the world. Come sleep with me instead."

I did.

As usual, we slept too much, so we were both wide awake at night. It was a perfect night, though. The air was moist and warm, and the half-moon hovered over the trees, and we used the moonlight to explore the rolling hills. The island was huge and smelled like many animals. Grouses and gophers and beavers and deer and weasels, but there were no wolves here, no strangers to bother us. This whole island was ours.

In the depth of the night, we came across a steep hill. I pulled Notch-Tail with me until we were at the very top, and as I got to the top, I tilted my head back and sang, for the first time in a very long time. Notch-Tail joined me. Our voices tangled and danced together until it was one single voice and then one single echo. This was a very nice hill on a very nice island. To the east, there was the mainland, too far and too dark to see. The ocean reflected the moonlight between the mainland and us, and I could see tiny white crests breaking the water surface. North and south, the island extended beyond the horizon, a blanket of green and yellow, and finally, to the west, there were hills and mountains, and then an infinite ocean.

"Sing again," Notch-Tail said. She waited until I started singing and she joined me. This time she changed her voice until it rumbled against mine, and all of a sudden, it sounded like many wolves had joined us. In the distance, a bird fluttered from the treetops, followed by a few others, and then it was quiet.

About the Author

Teng Rong is a Chinese-Canadian author living in Toronto. He grew up reading novels and he loves writing fiction.

Teng's favourite fiction books are *World War Z* by Max Brooks, *The Brothers Karamazov* by Fyodor Dostoevsky, *Unwind* by Neal Schusterman, *Silverwing* by Kenneth Oppel, and *Wolf Brother* by Michelle Paver. His favourite non-fiction books are *Fooled by Randomness* by Nassim Nicolas Taleb (and the other books in the *Incerto*), *Maps of Meaning* by Jordan B. Peterson, and *Outliers* by Malcolm Gladwell.

Teng has a B.Sc. in chemical engineering from the University of Calgary and a J.D. from the University of Toronto.

You can connect with me on:

🐦 https://twitter.com/TengRongAuthor

Made in United States
North Haven, CT
24 February 2022

16411840R00152